John Ford, Silvanus P. Thompson

Memorials of John Ford

John Ford, Silvanus P. Thompson

Memorials of John Ford

ISBN/EAN: 9783337400064

Printed in Europe, USA, Canada, Australia, Japan

Cover: Foto ©Andreas Hilbeck / pixelio.de

More available books at **www.hansebooks.com**

MEMORIALS

OF

JOHN FORD.

EDITED BY

SILVANUS THOMPSON.

LONDON:

SAMUEL HARRIS & CO., 5, BISHOPSGATE STREET WITHOUT.

YORK:

WILLIAM SESSIONS, 15, LOW OUSEGATE.

1877.

INTRODUCTION.

Amongst the instructions left by my beloved friend John Ford were the following relating to his Journals, bearing date 26th of Eleventh-Month, 1873.

"I wish my private Manuscripts of all kinds to come under no other eye than that of my dear friend Silvanus Thompson, until they have undergone his revision and selection.

"I have Journals kept at intervals from the Sixth-Month, 1820, to the present time. I have at various periods re-considered and recorded my reasons for the practice so long continued. Primarily the benefit to myself has been the motive. This benefit has been continually associated in my mind with the words of the Psalmist, lxxvii. 10, 'I will remember the years of the right hand of the Most High.' The reading over at times of these records of answered prayers—of constraining, restraining and directing grace—of help in extremities—of counsel in difficulties—of deliver-ances and blessings—of times of refreshing from the presence of the Lord—of heartfelt, personal love for a personal, ever-present, living Saviour—recurrence to these has often refreshed my spirit and cheered me to hold on my way. More especially at this late period of life, with fast failing bodily powers, these memoirs kindle feelings of lively grati-tude for the unnumbered mercies and blessings of the past, and help to cherish the confiding trust, that the same loving-kindness which has followed me all my life hitherto will keep me to the end. For these reasons and for others occurring among the memoranda I do not feel at liberty to destroy these memoirs and manuscripts.

"In addition to the foregoing, most of my memoranda are the records of efforts directed to the conscientious fulfilment of professional duties, in dependence upon Divine counsel and direction sought in earnest prayer, heard and answered, and followed by grateful, heart-felt acknowledgment. With these thoughts, I leave the disposal of these Manuscripts to the judgment of my dear friend Silvanus Thompson and to such friends as he may incline to take into counsel, after careful revision by himself.

"In coming to these conclusions, my desire is that whatever use may be made of the records whether private or more public, they may tend to promote the interests of Christian education and to the encouragement of all engaged in the solemnly responsible work.

"JOHN FORD."

I believe that the records of John Ford's professional career are well calculated to cheer and encourage others who are labouring in the same deeply important occupation, a calling in which trials and discouragements arise such as can be fully apprehended by those only who have had personal experience of them. It has appeared to me that the Journals also contain much that is valuable in the record of the strife maintained in the daily battle of life, by one in whom the work of Divine

Grace was eminently conspicuous in toning down and bringing into subjection much that betokened human infirmity.

Some readers may be disappointed that the extracts from John Ford's Journals do not contain more of the *details* of his professional life. It may be said in explanation that he was in the habit of keeping a separate " School Journal ;" but as this necessarily contained much of a personal nature respecting many now living, he destroyed a great portion of these memoranda a year or two before his decease.

It was my intention to include in these Memorials many of John Ford's " First-day evening Addresses " to his Scholars ; but finding that so doing would make the book undesirably large, I have omitted most of them, in hopes that if life be spared I may be able, from the abundant materials at my disposal, to prepare another volume to consist mainly of them. I am the more willing to adopt this course as John Ford himself contemplated their publication, and had made some preparations within a twelve-month of his decease for carrying out his design.

It will be noticed that the extracts of the Journals consist largely of records of mercies and " times of refreshing" rather than of failures or mis-steppings. In reference to this point John Ford writes : (4 mo. 23, 1865.)

"I dare not indulge in a morbid anatomy of thoughts and feelings, by a record of temptations yielded to or resisted. I know them but too well. But the loving kindnesses of my Lord through all the past, I am too apt in the cloudy day to forget, and thus to live below the privileges even of a poor, erring, sinful believer such as I am ; and so I record them still."

I have felt deeply the responsibility thrown upon me by my dear friend as to the disposal of his private papers. It has been my earnest desire to let him speak for himself, and to add only such brief explanatory and narrative matter as seemed needful. My acknowledgments are due to various kind friends and correspondents for valuable letters and other contributions that enrich the volume.

SILVANUS THOMPSON.

1, St. Mary's, York,
 9th mo. 26th, 1877.

CONTENTS.

I.

Yea thro' life, death, thro' sorrow and thro' sinning
  He shall suffice me, for He hath sufficed:
Christ is the end, for Christ was the beginning,
  Christ the beginning, for the end is Christ.

F. W. H. MYERS.

MEMORIALS

OF

JOHN FORD.

SECTION I.—ROCHESTER.

John Ford, the second of the five sons of Joseph and Elizabeth Ford, was born on the 21st of Third month, 1801, in the City of Worcester, where his father carried on the business of a baker. For some generations the family had been members of the Society of Friends.

At the early age of six years and four months, John Ford was sent along with his elder brother Joseph to a boarding School at North Newton, subsequently removed to Overthorp, near Banbury. Whilst there he lost his mother, who died almost instantaneously from an attack of apoplexy as she was waiting in the surgery of their medical attendant to consult him about her youngest child. On leaving Overthorp, after remaining at home a few months, he went to Ackworth School in 1811. Little is known of his course there, but from what information has been gathered from some of his

contemporaries, and the fact that he was appointed
a "monitor," he appears to have maintained a
respectable character in the school.* His principal
companion and friend besides his brothers, was
Thomas Pumphrey, also a native of Worcester, the
future superintendent of Ackworth School. The
close friendship between them continued till the
death of the latter in 1862.

Leaving Ackworth School in Third month, 1815,
at the age of fourteen, John Ford was articled for
seven years as apprentice to Robert Styles, a schoolmaster of Rochester. There is an almost total dearth
of information respecting him during the earlier part
of his apprenticeship. Happily in his twentieth
year he began to keep a Journal, which restricted
as it was in the earlier portions to the few weeks of
the annual vacation, affords some insight during
those years into his pursuits as well as his intellectual
and spiritual growth. Later in life, after making
abstracts of the contents of these early records, and
copies of portions of them, he committed the originals
to the flames. From this revised manuscript which
extends down to 1852 the following extracts are
taken :—

I have several manuscript records of the past. I have
often found it instructive, sometimes encouraging, perhaps
sometimes gratifying to self to read over these records.

---

* John Ford used to relate that the only time he was put into the "light
and airy rooms" at Ackworth, was (by an apprentice) for the offence of leaping
over a pool of water, left after a thunder-storm in the shed-court.

Sometimes too they have kindled love and gratitude in the recognition of the " arm unseen." It seems time to determine what to do with them. I feel hardly at liberty to burn them all, and yet there is much in them not worth preserving if even there is anything that *is*. Nevertheless I may perhaps still find instruction in reverting to the leading characteristics. Wherefore I propose to make an abstract :—

The earliest record is a holiday journal commencing 6th of Sixth month, 1820. I was then nineteen years and two months old. This summer Robert Styles, with whom I had been since the 25th of Third month, 1815, as an apprentice, gave up his school at Boley Hill, Rochester, to Richard L. Weston, and I was transferred with the rest of the stock. The journal extends to the 17th of Seventh month. It contains many traces of affection for several interesting boys, one of whom continues to this day an attached friend. With regard to occupations, it seems they had been various. Manual labour of many kinds was expected and performed by young men in my position. This system ended with the departure of Robert Styles and the accession of R. L. Weston and his wife. The journal then notes time devoted to French, Latin, Mapping, translating French into English verse, &c. In the way of amusements, riding, boating and cricket are included, also bathing in the beautiful Medway.

In this journal I see no trace or scarcely a trace of religious feeling. There is one memorandum of expression of thankfulness to God after a day spent very pleasantly as I then deemed it. Happily not one record is associated with the smallest recollection of any vicious propensity or act. I can feel grateful for this to-day, if I did not appreciate it then. Affection was my idol. I had been long isolated from all ties of consanguinity, and so fixed my affections on a few as

above noted with an intensity unequalled by any other sentiment till a higher love found place in my heart, and these
were in some measure subordinated. [1853.]

7 mo. 30, 1821.—Accompanied R. L. W. to London,
travelling by steamboat from Gravesend, the first time by
this then new mode of locomotion. [In this visit there is
notice of going to Westminster Abbey to see the Coronation
decorations, George IV. having been recently crowned.
Returned from London with twenty-two scholars. Thus
ends this second vacation journal. It appears to contain
some traces of a sense of want, some perception of a need of
patience, kindness, forgiveness, forbearance, &c.; but yet
scarcely an indication of where and how help was to be
obtained. Still the same absorbing affection for two or three
interesting and affectionate boys. The vacation was more
distinguished by frolic and gaiety than any previous or
subsequent one. Happily again there hang about it no
criminal recollections, except that of forgetfulness or ignor-
ance of that which can alone gild the past—the Love of God
in Jesus Christ. 1853.]

1822.—[I find notices of trains of thought in meetings
for worship that indicate the dawn of morning light;—also
of an intense perception of enjoyment in the beauties of
natural scenery. 1853.]

1823.—[Notices of solitary walks along the banks of the
Severn and in other beautiful localities in which mingled
with some sentimentalism, I see much of vivid enjoyment of
scenery—the harmonies and beauties of nature—(not ex-
tinguished now by double years) and then beginning to be
tinged with holier aspirations. 1853.]

6 mo. 29.—[The anniversary of my father's wedding.
All that remained of our family once more assembled in the

paternal home, the first time for sixteen years,—the last time! 1853.] My thoughts, turned to those whose place on earth shall know them no more: [my mother struck down by apoplexy in a moment in 1809, my eldest brother Joseph drowned whilst bathing in 1815] and believing as I do that the exchange has been for them a good exchange—earnest desires arose in my mind that I might by following their footsteps finally attain the desired haven: but the knowledge of my many deviations forcibly brought to my mind the language of Cowper,

> " But me, scarce hoping to attain that rest,
> Always from port withheld, always distressed,—
> Me howling blasts drive devious, tempest-tossed,
> Sails ripped, seams opening wide, and compass lost,
> And day by day some current's thwarting force
> Sets me more distant from a prosperous course."

7 mo. 10.—[A memorandum occurs at this date that seems to exhibit the sentimental merging into something better.] Walking along the Severn on a wet mizzling evening, spiritless and desponding, the beautiful lines of Moore occurred to me,

> " There's nothing dark, below, above,
> But in its gloom I trace Thy love;
> And meekly wait that moment, when
> Thy touch shall turn all bright again! "

Cheered and encouraged by this beautiful sentiment, I regained a more lively air and a lighter heart, resolving with humility and distrust of my own strength to pursue the path of rectitude.

[Another note of a lonely meditative walk, concludes as follows]:—How encouraging to the mind which conscious of numerous failings and frailties still wishes at times to keep the narrow road, is the following.

> " He reads the language of a silent tear,
> And sighs are incense from a heart sincere."

7 mo. 27.—Went to meeting with ——— this evening, for the last time perhaps at Worcester. It was a solemn meeting to me. I was enabled earnestly to desire for myself that I might be endowed with strength sufficient for the weight of my fast approaching engagements, and with that patience, meekness and condescension so requisite to one engaged in the arduous and important task of educating others.

1 mo. 13, 1824.—I frequently and I think with sincerity resolve to be more guarded in some particulars; and then in one short hour all seems forgotten as though it had not been. We are now commencing business again. Oh may He who was meek and lowly of heart graciously condescend to be my teacher, and be pleased to create a more earnest desire to become His scholar. I see increasingly the beauty of meekness, humility and forbearance. May I be more and more enabled to practise those excellent Christian virtues, and with reverence and tears I write, may the Almighty of His infinite goodness grant His blessing on my labours during the present half year.

6 mo. 9.—Private interview with a scholar who had given me much trouble. To a few words kindly spoken, he replied that he was extremely sorry, and that when he returned to school he would endeavour to avoid troubling me by his conduct. After this I took a walk in the fields, and though looking back on the half year just elapsed I find much, very much, to deplore, yet the remembrance of this interview and of one or two other times, created a feeling of humble gratitude, and a cheering hope that I was yet, though totally unworthy, an object of the compassionate regard of my Heavenly Father.

6 mo. 20.—Favoured to feel the spirit of supplication, and,

with tears confessed my many failings and entreated for pardon. I know whilst thus writing how very frail, how liable to err, how continually unwatchful I am, but I pray that I may yet be enabled to persevere.

During this vacation John Ford was engaged in teaching an interesting little boy, W. Curry Hillier; who subsequently became an architect, built a Christian church near the Jaffa gate in Jerusalem, and died there. Latin and Greek also occupied J. F.'s attention several hours almost daily; on one occasion $8\frac{1}{2}$ hours study are noted; on another, ten hours spent on Homer, Ovid and writing Latin prose.

7 mo. 27.—The holidays are now over. I am once more starting afresh. Oh may I not only start well but continue to run well. I know by mournful experience that I am utterly incapable of doing so by any strength of my own; therefore may I make it my more than daily endeavour to look unto the never failing source of strength. Of patience, humility and meekness I stand in peculiar need; may I so seek after these as to find them.

[The next series of memoranda relate to the school session. They abound in self-condemnation in reference to the want of patience, meekness and forbearance. In looking back on the period I can see that much of this arose from over-tasked physical and mental powers. The experience has been useful to me in my care of young men as Teachers. 1853].

8 mo. 21.—I have been on duty this week, and in some respects have been favoured to get through pretty well. Sometimes I believe when I make use of angry expressions and manner, it results in a great degree from an almost entire exhaustion

of the physical powers. [I am more inclined to accept that
excuse to-day than when I wrote it: that is, in looking back
at the modes of teaching, the circumstances of the school,—
the head having little authority,—exhaustion of spirits
acting upon a highly sensitive nervous system and a mind
consequently subject to intense feeling, account for these
outbreaks and the ever recurring lamentations over them.
The strife was maintained.   1853].

8 mo. 29.—Called on ———— ; asked to take wine : took a
glass: a second pressed: refused, but as ———— was peremptory
I yielded much against my will.   I will not flatter myself
that I shall for the future be able to resist earnest entreaty
to take a second.   I intend not to do it, and if I should I
will make a memorandum of it.

9 mo. 12.—I have destroyed several cantos of a poem,
which, though I have highly admired parts of it, I can no
longer retain with peace.

A subsequent entry records the destruction for the
same reason of a set of the works of the same author,
which had been a much valued gift.

11 mo. 8.—To-day after dinner I went up to my bedroom
and read a chapter in the Testament, and endeavoured to
prepare myself for the duties of the afternoon: but alas,
before the afternoon was half gone I got entirely out of
temper and was very cross.

In a retrospect at the close of the year 1824, the
following memoranda occur :

Convinced of the danger of conviviality, I some time
ago had resolved never to drink more than one glass of
wine at a sitting, but for want of firmness I have frequently

broken through my resolution.   One evening lately I supped
at ——'s : I drank one glass, resisted the second for a
time—gave way to banter—and drank three or four
more.   Another failing is I talk too much at random.   If
in the course of conversation an idea arises likely to excite
mirth, I almost invariably give it utterance.   I sometimes
omit to devote a little time at noon and in the evening to
retirement and perusal of the Scriptures.

New Year's Day, 1825.—With respect to employment I
am more and more convinced that the important one in
which I am engaged is the right one, and that to which I
am to look not only as the means of subsistence but as the
post allotted me to fill, so that with my present impressions
I think I should be unwilling to accept a situation affording
better pecuniary profits were such to offer.   With respect to .
the pursuit of knowledge, I desire to use all the diligence
and ardour that may consist with and subserve knowledge
which shall remain when tongues shall cease.

1 mo. 30.—I have endeavoured with some success to avoid
anger.   I have been frequently much provoked with ——
[a sort of boy Topsy, 1854] : but yesterday I had a little
conversation with him, apparently accidental, he being the
first to introduce it, in which his manner seemed once more
to revive my hopes.   I spoke to him in the spirit of love and
meekness, and I trust that the effect on both him and
myself was beneficial.

2 mo. 17.—This week I was on duty, and had some
delinquents to detain this afternoon.   I omitted to do it, not
wishing to dissipate any feelings suggested by the foregoing
topic [an· address to the boys on the death of a young person],
and desirous too of availing myself of the argument of
kindness.   In the evening some of them when retiring to

bed noticed it to me and said they would try to be good boys in return. I encouraged them so to do. I also spoke to ——— [the Topsy before noted] : he received my remarks kindly but he is too much like myself, he so soon forgets !

3 mo. 16.—The powerful ministry of Ann Alexander, who was visiting Rochester, had I believe a stimulating and encouraging effect on my mind.—[I completed my 24th year and my 10th of residence at Rochester about this time. Both these circumstances appear to have awakened serious thoughtfulness, and to have excited to renewed strife against all evil—a strife which possibly might have been more successful, had the Saviour and His love, and faith in Him,— and reference to Him and prayer expressly offered in His name been more frequent exercises of my own mind, and more frequent topics of the ministry. I trace much contrition of mind, much of prayerful exercise ; and yet possibly a misconception as to the mode by which peace of mind and a sense of reconciliation were to be attained : perhaps something of a " going about to establish " my own righteousness. And yet how gratefully I think I can say in reviewing these painful struggles, how gratefully now I can recognize the hand that led me through the wilderness, and that has kept me to this day.   1854].

[Will any eye ever glance over this page and gather encouragement from the following ? 1854]. 4 mo. 16.—Took a solitary walk after tea ; reflected with sorrow on the expired week because I have been extremely cross several times.

5 mo. 1.—This evening again, during a few solitary moments in the schoolroom whilst the boys were at supper, sorrow for the manner in which my time was occupied in meeting seemed to prevail. [This is one of the most frequently recorded difficulties of these my early days. They stand in

marked contrast with the notices of heavenly favour and enjoyments in the retirement of my own bedroom—in solitary walks numberless, and in silent hours in the schoolroom, of which after eight o'clock, I was often the sole occupant, sometimes till midnight and beyond. I believe there is a wondrous and most merciful adaptation in the Divine dealings with man, varying with his mental habits and constitution. To a mind of great power and able to control the imagination, and to concentrate itself upon the solemnities of united public worship—our silent meetings may be and doubtless are seasons of refreshing enjoyment. My mind was never such— but unconcentrative—a winged imagination too little subject to control. Highly as I estimate the privilege of public worship as beyond all price, much as I owe it, in the remembrance of instruction sealed on my spirit, sometimes by vocal ministry, sometimes by the immediate teachings of the Divine Spirit—and often as I can recall seasons in which I have been sensible of the Divine presence covering our assembly with a solemnity beyond the power of language to describe—yet the heat of conflict—the wrestling in prayer—the overwhelming sense of gratitude and love, the flashing train of thought and feeling too rapid and too deep for the poverty of language to express—these have been— they still are—the exercises, the enjoyments of brief moments of intensity in the solitary walk, in the silent chamber. 1854].

5 mo. 10.—Very unkind. Scarcely anything like meekness or gentleness in me. I feel this evening as if a line from Milton expressed my condition, "Exhausted, spiritless, afflicted, fallen !"

5 mo. 12.—This day I have felt the tendering influence of Divine Love: for this unmerited favour may I feel

grateful this evening.   [And so the conflict was maintained.
"I was brought low and *He* helped me."   1854].

6 mo. 13.—Though I think I have got through the half
year just closing better than any preceding one, I sincerely
hope that the next may be much better : there is abundance
of room for improvement.   Unkindness, to give it no harsher
name, has been too often the stamp of my conduct, though
I have generally been favoured to see my error, to acknowledge it or to make amends for it.   Oh that this spirit may
be entirely rooted out, and instead of it, the meekness,
gentleness and forbearance of our Holy pattern, Christ
Jesus, implanted.

7 mo. 10.—Thomas Pumphrey spoke in meeting, "Are
there not some amongst you who have heard a voice saying,
'this is the way, walk in it?'   I am certain there are such.
This is no other than the voice of Christ, calling, inviting
and alluring us to follow Him."   He went on to allude to
the calling of the several apostles as described Matt. iv. 18—22,
dwelling on the word '*immediately*'—no conferring with
flesh and blood—that we must be willing to follow Christ
not only to the Temple and the Mount, but also to the Garden
and to Calvary—that the same feeling of desertion which
prompted the words "My God, my God, why hast Thou for-
saken me?" sometimes attended His faithful followers.—Before
I came to Worcester I had a prospect of a requiring of a very
arduous and distressing character.   Since I have been at
home it has revived with great force, but I had hitherto
avoided it and endeavoured to get from under it.   It was
again brought before me whilst sitting in meeting.   I felt
something like a prayer for resignation, at the same time
wishing for some prospect of escape.—Just at this moment
Thomas Pumphrey appeared in prayer.   He prayed for

those who might be thinking the Divine requirings hard—
that they might be strengthened to submit to do whatever
the Lord might be requiring at their hand, thinking nothing
too trivial, but yielding implicit, unreserved obedience—that
those who had in some degree come out of bondage into the
glorious liberty of the sons of God, might be preserved in
deep humility—that those who had to drink of the cup of
affliction might witness His everlasting arms to be underneath
for their preservation.   Part of this seemed so applicable to
my state of mind that it appeared to me his prayer was
granted, and strength was given me to submit.   Great
tenderness of spirit was prevalent with me till the close of
the meeting, so that when T. P. shook hands with me after
meeting, I was obliged to turn hastily from him to conceal
my emotion.   I walked home with my dear father and did
what I believed to have been required of me, and found
inexpressible satisfaction, resulting from obedience, so that I
could have uttered the voice of thanksgiving which did
indeed rise in my heart!   [It was the simple acknowledgment of a fault committed years ago ; humiliating as it was
to an over-sensitive nature, it was abundantly blessed : few
things have seemed hard since : it was in some degree taking
upon me the yoke of Christ—borne since that day sometimes
restlessly and impatiently, but never I trust shaken off ;—
more and more meekly, more and more willingly may I ever
bear it !   1854].

9 mo. 18.—I was on duty last week—got out of temper
terribly on Sixth-day—better on Seventh. * * * * [Terribly
cross as I wrote myself to be, I can yet remember a maxim
that helped as a counterpoise—never to go to bed at variance
with anyone if it could possibly be prevented by a concession—
a kind word, a kind look—a friendly farewell—and so though
often terribly cross, I had a very large share of enjoyment in

the affectionate attachment of a large number of interesting youths.   1854].

6 mo. 12, 1826.—This day brings another half-year to a close.   The retrospect is perhaps less painful than that of many preceding ones.   Of all that affords pleasure in the review, of all the instances in which the spirit of love and kindness has checked the propensity to impatience or anger, the praise belongs to Him alone without whose aid I am nothing.   To Him I desire to return the tribute of a grateful heart for His innumerable blessings.   Notwithstanding my weaknesses and failings, Divine help has at times been very near.   The remembrance of it is transcendently precious. Love has increased in a remarkable degree amongst the members of our large family.   I do sincerely rejoice in the belief that many of my beloved young friends here have witnessed a growth in that which is supremely good.

11 mo. 30.—To-day after dinner, I thought of retiring to my room as usual for a few minutes, when a suggestion crossed my mind that it was of no use, but something like a solemn farce or mockery.   However I felt disposed to reject the suggestion and went as usual.   I read a few verses in the New Testament—one seemed to arrest my attention "Peter followed afar off."   I felt an earnest desire that I might still aim at following, though I felt myself exceedingly " far off." Tenderness and contrition revived ; I confessed my extreme unworthiness and asked for help.   Since then I have felt more cheerfulness and serenity than I have known for a long time.

Family troubles which need not be referred to more particularly, had for some years been casting their depressing shades over John Ford's path.

About this period they reached their climax ; and at
times they seemed almost overwhelming. Trials of
this kind were permitted to be his lot till far advanced in life. Yet it was evident that these
troubles were blessed to his spiritual growth, and
from his own deep experience he was enabled to
enter into close sympathy with others in their afflictions.

1827.—[In looking back on this time of deep distress, I
think I can thankfully acknowledge the preserving love and
mercy of my heavenly Father to me in that I was not also
a fugitive or worse. How often in those days did He forgive
and restore, and when " in sin and sorrow sunk revive my
soul with grace." I can dimly at least see too the wisdom
of the discipline of distress and sorrow. ".Who hath made
thee to differ ? " 1857].

1 mo. 7.—Dined with ———. In the course of conversation he applied the term mysticism to some sentiments which
I advanced. Oh may neither this, nor far sharper sarcasms
ever shake my confidence in Divine guidance even in small
matters. Those who earnestly seek it, will I believe never
be confounded. The prospect may at times appear gloomy
and events contrary, but in the end all will be found to have
been directed by Eternal Wisdom.

2 mo. 21. Let me put repining and murmuring far away,
and endeavour with heartfelt, humble resignation to say
"Thy will be done "! Oh may the gracious intents of
Divine Goodness in these multiplied dispensations of sorrow
be carried forward to their completion unfrustrated by my
perverse and unsubdued will. This evening I trust an

humble and resigned spirit is in a very small degree prevalent. Oh! I could even rejoice in these afflictions, could
cherish them as the choicest blessings, did they but humble
my proud heart. Oh! may they yet affect it! Neither wealth
nor honour, nor fame nor long life do I crave. Grant me O
merciful Father the true riches, and I will be even more than
gratefully content! "Thou hast been my help, leave me
not neither forsake me, O God of my salvation."

3 mo. 21. Entered my 27th year. Rose soon after six,
took a walk to the dell, read in my pocket Testament. Got
back just as the bell rang for school. Several times to-day I
have felt desirous to attain to a feeling of gratitude and that
gratitude might become a strong influential principle.
"If ye love Me keep My commandments." May I be
enabled to maintain the watch so that when the 27th year
of my life draws towards its close, it may present less cause
of regret in retrospect than its predecessors. If the silver
cord should be loosed ere that period arrives, may the day's
work have so kept pace with the day as that I may entertain a humble hope in the mercy of God through the ever
blessed Redeemer, our Lord Jesus Christ, that all will be
well.

5 mo. 15.—I could at times almost believe that I am in
my right field of labour, but my own many deficiencies seem
to forbid my labouring as I would for the good of others. How
can I recommend meekness, kindness, gentleness, humility and
the rest of that lovely Christian train, whilst manifesting
that I do not possess them myself? "Create in me a clean
heart, O God; and renew a right spirit within me. Then
will I teach transgressors Thy ways." Oh that I could with
David deeply feel the necessity of this and earnestly pray
for it; THEN indeed I think I could with some boldness
endeavour to teach.

This afternoon was perhaps the happiest I ever knew. I do not think I either said or did a single unkind thing. I felt grateful for the blessing. I am most sure it was not of myself.

7 mo. 26.—As I was leaving the school-room this afternoon, the thought occurred that probably the next time I should enter there, I should have commenced my solemn engagements again; and feeling the spirit of prayer prevalent, I paused, and on the bended knee and under a sense of my own utter inability to preserve myself, petitioned the Almighty to protect and guard me from evil, and to increase in me the love and fear of Him, my gracious God. Oh how precious is the spirit of prayer! Even now I would entreat the Lord to take away from me all evil tempers, all anger, impatience, ungentleness and unkindness, and to bestow upon me a humble, a meek, forbearing, forgiving disposition, and to be with me when tried and tempted.

10 mo. 24.—"I sometimes rejoice," says Henry Martyn, "that I am not 27 years of age, and that, unless God should order it otherwise, I may double the number in constant and successful labour." Such were his sentiments when at my present age, and what are mine? Perhaps somewhat as follows: "I am not 27 years of age, and am almost ready to faint by the way, and to long for the end of the journey. If I look forward to a continuance in my present field of labour, my heart sinks within me; unsubdued evil within, so frequently manifesting itself without, makes me fear that I shall be an unprofitable servant at last." [So I wrote in 1827. More than twice twenty-seven years have now passed over me and I am still in a like field of labour. I look back upon those early years of trial and of much severe self-condemnation, not only as useful discipline but as useful

experience. Much that tried me, impatience and its humiliating results arose from over pressure. Nearly all the moral weight of a school of more than sixty boys fell upon me. My days were sometimes 16, 17 and 18 hours—up before six—retiring between eleven and twelve—highly sensitive and easily excited nervous system—poor digestive powers—frequent headaches—ceaseless activity—all these combinations account for much that distressed me. They have taught me that early hours of retiring—cares and burdens better adapted to the ability to bear them—ultimate authority to appeal to in difficulty, would tend greatly to aid a young teacher to fulfil his daily duties with more peace of mind than was often my portion. 1858.]

3 mo. 23, 1828.—On sitting down in meeting to-day something very precious was felt—a perception of the full adequacy of the Saviour's sacrifice to atone for sin. This appeared of inestimable value. I felt the need of it and some degree of faith in its sufficiency. This was a strength to me through the day. A hope in eternal mercy seemed like a cordial under trials and discouragements. I find myself very unwilling to get up early enough to read, &c., before commencing. I am afraid it is idleness, and yet I feel very languid and unrested in the morning.

John Ford had now entered his twenty-eighth year, and he had been thirteen years a teacher at Rochester. The time for a change had arrived. William Simpson, the writer of the letter alluded to in the following extract, had formerly resided at Rochester, but for the last five or six years he had kept a boarding school in Lawrence Street, York. On account of health he was desirous of withdrawing

from the profession, and he applied to John Ford to
see how far he was prepared to become his successor.
Ten years previously Yorkshire Quarterly Meeting
of the Society of Friends had had under consideration the establishment of a boarding school under
its own control, "which would afford a liberal,
guarded and religious education, on moderate terms,
to the sons of Friends who were not considered
objects of Ackworth School." The project however was not then carried into effect. But now
when William Simpson announced his intention of
giving up his establishment, which had been carried
on in premises the property of the Quarterly Meeting
then considered eligible and commodious, the scheme
was again revived. After full consideration the
Quarterly Meeting decided to establish a school; a
committee of management was empowered to carry
out the details, and John Ford was appointed Head
Master or Superintendent.

3 mo. 28.—This evening I received a letter from William
Simpson of York, which may possibly lead to a new epoch
in my life. My first thoughts were painful as involving the
idea of leaving a place so full of beloved recollections, and
friends whom I love so truly, as well as so many dear ones
among the scholars, such altogether as I may never meet
again—giving up my beautiful flock to a stranger, and
disappointing some who had looked to my continuance here.
In the other scale I placed the idea of increased ability to
minister to the comfort of my dear father, whose residence
at York favoured this idea. Perhaps too some visions of

possible happiness floated before me. But alas! I *am*
and I sometimes really feel myself to be utterly unworthy
of the least of the Lord's mercies. I believe I can honestly
say in reference to this prospect, my prayer is that if not
right for me it may be frustrated.

3 mo. 31.—Wrote to W. Simpson to say I was willing to
treat with him. I did not come hastily to this conclusion,
not if I may say so, till I had sought for the direction and
committed the matter to the disposal of Infinite Wisdom.

6 mo. 10.—Another half-year has at length passed away!
How I long to be clothed with that spirit of kindness and
love which is

> "Ne'er ruffled by those cataracts and breaks
> Which humour interposed too often makes."

In reviewing the past I find abundant room for improvement,
and long for the time of commencing again, and making
under the Divine blessing a fresh effort to attain a little nearer
to the high standard which I strive to keep in view, and to
illustrate if possible in some degree the beautiful character of
a true Christian teacher. This is a high ambition, but a
worthy one I believe. That I may continue, though through
trials and difficulties, discouragements and infirmities, to
follow after, if so that I may attain, is my very sincere
desire.

6 mo. 15.—In my retirement in my bed-room, I took
up "Sacred Poetry" and found the hymn "There is a
fountain," &c. The sacred spirit of prayer seemed poured
upon me instantaneously; and prostrating myself as at the
footstool of the throne, I found more than usual freedom of
access, and poured out my prayer before the Lord, offering
also thanksgiving for the fountain opened, entreating that
I might experience its blessed cleansing power; pleading in

the name and through the merits of Him through whom alone
we have access by one Spirit unto the Father, even our Lord
and Saviour Jesus Christ.

9 mo. 13.—I spoke to ——— and ——— about disorder
in meeting, and from their conduct when spoken to I felt
much disposed to be angry ; but it happily occurred to me to
try the effect of a mild remonstrance. I did so; and it
succeeded excellently. I believe all three went away with
tears in their eyes. The thoughts of being about to leave
this beloved circle are very painful.

11 mo. 2.—First-day. Though about to leave to-morrow,
I called the boys and attended to scriptural instruction till
breakfast time. I attended to them at supper time and
heard them repeat some pieces of poetry. I lastly informed
them that I was about to leave. I expressed the regret I
felt that I had in too many instances departed from the law
of kindness and gentleness ; that nevertheless it had been my
endeavour to live in love with them and to promote their
interests in every way. I alluded to the time spent in
scriptural instruction, and expressed my wish that fruit
might yet appear. The deep silence that prevailed, and the
tears that many shed, surprised and affected me deeply.
They withdrew silently to the schoolroom and settled quietly
to their books. After evening reading I attended them to
their bed-rooms, and took leave of each boy separately. I
received fresh proofs of their affection : many shook hands
with me in silence and tears.

John Ford left Rochester the following morning,
and after staying a few days in the neighbourhood
of London, arrived at York on the 15th of Eleventh
Month, 1828.

SECTION II.

LAWRENCE STREET, YORK.

On arriving at York, John Ford became the guest of his kind friend Samuel Tuke, until the School opened on New Year's day, 1829.

Any account of York School would be incomplete without some notice of the important services rendered by Samuel Tuke in its establishment, and as an active member of the Committee of management during the succeeding twenty years. It was largely through his exertions and the deep interest he took in the cause of Education, that the Quarterly Meeting was induced to undertake the responsibility of the School. His eldest son, Henry, had been a scholar at Rochester, and it was in his visits to the school there that Samuel Tuke became acquainted with John Ford. How deeply the latter was indebted to the wise counsels and unvarying sympathy and kindness of his revered and honoured friend, cannot be told. "Amongst my choicest outward blessings," writes John Ford shortly after the school opened, " I number that of having such a friend as Samuel Tuke."

1 mo. 4, 1829.—A new era has opened in my life. A situation of great and awful responsibility has been exchanged for one still more so. Yet I cannot but believe in my best

moments that my post is of Divine appointment, disqualified as I feel for it. May faith be granted me to believe that "the Lord is nigh unto all that call upon Him in truth,"— that those who come unto Christ, He will in no wise cast out.

1 mo. 29.—I have had some favoured visitations of Divine goodness I think I may venture to say, and I do not know that the truly consoling and strengthening doctrine of the atonement ever presented itself so forcibly to my mind as of late. I think our evening readings have sometimes been condescendingly owned, and prayer has silently ascended on behalf of the flock that is given me.

2 mo. 22.—Let the fire do its work in me, there is much that wants consuming. Already I believe the name of Jesus is become to me increasingly precious, the blood of atonement, *God reconciled in Christ,* more frequently recurred to, and more highly prized : the necessity felt not of daily only but of hourly, yea continual supplies of strength to sustain and of grace to preserve. Oh mayst Thou who alone art able to keep us from falling, and to present us before His presence with exceeding joy, be near me so that I at last may be one of the happy number.

6 mo. 14.—First-day. I spent the day almost entirely among the boys and very pleasantly. They repeated poetry as usual and answered questions in Scripture before breakfast. In the evening I addressed them as about to separate. I began under a feeling of incapacity, but as I went on, a precious covering seemed spread over us ; several of the boys were in tears. It was worth a half-year's toil and watching to attain it. [Such was my first leave-taking of a beloved circle 29 years ago ; many a precious leave-taking has been

granted me since. May the last when it comes, (if it be not already passed) be thus blest! 1858.]

8 mo. 9.—Last Second-day evening my mind was much exercised with a prospect of vocal prayer (at reading time) for the Divine blessing on the commenced half-year. Several friends were present, and I put it by for "a more convenient season," but not without a feeling of condemnation. I have since prayed in private for strength to perform the duty should it be again presented. This evening after considerable conflict, I obeyed, and in a few words besought the Almighty to grant us His blessing. Felt a peaceful reward.

11 mo. 4.—(Referring to domestic troubles.) The clouds of last evening continued nearly all day—dispersed a little in the afternoon but gathered again towards night. Heaven is a blessed place! Oh that a mansion may be prepared for me there by redeeming love! *There* are no clouds—no surmisings—no distrust—neither pain nor sorrow nor sighing nor any such thing!

3 mo. 21, 1830.—I have completed my twenty-ninth year to-day. Though not under a very lively feeling, I have not been without sincere desires for advancement in the Christian course. I have no one here to notice the recurrence of the day and wish me well as on former birthdays, but if I have advanced one campaign nearer victory, it matters little if I still fight alone.

4 mo. 17.—I have often lately seemed objectless and lonely, often recurring to the scenes, the friends, the pursuits, the pleasures of the past! Then again better thoughts arise. I wish to tread patiently the path before me and to keep my eye fixed on the *end*. "Finis coronat opus." "Gad, a troop shall overcome him, but he shall overcome at the last;" may the latter part be as surely fulfilled in my experience as the

former has been !　Often has the troop of evil from within
and from without, overcome; but what a glorious promise,
" He shall overcome at the last."

2 mo. 22, 1831.—Oh when feeling that it is a painful and
sometimes dubious warfare, pressed from without by hostilities
of various kinds—the world, the flesh and the Devil in arms,
traitors in the camp threatening to surrender, a heart prone
to idolatry—feeling all these and more than these, who would
not long for the dawn of the glorious day of ultimate
freedom ! who would not long to be " absent from the body
and to be present with the Lord ! "

6 mo. 16.—The annual examination of the scholars was
conducted to-day.　I committed the cause to God in prayer
repeatedly, and during the examination in the Scriptures the
sense of His mercy and goodness was richly felt.　It expelled
all anxiety as to what might be thought by others.　Secretly,
and perhaps it should have been openly, I ascribed to Him
to whom alone it was due, all the praise.　Most unfeignedly
can I testify that I feel my love for my " beautiful flock "
increased; I look with pain to their departure, to our separation.　Oh that daily we may remember each other, and be
remembered and presented by each other before the Throne.

6 mo. 25.—And now they are all gone !　Oh the painful,
aching vapidity that comes over me in every interval of
employment !　The empty, noiseless play-ground, the absence
of every face that would expand into a smile or kindle one,
not a single thing left to receive or return an affectionate
word or look.　" This is to be alone."　Oh that all my
affections were set on heavenly things !

During the vacation of 1831, John Ford made a
tour on the Continent.　Crossing from Dover to

Calais, he travelled chiefly by diligence, visiting
Paris and Geneva, and the vale of Chamonix, and
returning across France via Rouen and Dieppe.
After he settled at York it was his custom to leave
home during the annual vacations as much as
circumstances permitted, not merely for the sake of
health and recreation, but being necessarily associated
chiefly with the young whilst the School was in
session, he felt strongly the desirability of mixing
as much as he could with others nearer his own age ;
and so by contact with those who lived in a wider
sphere, maintaining that freshness which, without
care, is apt to be impaired by confinement to " the
little world of a School."—For the same reason he
was glad to mingle in the social circles of his friends,
where his literary tastes and conversational powers
made him welcome.

1831.—[In Paris on my return, on the occasion of a grand
review in commemoration of " Les trois jours," I saw several
of the great actors in the past, destined also to illustrate
again in a few years the uncertain tenure of exalted rank—
Louis Philippe—Don Pedro, Ex-emperor of Brazil—the
Dukes of Orleans and Nemours, sons of Louis—Generals
Soult and Sebastiani. The Queen Marie Louise and her
other sons and daughters were in the balcony of the Palais
de Justice. Little Monpensier, eight or nine years old, was
dressed in the costume of a national guard. 1864.]

6 mo. 3, 1832.—A single case of cholera occurred to-day
in York. On the 13th all the scholars had gone home.
The city wears a most melancholy aspect. Hearses, mourning

coaches, tolling bells, assail the eye and ear continually. Great hostility is manifested against the medical men. " Burker," " butcher," " thief," &c., are lavished upon them ; but the spread of the disorder quelled a little these un-christian outcries.

6 mo. 17.—First-day.   Upwards of £60 collected in Meeting to-day, for the distressed poor in the cholera.   The city divided into districts.   Samuel Tuke and myself appointed for Walmgate.

6 mo. 28.—Drank tea with Thomas Backhouse at the Friars' Gardens.   We went on the City-wall which overlooks the Cholera Burial Ground.   The service was being read over a poor woman who twenty-four hours previously had been alive and well.   There was no mourner but the bereaved husband.   The numerous recent graves and one more preparing, raised feelings of sympathy with the afflicted, and a sense of awe in observing these outward signs of the Divine chastisements.

The contrast of the scene immediately below me, and that which met the eye in looking beyond it, was very striking. It was a beautiful evening—the sky as clear—the birds as musical—the slowly-sinking sun as splendid—the river as bright and tranquil " as if earth possessed no tomb"—nothing in the external aspect of nature to remind us of *Sin*.

FROM SAMUEL TUKE TO JOHN FORD.

York, 7 mo. 21.—The accounts for the last week of the disease in our City have been so favourable that we are (perhaps too hastily) pleasing ourselves with the hope that it is about to leave us at least for a time, and that our Schools may be permitted to re-open either at or very soon after the usual time.   As many of our committee are likely to be at Ackworth next week, we conclude to consult those who may be there on the subject of re-opening, and to issue a circular stating the decision. * * *

I am pleased thou hast enjoyed thy Westmorland tour. I recollect my own impressions on the first visit to those scenes of gentle sublimity and apparent peace. I dare say thou almost wished to tabernacle amongst them, and quit the toils and cares of an arduous public station. Solomon's result—vanity and vexation—is found however in this as well as every other search after peace—save *one*. Alas! that with so many this *one* should be the *last* they try, and that so many would fain try it when it is too late. I judge of thy hankering after a snug cottage by Grasmere water or in Patterdale, by my own *often longings* in former days when I used frequently to visit Westmorland, and was very wont to fancy that some *place* of peace was to be found other than by Siloam's brook, or beneath the shadow of that Rock which is so grateful to the pilgrim in a weary land;——— and *yet*, spite of experience, like the poor Israelites, I have often hankerings after the good things of Egypt, though they may take a more refined form than that of onions and flesh-pots.—Oh, how happy are those who like Paul consult not with flesh and blood, but are obedient to the heavenly message, and by a holy decision count all as loss and dross that they may win Christ.

.8 mo. 24.—After rowing about two miles up the river and back, I returned tired: before night I became very unwell with choleritic symptoms. C. Williams took prompt measures, and sent me to bed where I remained till the 27th. During this illness, knowing that the fatal cholera was in the city, I could not but look seriously towards a probable summons. I trust it was not insensible stupidity, nor yet the more fearful malady of a hard heart that enabled me to contemplate

a change without dismay. Death seemed fearful, but the
gloom reached not beyond. I examined the ground of my
hopes : it was not good works—nor full dedication of heart—
nor yet careful obedience—nor yet sincere attempts and
arduous struggles. It was a calm hope in Redeeming love
and mercy, not so much joyous as tranquil. I felt that I
could quietly commend myself and the result to God.
Though I often fall, sin is not my delight; it is my burden,
my grief, my abhorrence. I long to serve Christ more
ardently, more faithfully. Since I have known the Christian's
hope—and I dare not doubt that I do know something of it—
I can say with Cowper

> " I never trusted in an arm save Thine,
> Nor hoped but in Thy righteousness divine."

On leaving my bed for the first time, I enjoyed the unspeakable favour of a heart overflowing with gratitude, and was
enabled to pour it out before the Lord.

8 mo. 31.—I attended the evening reading, and read the
145th Psalm. My voice faltered at the verse, " The Lord is
good to all : and His tender mercies are over all His works."
It is indeed a blessed thing to be smitten. I would not
choose for myself unvarying health. Many times during
this brief cessation I have felt the love of God exceedingly
near, the Saviour in whom is all my trust, exceedingly
precious. My heart has been contrited in reverting to the
past, and expanded with hope in looking to the future.
May the remembrance of these things stimulate me to
persevere ! May I be preserved in watchfulness and prayer
hour by hour, till " well done " shall dismiss me into the
joy of my Lord !

12 mo. 31.—I have seen many of the parents this time :
they seem without exception well satisfied. I desire to be
thankful for this, and that I may be enabled to stand ap-

proved not only in their sight, but in His, whose servant, though most unworthy, I wish to consider myself in my station here.

At our evening reading, I alluded to the preservation from pestilence that we had experienced ; and in consideration of the goodness of God to us, invited all to unite in lifting up our hearts to Him in thanksgiving for His many mercies, and in prayer that He would continue His goodness to us and increase in our hearts daily the love and fear of Him. Solemnity seemed to cover us, and I trust aspirations did ascend and some renewal of covenant was entered into.   For myself I look to the new year with a trembling hope.   Something seems to whisper at times—it is of no use—things will go on as heretofore—a temporary resistance—and then a parley, and then a defeat—but still a better voice is at times heard saying, " fight on—take the whole armour—watch as well as pray—watch unto prayer."   Lord help me to say in Thy name, in dependance on Thy Holy Spirit's aid, " So I will," and then at the last day of all—though a troop may have overcome me at times, I may overcome at the last.

2 mo. 22, 1833.—Nearly two months have gone by since I noted down any of the fleeting events of a little-varied but conflicting journey.   I have indeed not done all that I would have done—and much, very much, daily that I would not, *that* I still do, but still I hope on.

5 mo. 16.—I breakfasted this morning with my friend John Phillips.*   I admired his varied and successful application of talent.   He makes his own barometers, and with such accuracy of construction that he says he can measure the height of a wall by them.   His thermometers are also his own manufacture and he has invented a new form of a self-registering

* Subsequently Professor Phillips of Oxford, the noted Geologist, at this time Curator of the Yorkshire Philosophical Society's Museum at York.

thermometer. He has a dipping-needle and one on which he observes the variation of the compass—this morning he says it is 25° west. He has a rain-gauge of his own contrivance which I intend to adopt. In his garden he has a stone tablet with a meridian line drawn upon it. He has telescopes—geological maps of his own delineating and colouring—he is a lithographer and has a turning lathe. I have enumerated these pursuits of my friend to stimulate myself to more diligence in science.

6 mo. 6.—I begin to look with painful thoughts towards the dispersion of my flock. Ill qualified as I am, and I make not the assertion lightly, yet I find so much happiness, even in the struggling, toiling, self-contesting life which I lead—so much pleasure in intercourse of various kinds with the boys, that I really look with sad forebodings to the dreary vacuity of the approaching recess. I have no other object yet in which I find a response to those feelings in which I delight—affectionate interest in the happiness and advantage of others, and to which I please myself with thinking that I do find some response in many by whom I am surrounded.

6 mo. 18.—The examination in the Scriptures was held this evening. It was attended, I thought with some evidence of Divine regard. A feeling of chastened pleasure during the progress of the evening's proceedings affected me deeply. In conclusion Samuel Tuke addressed the scholars. I felt pleased with the proceedings of the day. Much gratification was expressed by many whose judgment and sincerity were to be depended upon. Neither was I devoid of gratitude to Him whose help I had sought in prayer. Nor was this help withheld. I was enabled to go calmly and temperately through the arduous duties of the day.

1 mo. 13, 1834.—The close of last year and the commencement of the present have abounded with trials from without
and from within. I have pondered the step of quitting this
post, but I cannot lose the belief that this is my *right* post,
and that in no other could I expect to find peace; and that
here, through evil report and good report, I may have peace
within, if I do but keep a single eye to Him and His help,
who, I cannot but believe brought me hither.

4 mo. 30.—I got rid of a heavy load to-day in admonishing
an individual not of my household. I endeavoured to do it
faithfully. Few things that I remember have oppressed me
so much. I made it the subject of more than one prayer.
I trust that in setting forth the enormity of the sin in the
sight of a pure and holy God, I did though weakly and
imperfectly discharge my conscience.

1835. [Nearly a year passed by with only very brief
notice of incidents and almost no reference to the inner life.
In the early part of this year I frequently visited Stephen
Robson, then an invalid dying of consumption. His course
ended in peace. 1864.]

9 mo. 13.—Oh that desires and endeavours after true
holiness may increase in me ! I have no hopes of salvation
but in the unmerited mercy of the dear Redeemer, and I
long to show that I love Him by living near Him, and trying
to copy His example. A subject of personal interest sometimes comes before me, in the thought that " it is not good
for man to be alone," and yet the way does not appear open
for a change. My path in life has been so little of my own
choosing that I do not like to venture on my own contriving
in this: and yet I fear lest I should be looking for too
specific direction and may not be doing my own part. I
should rejoice in a little light on the subject. I can honestly

say I should prefer the Lord's choosing to my own, whether for single life or for the apparently more happy lot. May I which ever it be, attain to that name and place, better than that of sons and daughters.

12 mo. 26, 1836.—I have at times of late had so much pleasure in the company and conversation of the elder boys, that I have seemed almost to realize the "beau ideal" of preceptor and pupils. It is not that I assume credit to myself in that which afforded me so much pleasure. Hour after hour daily during the last week, I spent with six or seven of them in the library, with scarcely a moment's interruption of kind and cheerful freedom. They were engaged on their maps, I with the accounts.

1837.—An attack of influenza began in the school, 1 mo. 21, and occasioned great anxiety; yet mingled, as such periods have ever been in my experience, with the unspeakable mercy—the choice blessing, of closer communion with God, to whom the heartfelt tribute of gratitude did often arise on my own account and on that of the beloved boys, for His preserving care. On First-day the 29th, only seven boys out of forty-nine attended Meeting: that day week all were at meeting but four. I have several times lately, withdrawn for a few minutes to seek a little renewal of strength, by entering into the closet, shutting the door and praying to Him who seeth in secret, and have found at least a temporary calm and a little abiding sweetness. "Why art thou cast down O my soul? and why art thou disquieted within me? Hope thou in God: for I shall yet praise Him, who is the health of my countenance, and my God."

6 mo. 22.—The vacation began to day. I parted with regret with some who had greatly contributed to my happiness. I do not think I had ever had more enjoyment in my

D

work, in the company of the beloved boys. A large party accompanied me to Selby Monthly Meeting in the Fourth month and to Cottingwith in the Fifth. In the Fifth month I had a most pleasant visit from three warmly attached old scholars. I may never again stand so much in need of all those numerous little daily interchanges of kindness from those under my care, which so often cheered me during the last twelve months, but nothing can efface the remembrance of it. ["I may never again &c." quoted supra, refers to an event which was to provide a help-meet for me. My beloved Rachel and I exchanged vows the 30th of Sixth month, 1837, at Dewsbury. To me it was a peaceful, chastened, joyful day,—a joy which sometimes tears best interpret,—solemn, thankful joy. 1864.]

Rachel Robson was the daughter of Nathan and Rachel Robson of Darlington, and sister of Stephen Robson whose death is alluded to under the date of 1835. It was a union that was eminently blessed.— The frequent allusions to her in John Ford's memoranda render it unnecessary at present to say more of this beloved one, whose memory is still cherished by not a few.

7 mo. 28.—The first Meeting of the Friends' Educational Society was held at Ackworth to-day. I was appointed one of the Secretaries, colleague of Samuel Tuke and John Newby.

John Ford became one of the most active members of the Friends' Educational Society. The Papers he contributed excited much interest. One entitled "Influence and Authority," read in 1853,

and another in 1856 on " The Duties and Difficulties
of Young Teachers," may be specially mentioned as
of great value : both were printed by the Society,
and they have gone through two or three editions.

4 mo. 30, 1838.—Surely goodness and mercy have followed
me all the days of my life hitherto.　May my happy lot be
at last to dwell in the house of the Lord for ever !　What shall
I render unto the Lord for all His benefits ?　A little renewed
health after some weeks of frequent languor and pain, have
turned my eye once more to this record, and though I would
gladly have seen a few memorials of the many blessings of
the blank interval, I cannot admit though not registered, that
they have been unnoticed or unthankfully received.　Often
at various resting places in my pilgrimage I have felt the
language of the poet to be a not unfitting expression of my
gratitude; and to the other parts of his beautiful hymn, I
can fervently add a hitherto omitted stanza :—

> " Thy bounteous hand with worldly bliss
> Has made my cup run o'er ;
> And in a *kind and faithful friend*
> Has doubled all my store."

6 mo. 30.—To day my dear R. and I left home for Balby
near Doncaster.　My dear R. remained there while I travelled
a few days to recruit health.　On the 6th of 7th month I
arrived at Banbury, and met with a warm welcome from my
cousin Samuel Beesley.　In company with my cousin I
visited Overthorp, the first time since I left it, a little school-
boy of nine years old.　The next day I visited North
Newton, the village where the school was located when I first
went there a scholar in 1807, six years and four months old.
The houses at both places are inhabited, but the old school-
rooms are deserted depositories of lumber.　I paced alone for

a few minutes the old orchard, that first served me for a
play-ground. How vividly every little long forgotten circumstance was recalled ! I remembered how we cut our names
and injured some fine old elms, one or more girdled—our
consternation when the mischief was mentioned in the
Preparative Meeting (to which body the property belonged),
the alarm we felt when assembled in the school-room on
account of our evil deeds, expecting some sore infliction
which happily we escaped. Around me were now growing
five young elms, the successors of those which I at least had
innocently assisted in destroying. I remembered the house we
built like the one in Sandford and Merton—our gardens with
the wattled hedges—the cave not far off which one day
some of the more venturesome, my elder brother Joseph
among the number, explored with lighted candles.—I remembered too the river Cherwell where he was nearly drowned in
the spring of 1809—drowned at last in the Severn in 1815.
I passed along the fields through which I had so often walked
to and from Banbury meeting. It seemed as though all the
past, the very thoughts and feelings of eight years old came
over me again. Then recurring to the man of thirty-seven,
remembering the boundless, countless mercies of the intervening period, mercies which had followed me and surrounded
me, and marked my path from year to year, I wept tears of
thankful joy.

From Samuel Tuke to John Ford.

8 mo. 9.—Several times last week and again this morning
in thinking of thee and thy cares, these words have come to
my mind, " Be sober, and hope to the end." I am not going
to write thee a homily upon the passage : thou dost not need
to be told how much true strength there is in soberness, or
how much consolation in hope. I am sure in thy arduous

situation thou needs all the strength and comfort too which can be had from the Divine storehouse, and encouraging indeed is the thought that niggardly as man is in his poor gifts, our Heavenly Father loves to be asked and to distribute of whatever our largest desires after true good can ask of Him. Be sober then, my dear friend, and hope to the end. I do not yet despair that thou and thy dearpa rtner may reap some fruits from your present labour, which may prove that it has not been in vain in the Lord—only let it be in Him.

———————

4 mo. 19, 1839.—Accompanied the Directors of the York and North Midland Railway Company, by invitation of my kind friend Thomas Backhouse, on a short inaugural trip. In walking from the terminus towards the village of Fairburn I had an interesting conversation with the noteworthy George Stephenson, in which he unfolded his since well known theory of the geological storehouse of the sun's heat, our vast coalfields. His strong sense, his pure Saxon, his genuine Newcastle dialect, were marked characteristics of his discourse. George Hudson, then approaching the zenith of his power and fame as Railway King, was of the party.

[In the ninth month, 1840, Edwin Tregelles and Thomas Pumphrey paid a religious visit to the school. They spoke encouragingly to my dear R. and me, intimated an approaching time of trial, counselling so to live from day to day as to have no cause of self-reproach when trial came. They spoke very closely to the boys. In Tenth month William Janson, who left school in 1839 died after a very short illness. Somewhat distressed at the little apparent impression made upon several of the boys by this event, I said one First-day evening whilst addressing them, "perhaps it has not come near

enough to you." Within a very short period four of the
company were seized with fatal illness, and before the year
1841 closed were all summoned away. * * * One of them
arrived at peace through sore conflict. The other three had
found peace through their Saviour's love, before the time of
trial and sickness came. * * *

A few brief months ago all of them were in the full enjoyment of youth and health,—two or three looking with eager
anticipation towards the fair promising period succeeding
school-boy days;

> " supremum
> Carpere iter comites parati,"

prepared I trust through the alone merits and mercy of our
Saviour, and through the sanctifying power of His Holy
Spirit, for an inheritance eternal in the heavens. My dear,
kind, gentle Rachel was an inexpressible comfort to me and
these dear ones in this time of sore trial. She won the love
of the poor invalid boys and the lasting gratitude of their
parents. I believe the whole series of events was blessed to
the school, to the invalids and to ourselves. 1864.]

[I was taken unwell 12 mo. 3, 1841 with low-fever. The
half year had been one of intense trial. Many of the elder
scholars exercised no beneficial influence in the school: a few
of them a most injurious one. In looking back I cannot see
that either the teachers or myself neglected our duty. To
myself the half-year was one of continual conflict with the
known evil in the school. The manifestations of it in a few
were of a malignant character—a fearful want of love either
of God or man—unkind to their school-fellows—hostile to
the government. And yet there were a few who held their
ground, who if powerless to stem evil, kept clear of its influence. Their characters since have borne the same testimony.

Two of this small number have entered on their eternal inheritance.

During my illness, the result of long continued pressure, my dear brother Thomas Ford died at Worcester, on the 6th of Twelfth month. I was confined to bed and could only weep that I had not been with him and that I must leave him to strangers to inter. 1864.]

1843.—[In the summer vacation of this year, we spent some weeks with our cousin Sarah Wheeler at Bristol. We made several pleasant excursions—to Sidcot,—to the Banwell caves,—across the channel to Chepstow, Tintern, &c., and to the Cheddar Rocks and the Paper Mills. Here for the first time I met with William Tanner, little dreaming what a treasure of companionship and friendship was in store for me in him. 1864.]

To one of his Teachers.

11 mo. 26—I have not much to say in reply to thy little note, except to tell thee that it raised in my heart fervent desires for thee and for myself, that we may increasingly seek after watchfulness and prayer, for therein consists not only our own safety, but in no small degree the safety of those intrusted to us. That is, our *own* watchfulness over our *own* hearts is, I believe, blessed to them, and is as a hedge about them. So much for both of us : and now one word for thyself. Do not forget that one of the most pleasant offices of the great adversary is that of " the accuser of the brethren." Suffer him not in this capacity to gain an advantage over thee. Take thy burdens to the cross, (I can from some small experience testify that it is a blessed errand) ; and then if the accuser reproach thee, refer him to thy Captain, who will assuredly rebuke him.

12 mo. 31.—First-day evening. I felt some freedom and earnestness in commending to the boys the solemn thoughts connected with the closing year. My heart was lifted up in prayer for them and for myself. I enjoyed a calm and solemn feeling during the rest of the evening. Some of those "not lost but gone before" were very sweetly brought to my remembrance. My spirit was increasingly tendered, and under a sense of access I bowed the knee in solemn thanksgiving for the abundant mercy that has followed me all my life long, and which I thankfully believed was still continued to me. Humble confession of unworthiness,—of many transgressions,—was followed by earnest entreaty for forgiveness for the sake of Him who shed His blood for sinners. My friends, my brothers,—the boys,—the family,—my dearest— all were livingly brought before me,—and the language of intercession was raised on their behalf and the Divine blessing craved. The feeling of entire dependence, the utter renunciation of every plea but one, was the clothing of my spirit, and I was enabled to adopt the language,

> " Other refuge have I none,
> Hangs my helpless soul on Thee! "

Oh may this inexpressible favour, this contrite and humble spirit be oftener mine and increasingly prized. May the remembrance of this evening's song encourage me to press onwards! May the closing year find me lying down in peace to sleep in the blessed assurance, "Thou, Lord, only makest me dwell in safety"! May the new year begin with renewed dedication of heart to Him who alone is worthy.

1 mo. 14, 1844—First day. A little chastened pleasure this evening, although a laborious one, spent with the boys from tea time till near nine. I heard some of them repeat from Cowper's "Hope," and read to them Cowper's account of himself similar to the description of a condition in the

poem; "As when a felon &c."   I was led unexpectedly and
with deep feeling, to speak to the boys of the importance of
knowing that great and joyful change accompanying the
sense of reconciliation with our Father in Heaven through
Jesus Christ our Lord.

> "'Tis Heaven, all Heaven, descending on the wings
> Of the glad legions of the King of kings;
> '*Tis more.*"—

I pointed out how this might be attained by living from day
to day in the love and fear of God, cherishing every gentle
intimation of His Holy Spirit, welcoming it as an honoured
guest.   And now one more Sabbath evening is closing; how
many more may intervene between this and the dawn of the
never ending rest, the eternal Sabbath, I need not ask : sufficient to know that a "rest remaineth," and that Christ is
the way (the true and the living) to that rest.

I think I have lately experienced those times of refreshing
from the presence of the Lord, in which the Christian is
favoured to know his sins blotted out in the blood of the
Lamb.   In some small ability to believe this, and to pray
"help thou mine unbelief," I feel able to rejoice that mine
is a laborious allotment, and at times a capacity to labour is
granted, so that I can as now,

> "Forget my labour as I toil along,
> Weep tears of joy, and burst into a song!"

11 mo. 16, 1845—Seventeen years ago this day, I first took
my seat in York Meeting as a resident, an almost penniless,
friendless stranger.   "What shall I render to the Lord for
all His benefits?"   He has spared me hitherto.   He has blessed
me abundantly in basket and store, and has given me one of
His most precious temporal gifts.   And though unwatchful,
volatile, careless and sinful, He leaves me not but grants me
from time to time seasons of refreshment from His presence,

in which a lively hope in His mercy, for my Saviour's sake, fills my heart with gratitude to Him.   Oh that I might this evening, under some tendering sense of His love, renew my covenant with Him, who I believe assigned me my path and post here.   Oh that more singleness of heart and true allegiance were mine.   Forgive, O Heavenly Father, for the sake of Him who shed His most precious blood to save us, my many transgressions, my forgetfulness of Thee.   Help me to seek after, and graciously grant me more frequent and more fervent communion with Thee.   Increase in me the longing after holiness, the hunger and thirst after righteousness to which Thy blessing is promised.   Save me from lukewarmness and indifference.   Keep me humble and dependent upon Thee. Help me with increased diligence and with a single eye to Thy glory, faithfully to labour in this Thy fold.   And whether it may please Thee to continue my service here a few more years, or whether Thou mayst please to summon me away in the midst of my days, grant me for Thy mercies sake in Jesus Christ our Lord, to be found with my loins girt about and my lamp burning.

SECTION III.—BOOTHAM.

The period during which the School was carried on in Lawrence Street was now drawing to its close. Continued indisposition in the family in 1841, had directed attention to the sanitary condition of the buildings and of the surrounding locality. Previously to this, the visitation of Cholera in 1832 had been gradually forcing on the public mind throughout the country, the importance of good drainage and adequate breathing space for the maintenance of health. The small rooms, low ceilings, and narrow passages of the Lawrence Street premises were felt to be insufficient for the accommodation of so large a family ; whilst the proximity of a tract of low, undrained land called the "Foss Islands"— a name full of reminiscenses to old Scholars—was in the opinion of many sufficient in itself to condemn the locality. The managing Committee was empowered by the Quarterly Meeting to look out for more eligible premises. The result was the purchase of an estate in Bootham on the North side of the City of York, on which stood a mansion erected by Sir John Johnstone of Hackness near Scarborough. The nett cost including alterations in the buildings and the erection of School Rooms was about £4500,*

* Subsequent additions to the buildings, and purchases of adjoining property have raised the cost price of the Bootham Estate to £8494.

towards which by the liberality of Friends, dona-
tions were received amounting to £2679. The
School was opened in the new Premises in First
Month, 1846.

1 mo. 11, 1846—The last Sabbath day at Lawrence Street
after a residence of seventeen years.

I desire to commemorate this evening the merciful kindness
of our Father in Heaven to my household and myself during
our residence here. I attempted this acknowledgment in a
few words, at the close of our last evening reading under this
roof. May the remembrance of the tender mercies of Him
whose mercies are over all His works, go with us to our new
abode: and may we be enabled so to live to His glory as
that our hopes in His mercy through the dear Redeemer may
be strengthened from day to day. Help us, Heavenly Father,
help my beloved partner and myself and all our fellow
labourers to seek daily to Thee for strength and ability to do
Thy work! May our dependence be upon Thee alone. And
oh for myself, the weakest and unworthiest, keep me humble
and meek and sober-minded. Increase in me a longing after
holiness, lead me away from all self-confidence and self-seeking.
Qualify me more and more if it please Thee for Thy service.
Forgive all my past transgressions for Jesus' sake: and when
my work here is done, may Thy mercy be near to sustain me
at the last, and grant me a good hope that one of the many
mansions in Thy house may be prepared for me when my
earthly house of this tabernacle shall be dissolved in death.

3 mo. 21, 1847—I am forty-six years old to day. I have
been reading over some of the memorials of the past, and
have felt earnest desires that I might be enabled with
increased energy to pursue the heavenward journey. In

reviewing the past year I cannot but lament the want of earnest diligence, much lukewarmness and many sins of omission and commission : at the same time I recall many blessings;—peace and harmony, prosperity and health have been granted to the flock entrusted to my care. There has been less of apparent evil and more of what is hopeful and pleasing than perhaps at any former period. Oh that I could live up to a true sense of "what shall I render to the Lord for all His benefits?"

Among the blessings of the past year I would number a few days of illness in the summer. For several hours I had much pain, yet resignation and peace and some increase of filial love filled my heart. It was indeed good to be afflicted. I am now much relieved from the daily routine of teaching. Whilst I gratefully accept this relief and feel comforted and thankful in its results, may I be doubly diligent on other points, and turn to good account the increased time at my disposal to the truest interests of the school.

Life is rapidly hasting away. How are the great purposes of life being answered—the glory of God—the good of my fellow men—and my own eternal peace? Lukewarmness and indifference are too frequently my besetting and prevailing sins. Nevertheless I can thankfully acknowledge that at times I feel more earnestness of spirit, and also a measure of peace in yielding to little openings to call the minds of the scholars to serious thought. Our evening readings are some-times owned. I believe it was so this evening. May I more diligently seek after more frequent communion with my Saviour. I sometimes feel Him to be precious to me—my only ground of hope.

8 mo. 19, 1849—The vacation is over, the school opens to-morrow. I have been reading this evening the closing scene

of Dr. Arnold's life. He had just completed his forty-seventh year. I am in the midst of my forty-ninth. He could write "vixi:" I can write neither "vixi" nor "vici." He had no further ambition to gratify or rather, as he says, "I thank God *that* is fully mortified." He had no desire to rise higher in the world, but to step back from his present place. The reading of these things made me very thoughtful—very sad—almost to despondency. I have no wish to step to any higher station, but I do most earnestly desire to be found more faithfully, more zealously, and with far more singleness of purpose fulfilling the duties of my post, before called upon to give an account of my stewardship; that by increased fidelity and zeal and singleness of eye I may more testify of my love to Him whose preserving love and care have kept me hitherto. For the sake of Jesus Christ Thy dear Son, our Saviour and Intercessor, pardon, O Lord, all my past transgressions and sins and short comings; blot them out for His sake, O Lord, and let them be no more remembered against me. "Create in me a clean heart, O God; and renew a right Spirit within me." Kindle renewed desires for communion with Thee. Help my faltering resolutions—incline my heart daily to increased watchfulness unto prayer—endue me with kindness and gentleness, with wisdom and firmness to fulfil as in Thy sight from hour to hour my duties in this school and family. Help me to watch against every incipient temptation to evil in myself, that thus I may more effectually warn and assist those whom Thou hast entrusted to our care. If it please Thee, O Lord, bestow on my beloved partner and myself health of body and stedfastness of heart and purpose, that we may do for Thee cheerfully all the service Thou mayst require at our hands. Grant that we may be increasingly, each other's joy in Thee, O Lord! and if trial of any kind await us—sickness or separation, give us a good hope in Thy pardoning mercy, and help us to receive all as from Thy hand; "for the sake of Jesus Christ our Lord."

8 mo. 21—This evening feeling (perhaps unduly) perplexed, the passage of Scripture, suddenly (shall I say strangely) occurred to me, "The peace of God which passeth all understanding, shall keep your hearts and minds through Jesus Christ." It affected me forcibly, and led me silently yet earnestly to petition, that I might be enabled to live in so close communion with God as to know for myself this peace. I then remembered the lines :—

> " Soul, then know thy full salvation,
> Rise o'er sin and fear and care,
> Joy to find in every station
> Something still to do, or bear."

I prayed that my restless anxieties might be taken away, and that I might increase in patience and humility.

11 mo. 27.—Within this year my property has been reduced (by the Railway delinquencies of ——) by more than half: but I can truly and thankfully say, I have been freed from all pain or anxiety about it. We have unitedly sought for a thankful spirit for what is left—for the ability still to labour in this our appointed field—for a capacity to leave the things that are behind and to reach forth unto those that are before, and so to press towards the mark for the prize of our high calling of God in Christ Jesus.

1 mo. 9, 1850.—Our short vacation is near its close; the school reassembles on Second-day. May I take for my abiding memento, "Gird up the loins of your mind," and, "be sober and hope to the end." May I be enabled to keep from hour to hour a single eye to my Master, if I may. call my Saviour by this name—that so my constant aim may be to do work as for Him. I crave Thy help, O Lord, to lay aside

every weight and every easily besetting sin, that so I may
throughout the commencing year, run with renewed patience
the heavenly race, looking constantly to Jesus, seeking
conformity to His mind and will and image, laying aside
every inordinate affection, providing treasures that wax not
old,—treasure in Heaven that faileth not, where no thief
approacheth neither moth corrupteth.   May I seek oftener
than the day communion with Thee.   For Thy dear Son's
sake bless this school and family, and my beloved partner
and myself.   Whatever of anxiety or trial may be our portion,
keep us from sin, from all that could grieve Thy Holy Spirit,
and give us grateful and rejoicing hearts for all Thy many
mercies.   Amen!

9 mo. 28, 1851.—As years accumulate I find myself—as
others have been before me—less frequent in noting down
incidents and feelings marking the onward course of life.   It
is not that I have no mercies to record—no blessed seasons of
access to the place of prayer—no contriting sense of the
abundance and largeness of Divine Love—no humble confidence in a Saviour Lord.   It is not because I have none of
these to note down—thankfully I can say this.   Nor is it
because I have nothing to say of unsubdued self—of sin in-
dwelling still—of conflict—of defeat.   Alas this mingled
condition is too much mine yet.   Faint yet pursuing—
rejoicing too at times in a cheering hope of victory at the
last.   Weighed down sometimes with the formidable array
of responsibilities presented by my post here, and yet again
encouraged to work on, and glad that such a post is assigned
me.   I am often reminded that I hold life on an increasingly
uncertain tenure ; health is more easily disturbed ; slighter
causes affect it.   Oh may I increasingly, and even now as I
write, seek to dedicate the remainder unreservedly to the
love and fear and service of a long suffering and most
merciful God and Saviour !

To JOSIAH FORSTER, in reply to enquiries respecting the
course of religious instruction on First-days.

11 mo. 10, 1851.—Some of the intervals of First-day are
occupied by the scholars in committing to memory passages
of Scripture of my own selecting, illustrative of Christian
doctrine and practice. They also learn hymns and selec-
tions from Cowper's Task, &c.; these are repeated to the
teachers. I spend some time with the scholars assembled.
Each boy has his Bible and biblical atlas. They read to me
in turns. We endeavour to go through, although but
cursorily, the principal parts of the history, both of the Old
and New Testament. The course of reading is interrupted
by frequent questions, and by a variety of information,
historical, geographical, &c., illustrative of the period before
us: and as opportunity offers, remarks are made pointing
out the moral and religious instruction derivable from the
narrative. In the course of these readings, it is obvious we
must sometimes encounter passages which we do not read.
On these occasions, as I have felt ability to do it, I have
pointed out in general terms the lesson to be drawn, and
have endeavoured to show that all these things were written
for our instruction; at the same time warning against that
most fearful perversion of Scripture, which would seek to
gratify an impure imagination by reverting to these passages.
The propriety of this course has I think been proved by facts
which have come to my knowledge.

I mostly avail myself of time on First-day evening for
special remarks upon any circumstances which seem to
afford a good opportunity for illustrating Christian principles
and Christian conduct—sometimes by reference to facts,
which the school is not cognizant of, but which are known
only to myself and the individual alluded to but not named.

E

I have sometimes been a little encouraged by finding a boy dating his commencement of some good habit, or his abandonment of some bad one, from these First-day evening remarks.   *   *   *   *

The number of my assistants, and the ability, tact, good temper and kindness, and I think I may add the Christian concern which actuates them,—these circumstances combined, by diminishing occasions of angry feeling, afford proportionably more scope for the application of scriptural precepts and principles in conducting the discipline of the school. Appeals to those principles have not to contend with the feeling that both parties have equally violated them.

I recur with much pleasure to our little conference; it is very refreshing to find that we are not labouring alone in this great work, but that we have the kind sympathy and the wise counsel of our friends thus freely offered. If any suggestions have arisen in thy mind, or should arise on perusing this imperfect sketch of our proceedings and aims, I should feel greatly obliged by thy communicating. We are still but learners and are still glad to learn.

---

1 mo. 23, 1852.—The return of the scholars and the resumption of duties have been pleasant; and we have been permitted to enjoy a sense of our Heavenly Father's love, and an interest in Christ our Saviour. Last First-day evening, feeling helped in my work and believing that it was graciously owned, my heart was filled with joy and peace and thanksgiving.

On Seventh-day last I was enabled in patience and quietness to labour with a beloved boy, successfully I trust. This evening again with the same, and yet hopefully. I sought the Divine blessing on my labours, and when I found hardness yielding under kind and gentle words I could but rejoice. Among other blessings, privileges and enjoyments I number that of having as aids, three young men, and two juniors, all of whom kindly and efficiently co-operate with me. The attachment of the two juniors is particularly grateful to me. * * * * Till Adam Smith is still as a pillar and *buttress*. His strong sense, animation and good humour, combined with energetic and vigorous capacity for teaching, are of excellent service in his post. * * * * With all these and many unnumbered causes of thankfulness and gratitude, I have a partner beyond all expression dear, Heaven's most peculiar and most especial blessing to me, fitted to my every want, dearer and dearer every day, the frequent solace of my fainting spirits, my daily cheerer in my onward path. For all these what shall I render? The morning of life is over; it has ceased to be high noon; the sun has passed the meridian and is pointing westward : more faithful service, more constant love—more frequent communion, more watchfulness, more frequent prayer.—Grant me these O Lord : in Thy dear Son's name and for His sake I ask, all unworthy as I am.

3 mo. 21.—One more birth-day! Fifty-one accomplished years! The end nearer! How near? What preparation? What hope? What ground of hope? A quiet, thankful, peaceful feeling is my portion this evening. I sought and found some ability to advocate the cause of the Redeemer with the boys. The solemnity of our evening reading gladdened me. I acknowledged my sense of this, and pointed it out as a cause for thankful gratitude. Weak as is my faith, faint as are my hopes, wavering as is my allegiance, yet faith and hope and allegiance I still strive to maintain.

I read the hymn (at reading time) "There is a fountain." The last two stanzas, moved me almost to tears:

> " Lord, I believe Thou hast prepared,
> Unworthy though I be,
> For me a blood-bought, free reward,
> A golden harp for me:" &c.

I can truly say, in Christ and in Him alone centre all my hopes.

5 mo. 29.—I attended the Yearly Meeting in London and took more part in the proceedings than on former occasions. I felt it to be a privilege, though not without its snares, to be associated with the wise and good in two or three special services. In these I earnestly sought first, for that wisdom which comes from above, and also for humility, that self might be laid low and that all might be done to the glory of God. An unmerited favour (there can be none but unmerited) awaited my return home. All my fears and apprehensions of physical or moral evil were unfulfilled— neither ailment of body nor trouble in regard to conduct had occurred to report. I solemnly returned thanks for this mercy with soul and body prostrate before the throne.

6 mo. 13.—Another "last First-day" has come to its close. Quiet, peaceful thankfulness is my portion this evening. We had a short but solemn time at reading and a still more solemn pause at its close, when I felt constrained to invite all to unite in lifting up our hearts to God in grateful thanksgiving.

1 mo. 16, 1853.—Our short winter vacation of two weeks closes this evening. Once more about to engage in the solemn duties and responsibilities of my post, let the injunction, "work while it is called to-day for the night cometh," be ever increasingly present. The afternoon has

come. Twenty-four years of service here, may well remind
me that I am no longer a young man—even if other
symptoms did not sufficiently declare it. If bodily power
and mental vigour have passed their meridian, how is it
with the far nobler part, the immortal spirit? Longing
sometimes for rest—for more of the heavenly, less of the
earthly mind : enjoying at times (alas too seldom) a taste of
the blessedness of communion with the Saviour, and enabled
to trust in Him for time and eternity. Too frequently cold
and lifeless, I want more constant watchfulness, more
frequent and more fervent prayer. Whilst anxious and
seeking to be diligent in my care of others, I have too often
to fear "mine own vineyard have I not kept." May it be
my more than daily exercise to see to this: as a means let
me try to press through the obstacles so often in the way of
private retirement and prayer. "Careful and troubled about
many things" is my too constant condition. May the one
thing needful obtain a more decided earnest attention. * *
* * Often on First-day evening after the hour spent with
the scholars in which I have felt helped to speak perhaps a
word in season, what a blessed sense has been given me of
quiet peace. May I, now commencing my twenty-fifth year
of service, seek with ever renewed earnestness to maintain
the warfare—to take the whole armour of God—so that
whether permitted to labour longer, or called to give a final
account of my stewardship before the year closes, may I,
trusting in the dear Saviour alone—renouncing every other
claim—be found nevertheless with loins girt about and lamp
burning.

3 mo. 21.—A time of trial and perplexity has been ours
since I last wrote. For six weeks, hospital cares for thirty
patients in the mumps, distributed over that time—in one
instance fifteen at once—engrossed our time and thoughts.

* * * Duties besides those of my very responsible post
seem to increase upon me. My connexion with the Retreat,
with the Bible Society—the Museum—the discipline of our
little church—present claims upon time and thought, and
bring too their snares. "Rendering service" (in civil,
religious or scientific matters) "as to the Lord and not as to
men" is indeed a great attainment. Self and self-exaltation,
self-complacency and self-seeking would fain mingle with
and mar every good. I have been instrumental in promoting
a certain plan of action at the approaching Jubilee Meeting
of the Bible Society. Engaged to take a part in the proceedings, I feel truly desirous that I may keep a single eye
to the service of Christ; that no thought of self-exaltation,
on the one hand, no shrinking from service for fear of exposing
my incapacity on the other, may interfere.

6 mo. 26.—Long intervals between these memoranda cause
many links in the chain to drop. The Bible meeting just
impending when I wrote last proved a very successful one.
The Earl of Carlisle presided; the plan sketched was carried
out; nearly two thousand persons were said to be present;
the funds of the Society were increased, and I hope renewed
interest excited. This was cause of grateful thankfulness.
In the Fifth month I again attended the Yearly Meeting
and again found it a time of renewal of faith and hope, and
of increased attachment to our own little corner of the
Christian fold. Some little service seemed to fall to my lot
and some ability given to perform it. I was favoured with
good health nearly the whole time, freedom from headache
with only one day's exception. * * * *

This evening we have again an empty house. The scholars
left on Sixth-day. In reference to those who leave us this
summer I think we may look forward hopefully. I believe

that our morning and evening readings and our First-day
evening exercises, have not unfrequently been marked by
deep and solemn attention, whilst the truths of Christianity—
its duties—the spirit it inculcates—the love of Christ to us—
our debt of love to Him, were set forth, not without a sense
of help from Him, and that not unsought.   One of the elder
scholars on taking leave mentioned his grateful estimate of
the First-day evening Addresses.   May I derive encouragement from this incident, and give all the praise to Him
without whose help all such efforts are but

> " Tinkling cymbal and high sounding brass
>   Smitten in vain !   Such music cannot charm
>   The eclipse, that intercepts truth's heavenly beam."

With one solitary exception which looks like incipient
insanity, love and harmony and affection have largely prevailed amongst us all reciprocally.   No painful revelations
of the pestilence that walks in darkness have marked the half
year, nor yet indications that awakened suspicions of its
presence.

This evening though feeling to need relaxation and repose,
I cannot entirely dismiss a sense of vacuity and sadness that
" resembles sorrow only as the mist resembles the rain," at the
thought of the beloved ones dispersed and the sight of the
empty rooms.   The privilege of association with young
life—the power of exciting and the heart to reciprocate
affection, transient though it may be—are elements of daily
happiness, the peculiar advantages of my post.   With these
too are permitted at times to mingle the thought that my
beloved partner and myself may not only not have hindered,
but have helped some of the lambs of Christ's fold in their
early efforts, in the first buddings of youthful love for Him
their dear, their ever loving Redeemer.

The vacation now before us will soon be with the past !

Chequered as its predecessors it will probably be. The recollection of the last encourages the belief that even trials may be transmuted into blessings by the wondrous alchemy of the love of God in Jesus Christ.

Poor and empty—faith and hope and love not extinct but feeble,—I would fain come this evening before the mercy seat, and with the Intercessor there, for without Him I dare not go, acknowledge remissness, coldness, unworthiness, sinfulness—plead for pardon in His name—plead His most precious blood—cast all my cares down *there*—small and great—perplexities, anxieties, hopes, fears—and ask for one thing—ability to say, with deep and earnest sincerity, "Thy will be done." I would fain offer too, feeble and faint though it may be, a note of thanksgiving for innumerable and ever accumulating mercies that have followed me all my life long to this very hour.

To Josiah Forster.

8 mo, 22. 1853.—In reference to thy inquiries respecting religious instruction, I have been looking at a copy of the letter which I sent thee in the Third month. I do not think I can add much to the delineation of the plans pursued at York, as there detailed, nor have I seen reason to distrust or to modify those plans, considering the party who communicates and the parties who receive the instruction. The proceedings described in the letter referred to, involve a larger amount of direct viva-voce instruction, than I have seen or heard of in our schools in general. I rely for this on the testimony of some of my young men as well as upon my own observation. I do not mean to represent this circumstance either as a good or bad feature per se, but as a peculiar one in regard to the extent to which it is carried here. I may further observe that it is not so much the result of preconceived ideas as to

what might be best, as it has been the growth or development of time, experience and circumstances. I can readily admit the belief that had I attempted at thirty-two that which I am practising at fifty-two, in all probability the plan would have been a failure. Do not understand by this that I have any exalted idea of the efficacy of the plans I am now practising; all I can say is, that from time to time I am permitted a measure of peace in following them out, and am not altogether without occasional evidence of pleasant results. I believe that my plan of religious instruction is availing as far as it is the result of deep, heartfelt experience of the truths communicated, and as far as ability is sought and granted rightly to communicate it. These expressions appear to me to involve the idea of earnest endeavour to *live* these things as well as to *speak* of them.

I think it will follow from what I have written, that I could not venture to prescribe to a teacher, especially to a young one, to follow out a similar plan : it might be injurious entrusted to youthful zeal and inexperience. At the same time I am not sure that more of direct teaching would not have been practised by wise, judicious and religious-minded teachers, had they taken larger views of the liberty, the duty and the responsibility associated with the possession of the Truth.

---

10 mo. 31.—Four months have sped away since my last memorandum here. In the interval many things have occurred worthy of a passing note, if it were only to arrest a thought or a feeling that might instruct the traveller or enliven the yet remaining road. Last week was one of most painful labour—oppressing the spirits—exhausting the intellectual powers—followed of course by prostration of health. The moral " pestilence that walks in darkness," manifested

by some of its incipient symptoms,—happily incipient, not
rife—demanded prudence—promptitude—decision—adaptation. Again and again under a sense of extreme need, the
knee was bent in secret for wisdom and prudence equal to
the need. Last evening sitting alone—late—all retired but
myself—reviewing the labours of the week—the toils and the
help of the evening—feeling too though weak and exhausted,
yet a merciful relief from bodily pain of which I had had
much—I felt a more overpowering sense of the love of God
in Christ Jesus than was (I think) ever before my portion.
It absorbed all power of words: it was beyond expression:
bended knees and streaming eyes were the only external
evidences: thought upon thought, glowing, rapid, well-
defined, like lightning flashes in quick succession, passed
through the mind—entire confidence in the Saviour—that I
could in that happy moment trust Him without a single
mistrustful doubt for time and for eternity.

Last Seventh-day evening I brought my labours on the
aforenamed subject nearly to a close by an interview with
the members of the senior class, when though labouring under
the depression of indisposition, I was enabled in somewhat
general and yet in intelligible language, to press upon them
their responsibility in regard to the purity and delicacy of
thought and speech and act, which ought ever to characterize
the Christian schoolboy. Whilst thus appealing to them and
marking the beaming and beautiful countenances of some,
whose hearts I believe responded to the appeal, I felt the
love of Christ towards them so manifestly present, that the
sense of it nearly choked my utterance. To-day I have
finished this painful labour—tracked out the foe to I trust
his last lurking place—tried to do all that my hand found to
do—and then once more commended myself and my charge

to Him who assures us by inference, that whilst He keeps
the city the watchman shall *not* wake in vain.

11 mo. 21.—I have employed the evening hour from 10
to 11 lately in looking over and making an abstract of some
journals of vacations commencing 1820. I find some interest
in looking back at the unfoldings of character, moral, intellectual and spiritual, as indicated in these narratives. Last
evening having spent a little time in this way, I felt before
retiring a strong sense of that preserving love and mercy—
for some years "unseen " truly—that at length " conveyed
me safe and led me up to man ;" and more, far more than
that—led me to intercourse and acquaintance with the wise
and good, kindled in my heart love for them, and slow and
backward to learn as I was, taught me something of the
preciousness and excellence of a Saviour's love.

To WILLIAM S. LEAN.

12 mo. 19, 1853.—Thy continued interest in Bootham is very
gratifying to us. I think I may confirm thy supposition
that things are going on satisfactorily on the whole. Good
and evil are still manifest—and the evil does not predominate.
I have had again as on many past occasions, thankfully to
recognize that watchful providence, which does not permit
evil long to remain unnoted, even that class of evil which
emphatically walks in darkness. I have had to rejoice too in
the fact that among the senior scholars there was moral
courage enough, first to warn, and then to denounce to me
one of their number, who not satisfied with the negative
gratification of being wrong himself, must needs point the
sneer at one who was unobtrusively pursuing the right.
　*　　*　　*　　*　　*　　But these, dear W., are not
the things to discourage us : if there were no conflict there
could be no victory. I rejoice with thee in believing that

among those whom thou knew, and among those who have
since entered the school, there are some "honourable characters,"—and I will use this word in an apostolic sense—true
disciples, even though young ones, of our Lord and Saviour
Jesus Christ. ——, a new scholar, and —— whom thou
knew, are two of whom I could say with Dr. Arnold, " I
could stand hat in hand to them," so highly do I honour
every appearance of the meek and gentle and courteous
spirit of the young Christian. * * * * And
now a word or two on another topic—one of deep interest—
thyself. If thou told me that thou wast sensible of no
opposition in thy own heart—that thou found it perfectly
easy to live the life of a Christian, I should think of thee as
I should think of a school said to be cleared of evil—a little
paradise regained—I should think there was a mistake some-
where. And here let me remind thee, and if it be a repetition
excuse it, that thy Saviour was once exactly the age thou art
to-day. The record of Him forbids the idea that He was a
stranger to conflict—"tempted in all points like as we are
yet without sin." Mayst thou, dear W., ever increasingly
look to Him in every conflict, and may His loving spirit be
very near to strengthen and to help thee.

Thy mention of conflict—of willingness of spirit and
weakness of flesh, brought vividly before me my own early
days. When about two years older than thou art now, I
was in the thick of the conflict. The banks of the beautiful
Medway were to me the place where prayer was wont to be
made, and many a tear shed, over innate depravity, an over-
sensitive temperament, and many a besetting sin. Write
over all such scenes " Hæc meminisse juvabit!" The pain
and the strife and the heart sinkings will be forgotten in the
sense of that mercy and love which then at times unseen,
sustained. Thou wilt at length find, and mayst thou find it

earlier and more abundantly than I did—not ultimate victory but—success and progress.

I assure thee it was with no self-complacent spirit that I read thy encouraging remarks respecting our First-day evening exercises. They were often conducted by me under a deep sense of weakness, unworthiness and incapacity, and yet preceded at times by prayer, and followed by a tranquil feeling of peace and thanksgiving. To know that they were received and valued cheers my spirit and renews my trust. And thus it is that the members of Christ's Church (may I say of "the Church in our house," for I love the term), may help and encourage one another. There needs no apology for thy three volumes of notes. I am sure thou wilt not misapply them; and I am glad I never knew that they were taken till now. The knowledge might have been injurious once—now it is a little testimony which, in conjunction with a few occasional admissions made to me by the scholars, serves as a brook by the way.

12 mo. 31.—A letter from dear William S. Lean a few days ago moved me deeply. He mentions that he possesses three volumes of notes of First-day evening Addresses. I was humbled and yet pleased with this—glad I never knew it whilst it could influence my Addresses—thankful for it now as an encouragement to labour on. Is "non omnis moriar" altogether an unhallowed sentiment? Is it wrong to hope to live in the memory of the wise and good? Is it permissible to be pleased with the gift of ability to attract and attach the young? Are we to press after entire abstraction? Oh may I, if I must acknowledge that I still feel the force of these motives—seek with ever increasing earnestness to have them all baptized in the love of Christ, and all entirely

subordinated to His service. To my Heavenly Father, this
evening, through the ever dear Redeemer, his son Jesus
Christ, I would offer in the retrospect of the year heartfelt
praise and thanksgiving, and ask for ability to dedicate my
all to His service !   Amen.

The First-day evening Addresses mentioned in the
preceding letter and paragraph, formed a marked
feature in John Ford's course of instruction.   They
were usually given in the School Room when only the
Scholars and Teachers, and occasionally one or two
old pupils, were present.   The subjects were varied;
points of Christian truth—passing events of the day
and the lessons to be deduced from them—anything
that had awakened uneasiness regarding the flock—
and earnest invitations to accept the offers of a
Saviour's love.   Not a few of the old Scholars will
endorse the opinion of one of their number, who
several years after leaving school wrote as follows:—
" I think in looking back to the three years spent
at Bootham, that the times most impressed on my
memory were those First-day evening Addresses,
which often seemed so to touch and solemnize my
mind, that I wished to go to bed without speaking
lest the feeling should be dispelled."

12 mo. 31.—The year is nearly closed. All our scholars
have left.   Peace without and peace within, my dear R.
and I can acknowledge is our pleasant portion.   And yet
whilst quietness and repose are grateful, it is with no feeling
of delight that I hear no echoes of youthful voices. Pleasant

intercourse with them from day to day is so much a daily
pleasure, that the absence of it throws a pensive air over my
spirit. Perhaps the more so from the circumstance, which
not boastingly but rather with the deep humility of gratitude,
I may record, that I have been enabled from time to time to
minister to them of the things entrusted to me for their good.

3 mo. 21, 1854.—To-day I complete my fifty-third year!
Though poor and lifeless I can hardly let the day pass by
quite unnoted—if it were only to number my blessings and
deplore my ingratitude. A day of probation prolonged
whilst many contemporaries are removed—a measure of
health and strength still granted for daily duties—my
beloved R. though just now far from well, yet preserved in
a measure of health demanding thankful gratitude—able and
united officers—allegiance and affection still characterizing
the Scholars—all these and many more blessings are still
prolonged, loudly demanding more zeal, more constancy,
more earnestness, more singleness of purpose, more seeking
after frequent communion. May I bear these thoughts in
mind, and with more tenacity of purpose seek to realize them.
May the spirit of prayer be granted me for that aid without
which all effort is vain.

4 mo. 9.—Yesterday evening I was passing out of the
parlour to bed. I had felt for some time a want of capacity for
communion with God—not careless—but poor, very poor and
helpless. A feeling of sorrow and of longing flashed across
my mind as I was about to close the door. I turned back
under these feelings, kneeled down, and was favoured with
access to the throne, with thoughts and words and feelings
in unison, so that with a contrite heart and with tears of joy
and thankfulness, I availed myself of this glorious privilege
of access in the name of the dear Redeemer. Confession—

entreaty for pardon—for strength—intercession for my beloved ones—were offered under an overpowering sense of
Divine love and mercy.

This evening, without making any allusion to the foregoing, I set before the scholars the duty of availing ourselves
of such like offers of Divine love ;—that whilst daily seeking,
even under a sense of poverty, unfitness and discouragement,
for communion with God in the name of Jesus Christ, and
for His sake—we should avail ourselves especially of these
precious moments when invited as it were to the very
presence chamber.

To WILLIAM KITCHING, JUN.

5 mo. 19, 1854.—I was much interested in thy little review
of the past. It seemed to indicate to me something very much
the reverse of a careless or indifferent state of mind ; rather,
that condition which, seeking to profit by a review of the
past, both of its lapses and its successes, is earnestly pressing
forward. It is a rare felicity, seldom experienced by those
who engage in this world's warfare, never to suffer repulse
or defeat. Perhaps it is still more rare in regard to the
conflicts in which the Christian is called to engage. To profit
by repulses and defeats so as to renew the strife with fresh
courage, and with still firmer faith, is a safe and wise course.
It is cheering to me to believe that some such experience as
this has been thine; and I interpret thy expression of feeling
thyself again on " firm ground " to mean, that by watchfulness and prayer and by frequently looking to that loving
Saviour, who was tempted as we are, yet without sin,
temptation is successfully resisted. * * * * It is a good
omen of success in a calling, when we feel we prefer and love
it. This preference and love are absolutely essential to success
in the teacher. It removes obstacles, smooths down difficulties,

and gives courage in times of trial; I am therefore glad to find that thou still entertains these feelings in regard to thy future allotment.

---

7 mo. 2.—The session just closed has been one of some continued anxiety in regard to health. * * * The senior class has been a company of contrasts; high intellectual power, amiability, kindliness and religious thoughtfulness have been the characteristics of a few. On the other hand two or three have manifested very opposite tendencies, and have occasioned much care and anxious thought as well as not unfrequent painful labour. In reviewing the course pursued with both these classes, I may thankfully acknowledge that I have not withheld the language of kind encouragement from the one, and that I have again and again been helped in labouring with and for the other. Our evening readings and our First-day gatherings in the school-room have often I believe been owned by a solemnizing sense of our Heavenly Father's love in Jesus Christ.

With many symptoms of powers past their prime, may I yet not turn faint-hearted, but be willing to abide at my post till He who allotted it shall be pleased to grant a discharge. May my dear partner and myself be permitted to realize the promise, or rather to fulfil the injunction in which a most precious promise is involved, "casting all your care on Him, for He careth for you." "Cast thy burden upon the Lord, and He shall sustain thee."

To WILLIAM S. LEAN.

11 mo. 3, 1854.—In the first place, a few words about thy prospects. My dear R. and myself are much pleased with thy sentiments on this subject. Circumstances certainly seem

to point plainly towards the arrangement, and whilst we are
not to allow ourselves to drift in the current of circumstances,
irrespective of their tendency, yet when their tendency
appears to be in the right direction, when no manifest duty
is neglected in following them out, we may commit ourselves
confidingly to our Heavenly Father's care, trusting that He
will lead us on safely if right, and arrest our course if it is
wrong. I can gratefully record my own experience of the
safety of thus accepting openings of service, in preference to
attempting to cut and hew them out for myself. Therefore
far from disapproving of a decision in which thou hast the
very important element of thy father's and mother's approval,
I shall trust that it is a right decision, and that it may prove
a field of service, and lead to fields of service in which those
who love thee will rejoice to see thee labouring. Thy letter
appears to contain evidence that thou hast given the subject
a very careful consideration, and though we felt sure thou
wouldst so consider it, yet it is a satisfaction to have these
proofs of it. Entering upon a new engagement in the spirit
indicated in thine is I believe a safe course, and one which
will bear reverting to whatever may be the result. * * *
When I feel as though I could rejoice in the aspect of a School,
I find something of that "trembling" mixed with it, of
which the Apostle speaks. I think I feel a little of that joy
just now. I may be mistaken, but I believe that for several
years we have not had so unexceptionable a Senior Class—
open, confiding, generous, intelligent,—and several I believe
serious-minded. The only one of the lot whose antecedents
would make it folly not to be somewhat mistrustful, has so
conducted himself since the vacation, that I took an opportunity of his coming to the Library a few days ago, to tell
him that I had entertained the belief that he was making
better principles the guide of his conduct, and that I wished

to encourage him so to do. He did not look as though conscious of unmerited confidence. A flush of pleasure, with
something of the grateful in it, adorned his not unintelligent
face, and strengthened my hopes.

---

12 mo. 31.—My First-day evening labours, of which I
have kept a record, have again and again been blessed with
a spirit of prayer before engaging, help whilst labouring
and peace in retrospect. For all these and many more.
favours and mercies what shall I render? Poor, empty,
cold and lifeless—this evening I would at least acknowledge
my indebtedness; and confessing poverty and penury, yet
seek to come just as I am, a poor petitioner but having an
all-powerful Advocate. What would I have? Pardon for
His sake for all the sins—omissions and commissions of the
past—pardon for the want of earnestness in asking—pardon
for a want of a sense of thankfulness and love and gratitude
for so much and so many kindnesses—faith to keep alive in
the hour of depression.—O Heavenly Father, for Thy dear
Son's sake forgive.—Help me with increased vigilance, fidelity
and alacrity (leaving the things that are behind) to press
toward the mark for the prize. May a sense of Thy love
still extended to my dear partner and myself stimulate us to
more devoted service, if permitted still to serve in the coming
year. "Create in me a clean heart, O God; and renew a
right spirit within me." Enable me to lay aside every
weight and every besetting sin, and with a single eye to Thy
service, to Thy glory, to commence the new year. For Thy
dear Son's sake, our ever living Advocate, accept my poor,
cold, lifeless, not insincere evening prayer: for His sake
pardon its very coldness and lifelessness, and accept it in
Him. Amen.

1 mo. 14, 1855.—To-morrow commences another six months' session. Though daily watchfulness and more than daily prayer must be mine, in order to maintain the daily warfare, first for myself, and then as delegated guardian of others, yet now on the eve of commencing I would earnestly pray for the guiding, protecting, controlling and loving care of my Heavenly Father in the name of His dear Son, to guide and to guard and direct and help and strengthen and preserve my beloved partner and myself through the session.

I travelled with three friends lately, each of whom denounced the system of the school in which he had been educated—each different—each among Friends. One of them said that what good might exist in those subjected to such training, was in spite of, not by favour of the influence of school—in short that evil was predominant. I listened with silent concern, querying what will be said of York training—what under-currents of evil will be the theme of the men twenty years to come. I think it will be of under-currents only that they will be able to speak. In some recent fearful conflicts with evil, I had reason to believe it was only an under-current—that it was limited and recent. May I be kept in that prayerful vigilance from which even under-currents shall not be long concealed, and endowed with true wisdom to track and to arrest their course. I would fain hope even now, that it might be said *evil* was in spite of, and not by favour of the influence of the school— that the good have a fair chance—that evil is in a minority. Heavenly Father help us still for Thy dear Son's sake, our only Saviour.

2 mo. 26.—Since I last wrote in these pages a depth of sore trial has been permitted us in the breaking out of scarlatina in the school. This is the thirty-eighth day since

its first appearance, and we have still three patients in the nursery. In the interval I have been very unwell. My beloved partner has been able to fulfil her usual daily duties, though sometimes faint, weary and almost desponding : and yet both of us have been enabled from time to time to renew our confidence in our Heavenly Father's love and care.

3 mo. 18.—Since I wrote last, illness increasing, the. Committee resolved to disperse the school, and all that were well left us on the 9th instant. Twelve invalids remained ; they are now reduced to two still with us. Two months' tension has produced its not unexpected effects, abated health and prostration of spirits.

3 mo. 21.—This evening our kind and able committee met once more to consider various circumstances connected with the state of the school. I was present, and in the course of the discussion expressed my apprehension that my beloved R. might not be equal to the post she now occupies, except at a cost that I was not warranted to incur—that I could see no medium between continuing as at present, or entirely withdrawing—that I was not prepared peremptorily to withdraw, but after having stated these views we were satisfied with placing ourselves in the hands of our friends, and for the present to abide by their judgment, trusting that we should be adapted to the burden, or the burden to us; or that way would be more plainly made for our release. The will of the Lord be done !

To WILLIAM KITCHING, JUN.

(about to enter the school as a Junior Teacher.)

7 mo. 26, 1855.—I had intended to converse with thee a little on the subject of thy last letter, when at Ackworth ; but my ability to converse or indeed any other ability was

very limited, quite unequal to ordinary duties. However I do not know that I should have had much to say, except to express my wish to encourage thee to look hopefully forward. * * * * * The right fulfilment of a Teacher's office consists less with the extent of his attainments than with his aptness to teach, the largeness of his sympathy with youth, his love for them, and above all, the love of Christ ruling in his heart and regulating all his proceedings. I look forward with pleasure to thy joining us; and I believe it will be the study of my dear R. F. and myself to do what we can to make thy path pleasant and happy.

On the 3rd of Ninth month I went to Scarborough. I had been extremely unwell. A few days' residence at Scarborough produced a surprising change. I returned home on the 7th. On the morning of that day immediately after breakfast I ascended Oliver's Mount. It was a glorious morning—an almost cloudless sky. I was too early for the crowd of visitors. I reached the summit, retraced the ground almost to the level of Seamer Mere, then returned to the top, walked round the whole drive, and only encountered one set of Tourists just as I had completed the circle. Whilst alone on the summit, struck with the beauty, seclusion and extent of the scene—the blue sky—the expanse of sea—the freshness of the morning air, and superadded, the sense of renovated health,—my heart I think I may say overflowed with gratitude and love. I was constrained to bend the knee on the turf. Prayer and confession—and a sense of pardoning mercy—and heartfelt thanksgiving in the name of the dear Son of God—a renewal of covenant—a fresh desire to love and to serve—all these rendered it a consecrated spot and a consecrated moment, never to be forgotten. The

God of nature and the God of Grace—the great Creator,
and the loved and loving Saviour seemed in some sense
realized.   The scene brought to my mind,

> " From the blue rim where sky and ocean meet,
> Down to the very turf beneath thy feet,
> All speak one language, all with one sweet voice
> Cry to the universal realm, Rejoice ! "

12 mo. 30.—Lifeless myself, dry—empty—hard—the
opening of these pages has revived past mercies, and kindled
some little feeling, some renewed sense of gratitude.   The
year almost closing has been marked by mercies innumerable :
among those mercies I enumerate the capacity to perceive,
to acknowledge and to enjoy them.   Many of them have
been connected with sore trials—songs of praise and deliverance.   Some of them have been connected with deep concern
for others, and permission given and access granted to petition
for them at the footstool of the throne in the dear Redeemer's
name.   The verbal mention of my young friends and of
some who are not young, has seemed to intensify prayer and
intercession.   And now twenty-seven years of service have
nearly closed : but few can remain, possibly very few.
" What is that to thee ? follow thou me."   May I receive
and appropriate the admonition and the command—seek
still to occupy—more diligently, more faithfully, with less
of self-seeking—more of singleness of heart as unto the
Lord.

1 mo. 20, 1856.—At reading time after some conflict—
not a little—I bent the knee, and was strengthened to implore
in the name of the dear Redeemer the blessing of our Heavenly Father on the session just commencing—that He would
guard us against every inroad of evil—that He would imbue
the hearts of the beloved young ones assembled, with the
love of Him and of their dear Redeemer—that He would

so fashion them by His Holy Spirit that they might be His
for ever. I had peace in this offering.

Soon after the re-assembling of the school, measles
broke out, and many of the boys were laid by in
the complaint. All went on favourably for a time
till one of the scholars, the son of Henry Bewley of
Lota, near Dublin, became a cause of anxiety.
Before he was seriously unwell, an inmate of his
father's family had come to nurse him. Alarming
symptoms coming on, his parents were telegraphed
for, but they did not reach York until some hours
after his peaceful close. John Ford thus alludes to
this severe dispensation :—

2 mo. 21.—Since I wrote last a time of deep trial has
been allotted us. "Fire and hail, snow and vapour, stormy
wind fulfilling His word." This may not unaptly characterize
the events of the last three weeks. All these are called upon
by the Psalmist to praise the Lord. May such be the blessed
results of this dispensation. *   *   *   * Sleepless-
ness, watching, anxiety, deep sympathy with the bereaved
parents, the very delicate health and the distress of my dear
R., bore away all refuge except one, and that did not fail:
again and again prayer was found to be a hiding place.
*   *   *   *   * After the funeral, in the Meeting
House after much conflict I bent the knee in prayer. My
feelings were wonderfully calmed by this offering.

To THOMAS PUPLETT.

2 mo. 26, 1856.—Whilst we have been sensible on many
occasions during the last two weeks of the visitations of our

Heavenly Father's love to our own beloved circle, it gladdens our hearts to know that this blessing has been extended to other circles in connection with the same sorrowful event. Some more wondrous connecting influence than that of the electric wires, might seem to have subsisted between Ackworth and York last First-day evening. In the course of our engagements in the school room, the *missing one* (though no new topic) was incidentally alluded to, and yet another of the many lessons offered for our instruction was pointed out. The deep and touching solemnity that attended and followed— a silence that no one seemed willing to break—cheered my heart again, with the belief that the love of our Heavenly Father was especially extended to the youthful company before me—to all of us.

I am glad that the invitation to seek communion with God, in prayer offered in the name of His dear Son, was extended to your interesting flock. I have found myself drawn frequently of late, both before and since our late loss, to press the invitation here, and on more than one occasion the *united* spirit of prayer has been granted us. Whilst "Non nobis Domine" is the inmost sentiment of our hearts, we may tell one another of His loving kindness and tender mercy.

We have had several interesting letters from Dublin. One from the father of the beloved boy, whilst it bears evidence that their hearts at times feel their desolateness, yet expresses the earnest desire that the event may be the blessed means of drawing many young hearts to the Saviour. "*He* can do it," he says, "may He give us faith to believe that He will."

In addition to our anxieties, our sorrows were not merely sympathetic. We truly mourned the loss from our circle of a good, a bright, intelligent, loving and lovely boy—one

whom we thought it would be a delight to train for his
Master's service on earth, and He has early transferred him
for service in Heaven. Besides an evidence sealed on our
spirits that he is safe for ever—an evidence which I dare not
call in question—we have the confirming testimony of his
previous life and conduct, of his patient and thankful
demeanour in sickness, and of the peace which hovered over
his dying bed. His pleasure in listening to, and his affirmative responses to the beautiful hymn, " How sweet the name
of Jesus sounds," and his emphatically earnest reply to my
dear R. F.'s enquiry, " Was not his Saviour near him, was he
not sensible of His presence and His love ?" "Yes, indeed I
am!"—all these considerations remove all thoughts of gloom
in remembering this beloved child.

---

3 mo. 10.—Last Sixth day the quarterly Committee met
at Bootham to consider the best arrangements for the carrying on of the School. Members of the sub-committee had
already conferred with me.   *   *   *   * For myself
I may say as I have already said to the Committee, that I
place myself in their hands, to carry out cordially and
earnestly such plans as they may deem most likely to promote
the benefit of the School.

Ten years ago my property was larger than it is to-day.
Perhaps I once indulged the idea that I might be in
circumstances to quit this post, and might be permitted
peacefully to quit it with an adequate competence, by the
time I had arrived at my present age. It seems to be not so
permitted—not my will, but that of my Heavenly Father
be done ! I had once thought that when my time of dismissal came, it might be an entire dismissal—that a successor
might be found who would revise and reform and renovate,

and that I might be permitted to find an abode elsewhere, leaving the field clear for new and better men and measures. It seems it is not to be so.—I am told that there is a general wish that the system of management should remain unchanged—that there is a general desire that my successor should be of my own training—that R. and I should continue to render such service as we can, and await the unfoldings of events and times. To this I would repeat, even so "Thy will be done!" A little ability to render service whilst required, a willing heart to render it—a heart to render it as to the Lord—industry, fidelity, courage, faith, true-hearted allegiance—all these I need. Bestow them upon me, O Heavenly Father, for Thy dear Son's sake. Amen!

3 mo. 21.—The difficulties always attendant upon the introduction of new officers, make me look to the future as not involving relief; perhaps as tinged with sombre uncertainty, not to say gloom. If trial still awaits *us*, or awaits *me* only, may I be enabled to accept it as the appointed discipline of a Father's love. If it draws me nearer and nearer to Him, if it should prepare and strengthen me for further and more faithful service, it shall be indeed welcome. Even now in reverting to the trials of the last few weeks, and calling to mind the "joy unspeakable" of free and frequent access to the throne of Grace—the realization of the love of Christ—the delight of seeking and finding a sense of that love, with body, soul and spirit prostrate—I could exclaim with the Patriarch of old, "oh that it were with me as in days past." If less of sensible enjoyment *is*, and *is to be* for a time my portion, may I be kept faithful and watchful so that I may lose no opportunity of access in prayer, by carelessness or indifference.

To-night, remembering the innumerable mercies that have marked every year of my life, I would ask for an increase of faith and love, a deeper sense of the immense debt of gratitude due for the purchased salvation; and hence more constancy, fidelity and diligence in service if still permitted to serve : and if before another birthday should come round my term of earthly service should have closed, may I be permitted to entertain the hope, that for His sake who died to save us and who ever liveth to make intercession for us, I may (most unworthy as I am) be accepted in Him. Amen.

6 mo. 22.—Our scholars all left us on Sixth-day, and another vacation has begun. We parted with our two faithful aids, Till Adam Smith after nearly fifteen years of service, and William Robinson after three. It was not without much emotion, that my dear R. and myself took leave of these beloved friends. * * * * Prevented going to Meeting by indisposition, incapable and needing rest as usual at this time, yet also as usual feeling the silence and vacuity of the house and grounds, I am poor and depressed this evening, and yet not without a thankful remembrance of past mercies, nor yet without some trust for the future.

* * * * I believe that on several occasions lately I might without presumption, without running not being sent, have said a few words in our Meetings for worship. Fearfulness and faithlessness have prevented. I earnestly desire to be preserved on either hand. The gospel is livingly and frequently preached in our Meetings here at York; but that is no excuse if an offering be really required : again, " who hath required this at your hand " is a very solemn question. "Make my way straight before Thy face." Help me to be faithful and obedient ! I have often had to acknowledge thankfully the help afforded in my First-day engagements

with the scholars—a gift entrusted to me for them ; a measure
of the same feeling has attended me at times in Meeting.
Keep me from mistakes either of utterance or of silence, O
Lord !

7 mo. 6.—This morning early in the Meeting the text
" Even so it is not the will of your Father which is in
Heaven that one of these little ones should perish," came
before me.—There were many little ones present—and after
much conflict and many fears, I ventured to quote the text
and offer a short comment.   I believe that the enemy of all
good, the accuser of the brethren tried to discourage me after
this engagement.   I laid my case before Him whom I would
gladly claim as my Master, and His peace that passeth all
understanding filled my heart with gratitude and my eyes
with thankful tears.

Last Third-day I went to Ackworth to attend the General
Meeting and the Educational Meeting.   I read a paper on
" The Duties and Difficulties of Young Teachers."   I may
thankfully acknowledge the help granted in the preparation,
as well as the acceptance it seemed to find, and the precious
solemnity that followed its conclusion.

8 mo. 3.—Another vacation closes to-day.

> " What tho' the day be never so long,
> At last it ringeth to evening song."

And so with our brief vacation.   And so at length with the
brief term of mortal life.   With what evening song shall
that hour be greeted which marks its close ?   " Worthy is
the Lamb that was slain."   Oh if through wondrous mercy,
ability should be granted to unite at last in that glorious
anthem, welcome the evening that closes with such a song—
welcome the dawning of the succeeding day—" for there
shall be no night there."

10 mo. 17.—In the course of the evening, I had interviews
with ——— and ———. I remonstrated with ——— on the
unkindness of the procedure as regarded myself, the years I
had watched over him, &c. He was greatly moved—acknowledged his obligations and spontaneously said he was sorry he
had troubled me, and that he would try to avoid doing so. I
could not observe without emotion the tear stealing down his
fine face. The depth and sincerity of his feelings were manifest
in the expression of his countenance, and his whole demeanour.
Oh! how worthless are penalties compared with scenes and
emotions like these!   How efficacious is *Christian* discipline.
In the evening I met the assembled school exclusive of
the senior class.   I addressed them on the prevalence of evil;
comparing some form of it with Cholera, Scarlet fever,
Measles or some other deadly disease: a matter not for
punishment, but for sorrow, repentance, seeking for pardon
and for strength to resist future temptations.   At reading
time I read Ephesians iv., 22—32, and at the close, the
words of our Lord occurred to me "If two of you shall
agree on earth," &c.   I remarked that I had felt encouraged
by the remembrance of this promise—that I believed more
than two, this night are prepared to ask for the grace of
repentance, for strength to resist temptation, for the preserving
hand of our Heavenly Father to keep us from evil—that I
should seek for ability to do so, and I trusted that others
would accept my invitation to unite in it.   A solemn pause
ensued.

10 mo.   .—An interview with ———.   I reverted to his
past history—that I felt it hard as the close of his term
approached, and as that of mine could not be far distant (as
resident), conscious as I was that I had deserved to win his
allegiance and affection; that I should thus have to remonstrate

with him. "Thou hast won it, John Ford," he replied, with deep and earnest emotion. I could not but be greatly moved by such a speech from such a boy. It once more renewed my faith in efforts to maintain a spirit of allegiance, by Christian courtesy and gentleness and by appeals to the better nature.

11 mo. 12.—This morning in Meeting my mind was deeply affected with the evil manifestations I have lately had to encounter in a few of the scholars. It occurred to me

> "Thou art coming to a King,
> Large petitions with thee bring,"

and I felt as though I could pour out my soul in earnest petition for the powerful interposition of omnipotence, to aid in the warfare, to endue with wisdom, and every other requisite, those who keep watch and ward : to visit the hearts, contrite the spirits, and attract by His love the flock entrusted to us. It was a precious time of earnest, silent intercession.

This evening, I went, after the candles were put out, and sat down in "Number ——" bedroom. I told them I had felt inclined to come and offer them a kind word of counsel—to strive to make the bedroom a sacred place ; a place where neither in word nor deed, anything should occur of which they could be ashamed: the blessedness of falling asleep with a peaceful conscience, after a little lively conversation such as no one could blush to hear :—a review of the day's doings as in the Divine sight : condemnation, if need be, of wrong,—and then closing their eyes to sleep under a sense of their Heavenly Father's love. I felt peace in making this one more effort, a sense of love to the eight inmates of the room. A remembrance of the morning's intercession, encouraged me to take this step. Be pleased to bless it, Heavenly Father for Thy dear Son's sake !

11 mo. 23.—Since I wrote last I have had to pass through deeper trials and more arduous service in regard to some of the senior scholars than has been allotted to me for many years. I have often prayed that evil might not be permitted to lay us waste, but might be brought to light—and so hath it been : and through pain and grief and depression, physical and mental, and with many prayers, I have striven to maintain the conflict, to maintain it too in that spirit which I have so commended to others—the spirit which would win and restore,—and many a time have I had to acknowledge with tears of joy the help thus afforded. Many a time has the sorrowful countenance and the trickling tear of some whom I would fain win over to Christ, moved my deepest sympathy. They forget—they are careless—thoughtless. Is that strange ? Oh may I be preserved from faithless unbelief in the efficacy of true Christian discipline, the voice of gentle suasion and love !

Thrice since I wrote last have I opened my mouth in our Meetings for worship, I did so to-day. Hesitating to speak, yet afraid to keep silence I have spoken. I have heard no other than the voice of encouragement from my friends. Whilst willing to say " Here am I, send me," I shrink from the responsibility and sometimes from the inquiry, " Who hath required this ? " Heavenly Father, keep me humble, watchful, willing—keep me from all self-seeking in Thy service—give me a thankful, grateful heart for all Thy mercies—that so, honoured by permission to serve Thee here in this the flock intrusted by Thee—or in the assemblies of Thy people, I may be stimulated to more faithful allegiance, and know more and more of Thy sustaining and contriting love.

12 mo. 31.—Our school broke up on Sixth-day.—It is

long since I had so laborious a half-year : it is not often that I have felt so discouraged at the supposed lack of fruit of labour. I ought with renewed thankfulness to acknowledge that in the administration of the discipline, in meeting the various forms of evil manifest from time to time, I have been preserved from procedures that would give me pain in reflecting upon them. Moral suasion, appeals to the highest principles, urged with kindliness of tone and manner, have been my weapons ; and again and again I have brought my cares and fears and despondencies to the mercy seat—not in vain.

My beloved R. is still an invalid confined to her bedroom and parlour—a patient, thankful, cheerful prisoner of the Lord—comforting me many a time by her sweet, gentle, confiding, loving spirit—privileged often I believe to know what it is to rest on His bosom. A few more minutes will bring in another year. What it may bring with it matters little if it only finds us with our loins girded about and our lamps burning, and we ourselves like men who wait for their Lord. Weary, faint-hearted and unequal to the service, and longing, oh how earnestly, perhaps selfishly, for rest, I have often been of late : perhaps I am so now, and may be so when about to engage in the service again ; and yet I think peace has been my portion if not enjoyment. Increase my faith. Teach me to endure hardness. Oh keep me from a murmuring, a discontented spirit. Help me from day to day and from hour to hour in the constant warfare against evil in myself, and in those committed to my care : and to all these blessings add, O Heavenly Father, for Thy mercy's sake in Jesus Christ our Saviour, a sense of Thy love and of Thy protecting and sustaining care. Then preserved by Thee in this field of service, or dismissed from it for other service elsewhere, or called to render an account, a final account of stewardship—may a humble hope in Thy mercy through Him, whom I would fain love and serve with my whole heart, gild the closing scene. Amen!

1 mo. 12, 1857.—Never did the 34th Psalm appear so beautiful, so full of comfort as it did to me this evening. With a heart full of grateful emotions I felt invited to appropriate some of the gracious declarations—the promises—the blessed experiences—announced in several verses.

3 mo. 21.—Seven years at home—seven years a school-boy—twice seven a teacher—twice fourteen Principal—fourteen years at Worcester—fourteen nearly at Rochester and a little more than twenty-eight at York—making fifty-six in all—have brought me to the present day, my fifty-seventh birthday, and my present position. "Surely goodness and mercy have followed me all the days of my life," and at times a good hope (not a vain confidence I trust) is granted, that "I shall dwell in the house of the Lord for ever." A hope inspired by a sense of the pardoning mercy of God in Jesus Christ.

The time since the vacation has been less marked with trial and conflict than some previous months. I fear less marked too by frequent, earnest application to the mercy-seat. How precious nevertheless are the recollections of running thither with childlike confidence, to pour out troubles and sorrows and tears before a loving and merciful Heavenly Father, emboldened so to do by confidence in an ever living advocate, and in that confidence, realizing at times the assurance, "the Lamb which is in the midst of the throne shall feed them,"—and "God shall wipe away all tears from their eyes."

4 mo. 12.—I have been fearful lest the condition of our Meeting with regard to vocal offerings should induce me to keep silence unprofitably. I have tried to rest on, "what is

that to thee ?" May I be enabled faithfully and entirely
to obey the annexed injunction, "follow thou me."—In
looking towards the future, no way seems to be opening
for release from service in the school; and yet at times I feel
unequal to the cares and anxieties: they press more heavily
on my health and spirits than they once did. I would fain
trust it all to my Heavenly Father's disposal, and seek just
for help from hour to hour to do the hour's service.

To ———

4 mo. 27, 1857.—I was much interested in thy account of
thy two pupils more particularly in reference to thy little
friend. I was glad indeed to find that thou hadst found
access to his understanding and his heart on the most important of topics. In my late attempt to aid young teachers,
it was no mere piece of sentiment when I pointed out their
opportunities of cherishing in their young friends the love of
Christ: it arose from a deep conviction that knowing something of that love themselves, (if happily they do) they will
long to communicate it, and from a deep conviction too that
there are in the hearts of many little boys and older ones too,
at times, undefined longings which some perception of this
love can alone satisfy—a condition of mind which gratefully
and lovingly accepts as in the case of thy cherished pupil, a
word however simple, addressed to these aspirations of the
immortal spirit kindled in the youthful heart by the influence
of the Holy Spirit of God.   *   *   *   *

The morning of life—high noon—afternoon and evening—
each of these periods has its service. Mayst thou in this thy
morning, my dear young friend, and we too who have
arrived at *afternoon* be faithful, true-hearted servants. I
sometimes feel as though repose would be grateful. My turn
may perhaps some day come for a change of service. Welcome
that or any other allotment only let it be a Father's ordering.

BOOTHAM AND ST. MARY'S.

Though Rachel Ford since the summer of 1855 had resigned her duties as housekeeper to Sarah Robinson, whose efficiency relieved her from household cares, her increasing delicacy and the state of John Ford's health also, made it evident that the time was at hand when substantial relief from the constant pressure of their position must be afforded them. The way opened somewhat suddenly. A house in the immediate neighbourhood of the School well adapted to their requirements, became unexpectedly at liberty. After consulting with their friends the whole subject was laid before the Committee. With its entire concurrence, arrangements were made for them to remove to their new residence, No. 7 St. Mary's, at midsummer;—that John Ford, whilst relieved from some of the duties which he had hitherto discharged, should retain the post of Superintendent, and that Fielden Thorp, who as scholar, junior teacher and assistant master had been associated with him for several years, and for whom he entertained a deep affection, should become resident head Master at Bootham.

In reference to these changes John Ford thus writes under date 5 mo. 3, 1857:—

* * * * Embarking on new and somewhat ambiguous duties, or relationships in regard to duties, Rachel and I have been mostly enabled to rely quietly, hopefully and I believe thankfully on our Heavenly Father's love and care.

6 mo. 21, 1857.—Since I last wrote another vacation has commenced. The general kindness and loyalty of the scholars and the entire good feeling subsisting between them and the teachers, have been very gratifying features of the close of the session. I do not know and I find it difficult to estimate the amount or the nature of the change contemplated in our non-residence. The prospect has invested many things with some of that feeling of mournful interest which attends the doing of a thing for the last time: in some degree it is so; but I earnestly desire to regard the change as occurring in the ordering of an ever kind and merciful Heavenly Father, assured that if so, all will be well. If it brings its peculiar trials, may faith and patience equal to the emergency be granted; if a little less pressure and burden, may all so gained be consecrated to the best of services.

To RACHEL FORD.

Dewsbury, 6 mo. 30, 1857. * * * * Twenty years ago to day! Twenty years marked by mercies fresh every morning from our Heavenly Father, and by ever deepening love for each other! May ever deepening love for Him who has so loved us and blessed us be our experience to the end— and willing-hearted service whether it be to *do* or to *bear.* Farewell, dearest. In abundant love,

Thine ever,
JOHN FORD.

---

7 mo. 5.—To night probably for the *last* time I am making a memorandum under this roof. My term of non-resident

Superintendent has already commenced " de jure ; " before I
write again it will probably have commenced " de facto." The
eleven years and a half spent here have been marked by many
mercies, those of this very day not the least.   Perhaps I never
felt myself to stand more in need of pardoning mercy—never
wrestled more earnestly and importunately for it—never felt
more of its unspeakable preciousness.—A trial, (reckless evil
in another) crossed my path *unexpectedly* and *suddenly* yesterday, and found me unprepared.   Last evening and again to
day, the grace of repentance—the spirit of earnest prayer and
supplication with many tears has been in abundant mercy
granted me.   The sense of reconciliation—pardon—restora-
tion—renewed love, has again and again overwhelmed my
spirit.   The evening Meeting was a very precious time ; and
now again in the solitude of this large house with its two or
three inmates and my beloved R. retired, I have again to
acknowledge the rich sense of our Heavenly Father's love
contriting my spirit.   Oh that henceforth by continual watchfulness, by seeking to take the whole armour, the attacks of
an unwearied enemy, the outbursts of remaining evil, may
be successfully resisted and repressed.   Oh that I may never
utter another unkind word.   May the remembrance of yesterday's pain and to day's pardon be an additional safeguard.

RACHEL FORD TO BRIDGET THOMPSON.

7 mo. 14, 1857—I came to St. Mary's after tea last evening,
and soon felt very comfortable ; and on our little company
sitting down together for the first time for the purposes of
family worship, there did appear such an overshadowing of
heavenly good as quite to tender our spirits ; and my dear
husband was constrained on bended knee to offer the tribute
of thanksgiving, and to petition that the same mercy and
goodness which had in an especial manner followed us all

our lives long, might still be continued, keeping us watchful, and prayerful, with willing hearts doing all that may be called for at our hands: and that whether our sojourn here together might be longer or shorter, at the end an entrance might be granted us into the kingdom of our Lord through the mercies of His dear Son, our ever living, ever loving Saviour.

To WILLIAM KITCHING, JUN.

7 mo. 15, 1857.—We have got into our new house, and I am glad that it has been accomplished without much fatigue to my dear R.; and I think I can say I am truly thankful to see her so entirely pleased with the change, not finding a single discomfort in her new residence. It was indeed time, with her delicate health and long service, that she should be relieved from all feeling of responsibility in the large family over which she has presided for twenty years. But if *responsibility* on her part has ceased, *interest* has *not* ceased, nor perhaps *service*—that service which I believe she has often rendered, of earnest prayer for the blessing of our Heavenly Father on the labours of those called to more active service. I shall be glad to meet you all once more and to unite with you in caring for the flock. I account it a singular happiness to be united with such—with able, kind-hearted, earnest, young men—with whom associated, it is sometimes joy to be able to feel myself a fellow-servant with them, of our gracious Master. May our fidelity and love to Him, and our love one to another, as His servants, increase and abound.

----

9 mo. 11.—We have now been several weeks in our new house, and have much cause for thankfulness and praise for the sense of peace and repose often granted us. To me it has

been an especial cause of grateful thanksgiving that my
beloved R. does so enjoy the change. We have both at times
I think had our trust renewed that the change in our position
has on it the stamp of Divine ordering. My interest in the
school and in every individual in it is not diminished. It is
pleasant to find that I still have a place with all its inmates.
Whilst enjoying the quiet of St. Mary's, I miss perhaps most
of all the evening readings at the school. Brief as they
mostly were, they were often times of refreshment of spirit.
Thus far efficiency and harmony and united interest continue
to characterize the officers, and affection and loyalty the
scholars. * * * *

I think my health has improved since the change of residence. I find it more difficult, in my position between the
two houses to maintain steady, uninterrupted, literary labour
—some books and means being at one house and some at the
other. I must guard against desultory and indolent habits.
I hope to see more and more plainly what is my allotted
service—what new duties belong to my new circumstances—
what old ones to be more diligently prosecuted—what belongs
to the public, what to the more private service—what to the
moral, the intellectual, the spiritual. Watchfulness and
frequent prayer—diligence—perseverance—faith—these are
some of the means towards the fulfilment of "occupy till
I come."

10 mo. 14.—Especial private prayer this evening for some
of the thoughtless, yet beloved ones at Bootham. Again let
me plead O Heavenly Father, in the name of Thy dear Son.
Visit their young hearts—show them their thoughtlessness
and their forgetfulness of Thee—show them their need of a
Saviour—draw them to Him—give them to feel the love of
Christ inviting them to come unto Him. Suffer them not to

be hardened by the deceitfulness of sin. And for the whole
school and its unworthy head, withhold not Thou Thy tender
mercies from us. Thou hast been our help: for Thy dear
Son's sake, leave us not nor forsake us, O God of our Salvation.

12 mo. 6.—I have made some change in arrangements for
First-day, which occupy more of my time at Bootham with the
scholars, and more in preparation. Besides the ecclesiastical
history in the morning I have the senior class separately in
the evening on points of Christian doctrine. Thankfulness
should be the clothing of my spirit this evening for the help
graciously afforded in these services—thankfulness to Him
whose tender mercies are over all His works.

In the Second Month of 1858 a sharp rheumatic
attack of four weeks' duration, confined John Ford
to the house, and much of the time to his bed. He
thus writes in reference to this period :—

My head was preserved in perfect clearness. My memory
was more than usually clear and active. When I could
neither read nor listen to reading from weakness, psalms—
chapters of Holy Scripture—long passages—hymns—pieces
from Cowper—passed gently and quietly through my mind—
just trickling through, leaving a refreshing dew as they.
passed. Hymns and verses long unused to be thought of,
recurred. I went through many of Dr. Watts's "Divine
Songs," learned more than fifty years ago. Sleepless hours
were often thus charmed. Prayer and thanksgiving were
often graciously granted me.

6 mo. 13, 1858.—The last Sabbath of the Session. I gave
one more lecture, the 30th on Church History. After the

evening reading, in addressing the boys I said I could
publicly acknowledge a sense of thankful gratitude to our
Heavenly Father, for His preserving love and mercy extended to this family since the commencement of the session.
I believed there were those present who could unite in the
sentiment. I remembered that at the commencement we
had asked for this extension of love to us, that we might be
kept from sinning, kept in the love and fear of our Heavenly
Father. If there were young hearts present sensible of this,
they could so unite. Let them carry this feeling home with
them, and let the fruits of it be seen in increased kindness,
gentleness, unselfishness, affection ;—these would be proofs
that so it had been with us.

I came away once more from this interesting and beloved
company with a thankful heart, and yet with feelings a little
saddened—even yet after nearly thirty years of labour, at
once more parting with them, with some perchance to meet
no more. Continue Thy loving kindness to them and to me,
to my beloved partner and to all who are dear to us, for Thy
Son's sake, our ever living advocate with Thee. Amen !

9 mo. 19.—The past week has been one of sore trials.
Trials arising, I think I may venture to say, in answer to
prayer. I have often asked that evil may not be permitted
to *prevail* amongst the scholars. Evil very recent became
known, and I was helped to grapple with it. To day a
tender and prayerful spirit has been in mercy granted me.

12 mo. 7.—I gave my fifth lesson on Church History at
the Mount School. Last evening and this evening I spent
some hours in preparation ; and before setting out I felt
drawn to engage in prayer. I accepted the invitation, and
found prayer once more to be a very precious thing. Pardon

in the name of Christ—the aid of the Holy Spirit—the anni-
hilation of all self-seeking and self-sufficiency—permission
to serve, and direction when and how,—such were some of my
petitions, and I believe they were granted.   Interest seemed
well sustained during the lecture; and after the reading of
the Scriptures I addressed the girls.   I returned home with
a contrited and grateful heart.   My prayer is still, "make
me as one of Thy hired servants."

1 mo. 25, 1859.—This evening after many hours of
research, thought and writing, I have nearly completed my
second Lecture on Church History, to be read next Fifth-day
evening.   Looking forward to the preparation of one or two
similar Lectures—somewhat despondingly—not unwilling to
work and yet at times longing for rest—a very precious sense
of my Heavenly Father's love in Christ my Saviour was
granted me—a rich overpayment of all toil—a little evidence
that it is a service for Him.

To WILLIAM S. LEAN.

3 mo. 15, 1859.—Thy residence in Kent and thy mention
of Rochester brought up a numerous and busy train of reminiscences of the joys and sorrows,—the hopes and aims all
glowing—the poetry and the friendships of that bright period
of life through which thou art passing.   From the age of
fourteen to twenty-seven, my home was on the banks of the
beautiful Medway.   The window near my desk, about one
hundred feet above the river, commanded a broad expanse of
near a thousand feet of water immediately below, and the
windings of the stream were visible between the chalk downs
for two or three miles.   The opposite shore soon rose to considerable elevation, crowned by the woods of Lord Darnley's
domain.   The window looked due west.   Imagine the most
glorious sunsets thy fancy can paint, and confess that they

cannot equal those which now through a long vista of years,
I see along those hills and mirrored in that resplendent river.
Excuse this natural burst of enthusiasm, the vibrations of a
chord touched by thee.   I could almost personify that river
and say,

> " Never can that heart forget thee
> That has felt a love like mine."

But it was not the river, the woods, the hills, and the sunsets, that formed the charm.   Early friendships, not yet all
severed, and higher and holier things than these are associated with those scenes.   There some of my earliest vows were
made—the river-side was the place of many a prayer.   Do
not wonder at this train of thought.   Future years will
perhaps explain it to thee when looking back upon Blackwell
and the Tees, or the less picturesque York and its Ouse. The
poet says "Let the dead past bury its dead;" but there are
things of the past—living things, which it would be a sin to
bury.

---

3 mo. 21.—In the Meetings at York and at Wakefield
last week, the young, the children have been the objects of
my concern and love.   On these occasions, and especially in
my First-day evening engagements at Bootham, freedom of
utterance and a sense of a Saviour's love to them, have been
granted me in answer to prayer, accompanied with a
commission so to speak.

May this my fifty-ninth year, if spared to complete its
round, be more faithfully—earnestly—constantly devoted to
the best of services, the best of masters—loving service to
Him who hath *so* loved us!—service preparatory to that
blessed condition where His servants shall still serve Him,
and see His face, and fear no more the mingling of sin or
sorrow or unsuccess !

5 mo. 8.—A blessed evening at Bootham. After reading, I withdrew to the silent Lecture-room,* and there was enabled to pour out a thankful heart, and again to present many beloved ones in prayer to a merciful Heavenly Father in the name of His dear Son. Before I left the room a poor boy came to see me, oppressed with a feeling of prevailing sin. I gave him counsel, entreating him to apply for pardon and for strength, and to let no temptation of Satan prevent him from so doing. The evening closed with a very thankful heart for the mercies of the day.

To William S. Lean.

5 mo. 11, 1859.—Since I wrote to thee my dear R. F. has slowly and gently, step by step declined still further in health. Her voice is generally reduced to a whisper : she still comes down stairs : but yesterday, for the first time was carried up in the evening, the effort of walking up being no longer in her power, finding her strength and breathing utterly exhausted by the effort. She enjoys the change down stairs, and I hope she may be permitted to enjoy it for some time, as we have arranged means for carrying her up, and down also if that should become needful. She was much pleased with thy sweet reference to her condition, in thy letter. She is still preserved in quiet, peaceful trust, and sometimes her spirit can rejoice in God her Saviour. On Second-day evening she expressed this sentiment in the words of that beautiful stanza :

> " What thanks I owe Thee and what love ;
> A boundless, endless store, &c."

Though my heart is often heavy, and the thought " I must

---

*After removing to St. Mary's, the Lecture-room (since altered into the Dining-room) was occupied by John Ford during the hours he was at Bootham. It may be well also to explain, that whilst the First-day evening Addresses were usually given in the School-room, the reading of Scripture with the assembled household was conducted in the Dining-room, before the boys retired to rest.

finish my journey alone" makes me very sorrowful, yet at times the unutterable love vouchsafed to her, realizes in me something of the Apostle's experience, "sorrowful yet rejoicing."

---

6 mo. 1.—The shadows seem deepening. My darling wife is very ill. Looking at her pallid and worn face this evening as I sat by her bedside, I could not repress my sorrow, much as I feared to distress her. At length I read to her a passage of scripture on which I had casually opened, ending with, " for we know that if our earthly house of this tabernacle were dissolved." This and some of the precious declarations in the preceding verses, " the light afflictions"— the " far more exceeding and eternal weight of glory," seemed, under the Holy Spirit's influence to open the way for thanksgiving and prayer on the bended knee, for and with my beloved and myself. Oh what a blessed, soothing, calming, confidence-restoring thing is prayer! * * * Oh if this most precious treasure—this most tenderly beloved one be taken from me, may I be permitted to fill up the brief period of separation (till I rejoin her before the throne) in faithful, loving service of my Heavenly Father and Redeemer!

7 mo. 3.—The tender bond of twenty-two years is severed. Yesterday evening my darling wife entered upon her heavenly inheritance, purchased for her by her Saviour's most precious blood. Most gently and tenderly has her Heavenly Father dealt with her—gently sloping the way to her and to me by a most peaceful and painless illness. It was the most peaceful close—not a motion to indicate the parting moment. Though there was no opportunity for a parting word, yet the last week was one long farewell. Morning by

morning I read (and evening by evening) a few verses of
precious hopes and promises, to which her response often
was, "how beautiful"—"how precious"—"how comforting."
Her spirit too, often united with mine when I was enabled
by her bedside to pour forth words of thanksgiving and
prayer.　To-day I have again and again, especially in our
morning reading with my two poor weeping servants, and
again this evening at reading time,—found refuge and peace
and comfort and light in humble, heartfelt prayer, so that
I felt as though I could adopt the beautiful language of the
prophet, "The Lord Jehovah is my strength and my song ;
He also is become my salvation."

At the time of her decease Rachel Ford had
completed her fifty-seventh year.　Her remains
were interred in Friends' Burial Ground, York,
on the Eighth of Seventh Month.　On the evening
of that day the following sketch of her, drawn up
by John Ford in the interval that had elapsed since
her death, was read to a large company of relations
and friends assembled at the School.

The instruction to be derived from the less conspicuous
and the sequestered walk of the faithful disciple of Christ,
though less obvious and less easy to set forth, is perhaps not
less valuable than are the lessons to be drawn from a life of
active service,· in a wide and public sphere.　Some such
instruction seems to have been bequeathed to her friends by
the late Rachel Ford.

She was the daughter of Nathan and Rachel Robson of
Darlington, both of whom were taken from her in comparatively early life.　She had also to mourn over the loss

of two brothers and two sisters all summoned early away.
Thus she became acquainted with sorrow. Till her marriage
with John Ford in 1837, her life was of a somewhat
chequered character. She filled various stations of usefulness,
largely securing the esteem and affection of the kind relatives
in whose families she resided. Many of these have testified
to the early maturity and soundness of her judgment and to
an unvarying kindness—

> " Ne'er roughened by those cataracts and breaks,
>   That humour interposed too often makes."

Though she shrunk at first from the prospect of the grave
responsibilities involved in the proposed connection in
marriage, yet once satisfied it was of the Lord, she entered
on the union with all the warmth of the most tender affection,
and in humble confidence, that ability equal to her need,
would be granted to her, to fulfil the important duties
devolving on the female head of a large school. Though
constitutionally of very delicate health, she decidedly declined
the assistance of a house-keeper, preferring to have direct
and immediate personal intercourse with every member of
the large family, whose confidence, esteem and love she soon
secured. The attachment of numerous domestic servants,
extending over twenty years of active superintendence of
the school, testified to her love and care of them. A kind
word of counsel to the young, the wayward, and the careless,
forbearance to such—encouragement to every effort to amend—
wisdom and prudence in arranging differences, and the silent
influence of her own quiet spirit—were means blest in a large
degree, to the maintenance of harmony, and of efficient
service. The time of paying the half-yearly wages was
made by her an opportunity of evincing her interest in her
servants' welfare. She made a point of seeing each separately,
and many a word in season was thus imparted. In more

than one instance, she had in her domestics, those who, like
herself, loved their Lord, and manifested that love by a
careful, humble, self-denying walk.   These were dear to her
in the bonds of christian love.

More than twenty young men, as teachers and junior
assistants, partook of her care and kindness in the course
of her twenty years of service.   These too were the objects
of her especial interest.   To secure their physical comfort, to
make herself readily accessible to them, to minister to them
in illness, and by tender sympathy to cheer them under
discouragement, marked her line of conduct towards them.
The supper-table, round which they assembled when the toils
of the day were over, will be remembered by many of them
as the scene of tranquil enjoyment, to which she contributed
by the influence of her gentle spirit.   Nor were they uncon-
scious of this influence nor ungrateful for it.   One of them in
a letter written the day before her death says, "Her delicate
kindness to me during my sojourn at Bootham, and the
sweetness of her meek and quiet spirit will never be forgotten
while memory lasts."   Another who partook of her tender
care and interest for three years and a half, in a letter dated
two weeks before her decease, writes: "I have a vivid
remembrance of the thrill of feeling that went through me,
as my heart responded to the remark of a friend on the
occasion of Rachel Ford's appointment to the station of
Elder: He said, "Though there might not be the zeal of a
Peter or the boldness of a Paul, yet there was in her, the
ornament of a meek and quiet spirit, which is, in the
sight of God, of great price."   Truly it is not to eulogize the
departed that these testimonies are adduced.   Her humble
estimate of herself would have made eulogy most repugnant
to her.   And yet now, "seeing no longer as in a glass
darkly," she would not blame the attempt to draw lessons

H

from her life, calculated, though in ever so small a degree, to
stimulate others to tread the path of dedicated and loving
service.

More than three hundred and fifty boys passed through
the school during the period of her administration. To these
individually she gave a tender and ever watchful care. The
little boy, fresh from his mother's side, soon found in her,
one whose sympathetic kindness made some amends for the
separation. To her they soon found they could confide their
little troubles, without apprehension of repulse. Before
increased delicacy of health interposed, she devoted a little
time after breakfast each morning, and every evening after
reading, to receive all comers, with every little ailment,
administering to their several wants, and thus acquiring
distinct, individual knowledge of almost every boy's peculiar
temperament of body or of mind. Few half-years passed
over, without one or more of the scholars being brought
under her notice, bereaved of a parent, a brother, or sister,
or other near relative. On these occasions her parlour was
the scene of many a soothing and comforting interview.
The hearts and the lips, even of the shy and diffident, were
opened on these occasions, in response to her soothing and
delicate kindness. But it was in periods of sickness whether
of individuals or when numbers were indisposed, that she
seemed peculiarly gifted to minister. She availed herself of
these opportunities, not only to exert the kindest care and
superintendence, in regard to all physical wants and alleviations, but by reading a short portion of Scripture by the
bed-side, and by the simple expression of religious concern,
she availed herself of the softening influence of sickness,
gently to lead to thoughts of a Heavenly Father's love and
care. The kindling eye and the bright response of one dear
boy, to her whispered suggestion of a Saviour's love, a few

brief hours before his sweet spirit left its earthly tabernacle, were deeply impressed on her mind, and comforted her in a time of sore trial.

Way was often purposely made for her to see and converse with poor boys in trouble, whether for minor or graver offences : her softening influence over these, was no unimportant part of the Christian discipline of the school.

Such is a brief sketch of what may be called the official life of our late friend.   In the spring of 1856, it was evident that her physical powers were becoming unequal to the duties of Bootham.   The way for release however did not fully open till midsummer 1857, when she removed with her husband to a private house, not far from the school. She most gratefully enjoyed the repose of this change, and said that she had not an earthly wish ungratified.   For the last two years of her residence at Bootham she was most kindly assisted by her friend, Sarah Robinson, to whom she became warmly attached.   She retained her interest in the school to the last; was always glad to see her friend, and to aid her with her counsel—not more cheerfully given, than kindly and thankfully received.

For the last three or four years she had been sensible of declining health and strength.   In 1855 at a time when scarlatina prevailed in the school, she wrote as follows to one whom she loved as a daughter, and who warmly reciprocated that love.   "*This* is of all things, the one I the most dreaded, and yet, now that it is come upon us, I feel enabled quietly to submit to it.   I look upon it as one of those permitted trials, intended to do us good."   About the same time she says, "I am very feeble, getting at times quite discouraged about my health.   I know however that all is ordered well and wisely.   I cannot say, as some do, that I consider sickness a sorrowful thing : my feelings are more in unison with the beautiful hymn, 'Chamber of sickness! much to thee I owe.'" On the second of the First-month, 1859, she wrote to the same loved one as follows: "In the unusual solemnity that seems to cover my own spirit, at the commencement of the present year, my thoughts have turned very lovingly towards thee and thine, with warm desires for your welfare every way. What I long for you is, that you may go forward in that way, in which I most comfortingly believe, you have taken not a few steps. Oh! seek to live more and more in that spirit, which will lead you to realize the frequent presence of the dear Saviour, whose loving hand is upon you for good." Whilst she could thus comfort and encourage her friends, her diffident spirit taking an humble estimate of herself, thus expresses her sense of the need of a Saviour. "I feel the beginning of this year a very solemn thing to myself. There is much work to be done before the warfare be accomplished. Earnestly do I crave to be enabled, as a poor penitent believer, to come to Him, who alone can availingly say, 'I will; be thou clean.'"

During her last illness, and shortly before its close, there was evidence of deep searching of heart, and of jealousy over herself, lest she should be taking up with a false rest. Though to outward observation hers had been indeed a blameless life, from her youth up, yet in solemnly reviewing her early years, she told a beloved friend that she believed every transgression of her youth had been brought painfully before her, and that whilst she could thankfully believe they were all forgiven, yet the remembrance of them had been affecting to her. "Quiet trust, peace, not joy," she said "was her portion." Her tenderly beloved friend Sarah Rowntree, visiting her a few days before her decease, says, "I found her bright and cheerful. Her heart seemed peculiarly alive to her many outward comforts. She directed my attention to a beautiful vase of flowers, sent her by a young friend, one of the junior teachers in the School, and remarked, 'I do see the kindness of my Heavenly Father in so abundantly supplying my outward wants;' to which I replied, that great as were these blessings, they were not to be compared with the blessedness of having a good hope of eternal life through the mercy of our Lord and Saviour Jesus Christ. She said, 'I cannot quite realize *that*.' I replied, 'But thou hast a quiet, settled trust?' She said, 'Yes, a quiet trust, THAT IS JUST IT'; 'and' added S. R., 'all fear of death is taken away?' 'Yes,' she replied, 'and if I were now just entering the valley, I believe I should feel no fear.'"

On another occasion she spoke quite cheerfully of having arranged all the little presents she wished to be given to her friends, and in looking forward as regarded herself she seemed divested of every anxious thought. She said it felt remarkable to herself, that she, who had always, according to her own estimation, been so weak in faith, should now, with the end in prospect, be so entirely free from anxiety, and able to trust all to the mercy of her Heavenly Father, whilst she hoped it might be permitted her to have a clearer evidence of her acceptance before the end came. Another much loved friend, Esther Seebohm, who visited her two days before her death, thus writes: "It seemed when I had the privilege of a few minutes, beside her, as if the end was very near, and there was nothing left to desire but an entrance into that rest, the sweetness of which she was already tasting: the fruition of that love, and peace, and joy, which the presence of the Saviour alone can give."

Although since her removal from Bootham, Rachel Ford's health had been most delicate, it was not till the spring of 1859 that increased anxiety was awakened. From that

time till her decease, painlessly and most mercifully, did
her Heavenly Father, slope the downward way, enduing
her with patience to bear the weariness of debility, with
sweet resignation to His will, and with quiet trust in her
Saviour.   Some of her dear friends who visited her, and
he who for twenty-two years had been the object of her
devoted affection, often partook of the sweetness of her spirit,
and felt the atmosphere of her chamber inviting at times the
utterance of thanksgiving and prayer, to the mutual comfort
of their enfeebled friend and their own.   Encouraged by
witnessing the sustaining power of Divine grace so beautifully
exemplified, their hearts warmed with the love of Jesus, and
feeling the promptings of the Holy Spirit, they did not
hesitate thus to enjoy the precious privilege of prayer.

At length with no other premonition than that of increased weakness, the end came.   On Seventh-day, 7th mo.
2nd, her kind medical attendant, Dr. Williams, called to
see her about nine o'clock in the evening.   He proposed
that arrangements should be made for sitting up with her
that night, *for the first time* during her illness.   He waited
while these arrangements were making.   Aware that he
was in the house, his patient desired he would come up as
she wanted to settle for the night.   On going upstairs he
saw that the end was near.   Her sorrowing husband, his
attached friend Joseph Rowntree, a kind friend who had
come to sit up with the beloved one, together with her two
maids, stood round her bed, and sweetly as a child falls
asleep, without the movement of a muscle, she slept her
last sleep; the cessation of the pulse alone marking the
period of final separation.

Her husband in concluding the preceding sketch, thus
expresses his personal feelings.   " Whilst I longed for a
farewell word from this my dearest treasure, my Heavenly

Father's most precious earthly gift, I see and can thankfully
acknowledge, His kind and loving hand in sparing us the
pain of parting words. Twenty-two years and two days of
most constant and most tender love, and much of most
precious united communion with our God and Saviour, had
been through His mercy our happy experience. Thoughts
of her eternal blessedness, a humble trust in that same redeeming love which was so richly extended to her, and a
hope that it may be my portion at last, are my stay in this
time of trial, and under a sense of our Heavenly Father's
love in Jesus Christ, I desire to say, 'Thy will be done.' "

In presenting their annual Report to York Quarterly Meeting, the School Committee thus record
their sense of the value of Rachel Ford's services
to the Institution, and of the influence for good
which she exercised over its inmates :—

"The Committee cannot close their Report without referring to the removal, by death, in Seventh-month last, of
their beloved friend, Rachel Ford, and expressing their deep
sympathy with her bereaved partner under this affliction.
Our late friend occupied the position of female head of the
Institution from 1837 to the summer of 1857. Gentle and
unobtrusive as was her character, we apprehend that it is
not easy to overrate the value of the influence she exercised
on the three hundred and fifty boys who passed through the
school during the term of her administration. In an extended variety of ways, but with great singleness of purpose
did Rachel Ford seek to promote the welfare of the household
in which she moved. In the painstaking selection and training of suitable domestic servants, in ministering to the
comfort of the teachers, and in furthering the harmonious

working of the family, by the silent influence of her meek, unselfish spirit she was peculiarly blessed. So long as health permitted, Rachel Ford cultivated a personal acquaintance— more or less intimate—with each boy passing through the school; her delicate attentions to them, in times of indis- position, whether of a trivial, or of a more serious character, not seldom won their affections; and seasons of trouble, arising from misconduct, from domestic bereavement, or from other causes, were often embraced by her as opportunities for gently introducing the word of counsel, or of comfort, and of extending the invitation of a Saviour's love. Whilst the Committee would wish to abstain from eulogising their de- parted friend, the remembrance of her example, and of the service she was enabled to render, has deepened their estimate of the value of the quiet, persistent, Christian influence which, in the home circle, or in the public Institution, may be ex- erted in the work of education by the female head of a household."

To an Old Scholar.

7 mo., 1859.—Apart from the immediate topic of thy letter, the tone of it interested me much. It is indeed a step in the right direction to feel the vanity of all terrestrial things, of all hopes and aspirations whose ultimate aim is bounded by time. The next best step is a positive one (not a negative). It is to discover that here, on this earth, amidst all its vicissitudes, its sorrows, its trials, and mutations, there is for every one a service for Christ. If we accept this truth—to seek to know what our own especial service is, and ask for ability to serve: then, whether the school or the college or the counting house—the path of science or litera- ture or commerce be our allotment, then—vanity and vexation of spirit will be no longer ours. We may serve Christ our

loving Saviour, testify our allegiance to Him in any one of the departments, and feel at times that His service is the joy of our life, and that it is a service unlimited by time, stretching over the boundless range of eternity.

———————

For some years John Ford had occasionally felt it required of him to engage in ministry and in prayer in the Meetings for Divine worship in his own section of the church. His communications were often brief; yet as they bore the impress of right anointing, his Monthly Meeting in Eighth month, 1859, in accordance with the usages of the Society of Friends, believed it right to record its recognition of his having received a gift in the ministry of the Gospel.

In the Eleventh-month of this year another bereavement occurred deeply and lastingly felt by John Ford. It was the removal by death of his beloved friend Joseph Rowntree, with whom for many years he had enjoyed close Christian friendship, and who from the time of the establishment of the Boys' School at York, had taken a warm and active interest in its management and welfare. The following letter written some years after Joseph Rowntree's decease, will best convey John Ford's sense of the loss he had sustained, and his high estimate of his friend's character.*

———

* Permission has been kindly granted to reprint this letter from the unpublished Memoir of Joseph Rowntree, printed for the use of his family only.

JOHN FORD TO JOHN S. ROWNTREE.

St. Mary's, York, 11 mo. 7, 1866.

My dear friend John S. Rowntree,

In compliance with thy request, I have been looking back over the long period of thirty-eight years, to the time when I first became acquainted with my dear friend, thy late Father.—His kindness to me, and his services to the school were so constant and unremitting, that comparatively few incidents have marked prominence in the record. In the the 7th mo., 1829, whilst on a visit to thy uncle, John Rowntree, at Scarborough,—(a visit arranged for me by thy Father, on account of a low condition of health, at the close of the first half-year of my labours in the school)—I received intelligence of the serious illness of my dear father, then at York. On my way to York, I was met by a message of his death. On my arrival, I found thy father waiting for me at the coach-office. It was an un-looked-for act of kindness, never forgotten by me, stamping his character in my mind, with a " dependableness " which I never henceforth found to fail, through the long term of thirty years. His last act of this kind to me, was only three months before the close of his life. It was an act of quiet, affectionate succour in a time of deep distress, standing by me, when ready to sink by the open grave of my dear wife, near the spot where his remains were so soon to rest. * *

In the early days of the school, then situate in Lawrence Street, my dear friend, and one of thy father's dearest friends, Samuel Tuke, was my almost daily counsellor in the affairs of the school. Even then, in times of emergency, thy father's ready aid was always at hand. This was especially the case when the cholera first visited York, in the Sixth month, 1832. And thenceforth, in all times of sickness,—

in the time of the scarlatina in 1855,—and in that of the
measles in 1856,—he largely shared our troubles, sympathised
with us in them, and often cheered our drooping spirits with
his affectionate, brotherly aid.

In all critical times,—times of discouragement from whatever cause,—thy Father was ever the dependable and wise
counsellor, as well as the constant and faithful friend. About
the year 1841, much anxiety began to be felt regarding
the health of the school, and doubts arose regarding the
salubrity of the situation.   In that year, five youths, all
under the age of seventeen, died at their respective homes.
They were all cotemporaries at school in 1840.   Four of
them, two of decidedly delicate constitutions, left school in
illness.   From this time forth, thy father entertained the
idea of removing the school to a more healthy locality, and
gave the whole force of his mind to its accomplishment.   I
accompanied him in the survey of numerous properties in
York and its vicinity, till at length the house and grounds
in Bootham were fixed upon, and finally entered in the First
month, 1846.   In this matter, whilst largely aided by the
counsel and personal service of many Friends from various
parts of the Quarterly Meeting, success was in a great
measure attributable to Joseph Rowntree's persevering firmness, and to the confidence reposed in him throughout the
Quarterly Meeting, as well as in various parts of the
kingdom, amongst the parents and friends of the Scholars.

*   *   *   *   *   *   *   *   *   *

I have already referred to the attack of measles in 1856.
This ended in the death of one of the scholars. Never was
thy dear Father's aid and sympathy more deeply felt and
appreciated. Suffering himself by reason of his near connection with the parents of the dear boy, an only son, he
nevertheless so helped us, as to prevent our quite giving way

under the pressure of this sore trial. After this event, the
failing health of my dear Rachel pointed to the necessity of
relieving her from all care of the school, and in 1857 we
left the house and removed to St. Mary's. The arrangements preceding this step, and those consequent upon it,
involved not a little of delicate management. In this Joseph
Rowntree's counsel and aid were most efficient. Difficulties
were overcome, the post of Resident Head Master was most
satisfactorily filled by my friend Fielden Thorp, the cordial
co-operation and harmonious working of all connected with
the school, was secured ; and the arrangements thus made
subsisted for eight years, till my final withdrawal in 1865.
The sound judgment and executive ability, which distinguished thy father in public life, were often observed by myself in
regard to the concerns of the school. To plan wisely and to
adapt means to an end, in execution of a purpose, were his
peculiar gifts. With far seeing prescience he anticipated,
and prepared to remove, all obstacles to completion. For
myself, that which most impressed me, whilst observing his
daily path for many years, was his entire Christian consis-
tency. In the last few years of his life especially, he seemed
to me as one living under a constant sense of the Divine
presence. No one can ever replace him to me. I love and
honour his memory, and at times am enabled to entertain
the hope, that through the same redeeming love, in which
alone he trusted, and which sustained him to the last, I may
meet him again.

I am, thy affectionate friend,

JOHN FORD.

To his brother Samuel.

12 mo. 30, 1859.—Stripping and bereavement may well

remind us that our own end cannot be far off. With desires
and prayers for myself that I may be found ready when the
summons may come, I mingle at times prayer for thee, my
dear brother, that thou as well as myself may find refuge
and security in Him who died to redeem us. He will accept
us both if we will but apply to Him and accept the offers of
His love and mercy. It is a comfort to me to know that it
is " not by works of righteousness which we have done, but
according to His mercy " that He saves us. If it were by
works I have no claim. Give these thoughts a little
consideration, my dear brother.

---

1 mo. 29, 1860.—An especial prayer for help for the
evening service at Bootham was largely answered. . My
heart glowed with love and earnestness whilst inviting the
beloved boys in the School-room to come to Christ. Much
of the same precious feeling was granted at reading time ; and
on withdrawing to the Lecture-room I was enabled to pour
out my heart in grateful thanksgiving, and then earnestly
to pray that every one who had been with us this evening,
with myself, might at last be found safe within the walls of
the Heavenly City, through our Heavenly Father's boundless
love in Jesus Christ. And thus though of late often exceeding
sorrowful, rejoicing is permitted.   " *Yet* I will rejoice in the
Lord, and joy in the God of my salvation."

Within the last few years the need of provision
for the further religious instruction of the young
people in the Society of Friends after leaving school,
had claimed the attention of many thoughtful
members of the Society. With a view of in some
degree meeting this want, various individuals engaged in the preparation of papers on points of

Christian doctrine, Church History, and other cognate subjects. In this service John Ford took a deep interest. His extensive knowledge of Scripture illustration and Church History, combined with a ready discrimination of salient points and great facility in composition, rendered the preparation of such Essays, a very congenial employment. To enumerate all that he wrote would be superfluous. Suffice it to say that the interest excited by these papers entailed on him the expenditure of no small amount of time and labour, in complying with invitations to read them in various places up and down the country. A memorandum shews that his essays on " Sacrifice," alluded to in the following extract, were read at thirty-six different places between the years 1856 and 1863.

2 mo. 26.—Last Third-day I went to London, and that evening and on Fifth-day, read to very large audiences in White Hart Court meeting house the essays on Sacrifice. On the alternate nights I read the same at Tottenham to a smaller but very select audience. They were well received by Friends of very different views. Much was said in commendation by individuals whose commendation was valuable. But I may gratefully acknowledge that the prayer to be preserved from elation was fully answered. Numbers of Yorkists and a few old Rochester scholars greeted me at the close of the meetings.

3 mo. 16.—To-day for the first time I paid a solitary visit to the grave of my dear Rachel. I stood awhile in sweet, tearful silence. It was a bright, sunny, spring-like day.

> " I saw around me the wide field revive
>   With fruits and fertile promise, and the Spring
> Come forth her work of gladness to contrive,
>   With all her reckless birds upon the wing ;
> And turned from all she brought, to *her* she could not bring !"

Many a time I recall her words, when I sat sorrowing beside her, forecasting my future loneliness, "I shall be with thee ;" and surely it is neither delusive nor sinful to believe that her gentle spirit is hovering near me. This at least *I know*, that she loves and adores the same God and Saviour, and that at His throne we can worship together,—I with tearful eyes and trembling heart and hope—whilst for her, God hath for ever wiped away all tears.

3 mo. 18.—I sometimes fear I am too continually sorrowful, and yet it is not a repining sorrow, nor is it a sorrow that prevents or (as I believe) mars my duties. I engage in them, pray for help in the performance, and thankfully acknowledge the help granted me. But in the silence and loneliness of evening I cannot restrain my tears. And yet they are not hopeless or desponding tears. Often are they mingled with thought and feeling intensely fixed on her, whose constant love cheered me for twenty-two years— day by day—hour by hour—and sometimes mingled with an overwhelming sense of the love of a merciful Heavenly Father and Redeemer, and precious thoughts of re-union where parting is never known.

To-day I think I have been helped in my service. In Meeting I engaged in vocal prayer. This at one time seemed too high and too solemn an engagement for me. Since my bereavement I have more than ever sought and found refuge and comfort and peace and joy in frequent private prayer : perhaps this has been the means of preparing me for this service in public. To-day as at other times on thus engaging in Meeting, my spirit was greatly tendered and contrited,

especially after I had resumed my seat, under a sense of the
condescending love of my Heavenly Father in thus per-
mitting me to serve Him. "Why," therefore, "art thou
cast down, O my soul?" "Hope thou in God; for I shall
yet (again) praise Him who is the health of my countenance
and my God!"

To a Relative.

6 mo. 2.—I am glad to find that thou art using, as I think,
the only means of safety—entire abstinence. When I say
the *only* means, I merely mean to imply that in the case of
long continued habits, all other means, humanly speaking,
are hopeless *apart* from abstinence. I highly value the means
referred to in thine; and in reply to thy request that I
would pray for thee, I may say, that since I saw thee, I have
done so many a time, and continue so to do. Join thine also.
Why are our lives thus prolonged? Just to give us a
prolonged opportunity to accept the offers of Divine love and
mercy so profusely offered us, *in* and *by* and *through* our
Saviour. "Come unto Me *all* ye that labour, &c." "Him
that cometh unto Me I will in *no wise* cast out." For no
reason or cause whatsoever—not for long years of forgetfulness—not for multiplied transgressions—not at the eleventh
hour. Therefore let us come in full assurance of His promise,
He will *not* cast out. Having come and received the promised
pardon, and life still prolonged a little space, our joy will be
to spend it all in His service—longing at times for the *rest*
of Heaven, yet still willing and joyful to bear, to suffer and
to serve a little longer on earth, if it were only to afford the
poor proof we can of our love. May some portion of this
happy experience yet be thine.

6 mo. 17.—In the School-room I referred to the closing

session. Aware from week to week of its approach what
would retrospection now present to us?—Opportunities
improved? Evil successfully resisted? Communion with
our Heavenly Father sought and through Christ obtained?
Had we all, scholars and teachers, sought to fulfil our
respective duties? Could we look back without remorseful
regrets?—I said I had often believed, and I would not
to-night abandon the belief, that often our evening in that
room had been owned by our Heavenly Father's love contriting our spirits, and lifting our hearts to Him in silent
aspirations of prayer, thanksgiving and praise. A solemn
pause ensued; and I kneeled and returned thanksgiving for
the preserving grace and the love and favour granted us, and
prayed especially for the young men about to enter on the
busy concerns of life. Thus ended one more series of these
deeply interesting engagements.

To ———

(a former pupil who was contemplating the resignation of
his membership in the Society of Friends.)

6 mo., 1860.—I was glad to receive thine of the 5th, and
much interested in its contents. * * * I am glad thou
hast had a conference with thy father, and that it was as I
infer in some respects satisfactory. I think it was both wise
and kind of thee to wait at his request for a year or so before
taking a decided step. I cannot but believe that honest,
earnest, prayerful inquiry, such as I trust thine is, will issue
in thy accepting those views of Christian truth, doctrine and
practice, which will be to thee the road to peace and happiness. And so believing, I feel sure there will always be,
between thy views and thy practice and my own, far more
points of union than of difference—always granting that the

I

love of Christ, faith in Him, and desire to serve Him, be the
foundation stone of all our hopes and all our confidence.

In looking at some of thy sentiments especially on that
regarding forms of prayer, it occurs to me that thy personal
experience may have had much influence in thy conclusions.
Happily placed as regards early training—little exposed to
temptations from without—a temperament and dispositions
tending greatly to make early life pleasant, and to secure
the warm attachment of thy friends—and possibly having
less of temptation to contend with from within than many
have had to encounter—amongst all these happy and favourable circumstances, I can conceive a conscience less burdened,
less alarmed with the sense of sinfulness and of actual sin
than that of a large number less happily trained and placed.

Those who are conscious of the very reverse of all this—
conscious not only of a sinful nature but of accumulated
unforgiven actual sin—to such as these when once aroused
to a sense of their condition, all *forms* of prayer give way to
the deep, earnest out-gushing of heart and soul that needs
no prompting, no exemplar. The particular want, the particular confession, the particular besetting sin, the ever recurring temptation—will find earnest, burning words poured
forth in the name of Christ. Moreover I believe that in the
next stage of the Christian life, when the joyful sense of
reconciliation with God through the blood of the cross—when
"being justified by faith, we have peace with God through
our Lord Jesus Christ," any words but our own, the fresh
spontaneous outpouring of our joyful spirits, will be altogether
inadequate to the occasion. We should no more think of
adopting other men's words than I should think when wishing
to write to thee, of adopting the Chinese plan of going to a
paid letter-writer, and telling him, "I have a dear young
friend in ——, write to him for me and tell him all that
is proper to tell him."

Perhaps I am mistaken in my imaginary description of thy past experience. Perhaps thou wilt assent to much that I have said, seeing I have applied my remarks more to the individual worship of the closet than to the united worship of the congregation. Nevertheless whatever path may ultimately be thine, I feel assured that the further we advance in the Divine life, the less we shall depend upon man and his doings, and the more we shall seek for ourselves direct, immediate intercourse with our Heavenly Father in the name of His Son, under the guidance of His spirit.

I am glad to hear that the tour is agreed upon. I heartily wish thee every enjoyment in it. The capacity for such enjoyment is one of the especial good gifts of God to the young. One element of this capacity for enjoyment will also I trust be participated in by all your party,—to see amidst all the beauties of wondrous scenery,

> " A ray of heavenly light gilding all forms
> Terrestrial in the vast and the minute;
> The unambiguous footsteps of the God
> Who gives its lustre to an insect's wing,
> And wheels His throne upon the rolling worlds."

8 mo. 9.—Formal opening of the school session this afternoon. The usual topics of address—truthfulness—kindness —and purity of language and conduct. Allegiance on their part—kindness and good government on ours.—Excuse-making, dangerous ground, closely allied to untruthfulness.— Minor details—cash accounts—cash kept in purse and pocket. —New arrangement at the gardens—washing place, &c.— Elder scholars—their duties towards the school generally— their power for good or evil, and consequently their responsibility.—Whilst every one should be placed on new ground till by his conduct he brought the past to remembrance,

there were some who would hold their places in the senior class conditionally.

11 mo. 4.—To-day is the anniversary of the death of my dear friend Joseph Rowntree—more missed by me than any one whom I have lost except my dear Rachel. His brotherly aid, his wise counsel, and his Christian example seem more precious than ever : now I miss them day by day. * * * I have found a little access in prayer in private, and a little help sought and obtained in the evening at Bootham. At the close of reading I remarked to the boys, " You have begun your merriment again, and I do not know that I have much to object to if it will continue a little longer ; but let me repeat one word, already said in the schoolroom. Before you close your eyes to sleep to-night—' Try to love Him— tell Him you wish to love Him—ask Him to help you.' " My own spirit has been tendered to-day by these simple words of Dr. Vaughan.

11 mo. 18. * * * This evening I was led to address the scholars in a rather unexpected way, but it would seem not inappropriately. One of the elder boys followed me out of reading to the lecture room, and told me of the difficulty he felt in doing, that which he felt the need of doing under the influence of what I had said in the schoolroom. I had no knowledge whatever of his recent circumstances in this particular. He came to acknowledge what was wrong, and seeking for help. I was glad to see him. I tried to en- courage him to more effort. My own spirit was tendered. I told him I had prayed for him. I recommended him to try to-night the simple prayer, " Heavenly Father, for Jesus' sake help me to put away unkind and angry thoughts and feelings." He left me I hope cheered and encouraged.

To ——————

(a former pupil to whom the letter on page 113 was addressed.)

12 mo., 1860.—In reference to the main topic of thy letter, whilst I regret the conclusion arrived at, I will not say one word to disturb thy "convictions," or to prevent thee from following that course which will ensure thee peace of mind and progress in the Christian life. I shall entertain the belief that we are both travelling in converging paths, that will meet at last in one of the many mansions in our Father's house—in the city whose walls are salvation and whose gates are praise, where sects and names and all the poor distinctions of time are utterly unknown and forgotten.

To see thee, as I believe, in earnest to become a true disciple of Christ, looking for salvation through His blood shed for sinners—His life given as a ransom for many—is a very delightful thing. As I journey on towards the end, whilst I love that section of the church with which my lot is cast, and am thankful that the religion of my education has become that of my judgment and affections, I feel more and more disposed to recognize as brothers in Christ, all who love Him and manifest their love by their allegiance. I am acquainted with such of various names, and find large common ground of union, and scope for united action. I find among these many who can accept much which once was more peculiar to Quakerism than it is in this day. If I speak of Peace, they can respond in the hatefulness and anti-Christian nature of war: they think truth-speaking better than oaths: they admit that every true believer is a priest: they condemn the vanities and frivolities of fashion: they admit that essentials are better than signs: they do not deny the right of any man who believes himself called to preach the gospel, wheresoever and whensoever he can without violating the good order of society. One trained in the Church of England—and whose religion cost him much—makes the following declaration, to which I apprehend any Quaker would subscribe :—" Baptismal regeneration, Church privileges, the sacramental system, confession, and priestly absolution may do for some people when in health, but no smile of joy from a sick man, would ever be the fruit of such miserable comforters in the last hour. When a dying man [and I would add a living man] can say or feel, ' I know that my Redeemer liveth,' he wants no more." And therefore I trust that whilst seeking enjoyment of the means of grace *elsewhere* as tending to promote the great end of life—reconciliation with God through Jesus Christ, and a daily hope of eternal blessedness,—all that is sustainable on scripture grounds in Quakerism will still be maintained by thee. I shall not cease often to think of thee with affectionate interest. Our conversation at St. Mary's eleven months ago, and the day at——— are remembered with far more pleasure than if on either occasion I had entered upon controversy. I believe the tenor of my intercourse with thee on both occasions manifested more concern as regards the end, than the means. I rejoiced then in the belief that thou wast in earnest, and that feeling attends me now.

Don't let this letter close our correspondence. Let me know from time to time how thou art getting on ; and if the gospel should be so preached in ——— Meeting, and prayer and praise be frequently offered, and thou shouldst find peace and progress amongst *us*, how glad I should be. And more than that—if feeling the want of these, thy own heart should be so filled with the love of Christ as that thy own mouth should be opened to speak of it and invite others to partake, there would be joy and gladness in other places than ———. If the young would but come to the rescue,

I believe they might find in Quakerism all that their souls
long for.

---

12 mo. 1, 1860. ——— [one of the scholars] came to
borrow money. I took the opportunity of offering a word of
encouragement to him ; expressed my pleasure that he was
occupying his leisure time profitably, and my belief that he
was also seeking after higher and holier things—peace with
God by Jesus Christ. He seemed moved : his face assumed
more of beauty than it would have been thought capable of
expressing—a thoughtful, gentle, chastened aspect, denoting
as I believe a response to the word. He very modestly
signified his wish to do as I had suggested he was doing.
At parting he thanked me.

12 mo. 2.—Yesterday afternoon I had a short visit from
an old scholar. He wished to tell me more fully and freely
of some of his religious difficulties. One is, he feels no joy
in believing, no answer to prayer : thinks under these circumstances prayer is a mockery. He believes in predestination
because he cannot reconcile free will and foreknowledge.
With all this, his conversation led me to believe that he has
a tender conscience, is leading a blameless life, is acting
under the influence of the spirit, is an object of the love of
Christ; but is looking for too much of sensible, perceptible
evidence and feeling. I felt much for him, and gave him
such counsel as presented itself adapted to his condition,
which I assured him was no uncommon experience—patient
continuance in well doing, perseverance in prayer, rejecting
all idea of mockery as a temptation of Satan, accepting the
invitations to pray so abundant in the New Testament,
remembering that the invitations are to *all* to come to Christ ;
that man can be lost only by his own act, that there is no

election of reprobation : that these great truths like a line
of light run through Holy Scripture. These things I set
before him. He left me, I hope a little refreshed. He
thanked me warmly. I remembered him in prayer in the
evening.

12 mo. 8.—Had an interview with the senior class.
J. S. Rowntree in Meeting had expressed his sympathy and
offered encouragement and counsel to those who watched—
some for long years—over the souls of others, "as those
that must give account." This reminded me of a deep
exercise of spirit last evening in my solitary bedroom, when
I bowed the knee in earnest prayer for the senior class especially, and for those who leave us. I remember but few
such occasions. I found this evening, as I think, my peace
was concerned in simply narrating these facts to the beloved
company in the senior class-room. A deep solemnity was I
believe granted us, and I kneeled in prayer for them once
more, then and there.

12 mo. 15.—In the schoolroom, a brief review of the
session.—A reference to our first meeting. Truth and kindness and purity enjoined—with what success? Our prayers
with them and for them to encourage and cheer them—our
endeavours to induce them to pray for themselves. Though
I had not looked to any such service, a solemn quiet seemed
spread over us, and I kneeled down and offered thanksgiving
for the blessings and mercies of the session, ending with
prayer for continued preservation. Dear F. Thorp gave a
faithful word of parting warning and counsel.—So ends one
more session as far as Sabbath evenings are concerned. I
think I might say in the quaint language of Job Scott,

> " A thankful heart I feel ;
> In peace my mind is stay'd."

12 mo. 23. * * At Meeting this morning, seeing a

number of young children present I addressed them especially. I quoted Isaiah, "He shall gather the lambs with
His arm, and carry them in His bosom." I was helped I
believe to adapt my words to the understandings of these
darling little ones. I had more than peace in the offering.
Oh that I had myself more of the spirit of a "little child."

1 mo. 15, 1861.—I have received an extremely sweet
letter from a young disciple. "It cheers my old heart,"
(to borrow an expression of dear William Forster's) to see in
him and in other Yorkists, signs of early dedication.

1 mo. 18.—I had a special interview with all the teachers.
I addressed them on several points connected with moral and
intellectual training, and in regard to the avoidance of all
that would interfere with or discourage the religious life in
any—quiet deportment when attending them in the bed-
rooms in the evening, avoiding light conversation, and if
possible, all penalty. I mentioned that I had seen a boy
who occasionally kneeled at his bed-side, look extremely
offended on going into his room, by a penalty very small,
just then announced to him for a very trifling offence. I
referred to the solemnizing effect on my own spirit by being
present at times when boys were thus kneeling. A little
silence ensued in the conference, and I felt bound to engage
in prayer for Divine guidance and blessing on ourselves and
our charge.

To HIS BROTHER SAMUEL.

1 mo. 22, 1861.—These engagements of service are not of
my own seeking; but when solicited to assist on the occasion
of gatherings of Friends, I do not feel at liberty to refuse. It
is becoming very common amongst Friends to have meetings
of Sabbath School Teachers on a large scale, and I have
frequent invitations to attend such. I do not complain of
labour or fatigue or expense, but rather feel glad if I may

be permitted to do a little service for Him who has done so
much for me. And when I feel for myself how precious a
thing it is to know something of peace with God through
faith in Jesus Christ, and feel too His preserving grace and
mercy in keeping me from sinning, and His pardoning
mercy when evil in any form gains the ascendant, I earnestly desire the same blessings for all who are dear to
me, and for none more than for thee. Whilst life and intellect are still ours there is hope for every one of us. If
we have not come in at the ninth hour we may at the
eleventh. Do come !

In the Second-month of 1861, John Ford attended
the interment of an old Scholar, Richard Ecroyd
Tatham, of Settle, who in his twenty-third year was
called away after a brief course of earnest, loving
devotedness to the service of his Lord. Deeply
interested in his former pupil, and in the part he
had taken in the establishment of the Settle Adult
Sabbath Classes, desirous also that the encouragement and instruction of such a life should not be
lost to others, John Ford willingly undertook the
compilation of a Memoir of his young friend from
materials furnished by his family. It was published
in a small volume entitled " The Sabbath School
Teacher ; a Memoir of Richard E. Tatham ;" and
it went through three editions in a short time.

To ———

(To whom the letters, pages 113 and 117 were addressed.)

Early part of 1861.—I am indebted to thee for thine of

the 10th and 28th. I must ask thee to attribute any delay
in replying, to any other cause than that of diminished
affectionate interest. In attempting to reply, I feel deeply
the inadequacy of correspondence to explain or illustrate the
important and interesting topics touched on in thine.

I am glad of thy first concession that "private prayer and
watchfulness are our most essential duty." Agreeing entirely on that point, and earnestly seeking to live in the
spirit of such a conviction, we shall not differ *widely* about
other matters, and shall most assuredly as I believe, meet in
heaven at last, and entirely agree in all things for ever in
perfect love, joy and peace.

In reference to public worship, (no form of proceeding
being set forth in Scripture) its arrangements seem to be left
to the judgment of the churches. Now the vast diversity of
conditions assembled in any congregation, seems to me to
militate against the idea, that perfect unity of thought and
of devotional feeling could be possible, and cannot therefore
be an essential circumstance. I should abstain from quoting
any passage of Scripture as a warrant for silence in worship :
I deduce the practice from the very nature of true worship
as defined by our Saviour, "in Spirit and in Truth." I can
conceive no better *preparation* for worship than silence.

When assembled for this purpose, each individual, as in
the Divine presence, examines his own heart—feels his various wants—his indifference—his sinfulness, and secretly
applies for pardon and for help in the name of Christ.

I believe worship to be an *individual* act—direct communion with God through Jesus Christ our intercessor and
mediator. Each individual in the congregation thus feeling
his own particular needs and thus applying—the whole
congregation is engaged in the most solemn and most acceptable worship in spirit and in truth. A solemnity spread

over a silent meeting at times—seems manifestly. to own this worship. Ministry of the word faithfully exercised, whether in prayer or in proclamation of Gospel truth, is a most valuable auxiliary to this public worship—a means for the edification of believers, and for the conversion of the unregenerate. I fear that a set, appointed, pre-arranged course of prayer and praise, interferes with this individual worship, and tends to foster a mistaken idea that to listen attentively, to be present at these services is worship—when not one thought of the individual heart may have been directed heavenward.

In reference to prayer, I think I must renounce the authority of Holy Scripture, if I conceded that true and acceptable prayer could ever be offered without the aid of the Holy Spirit of God. The very first thought of the awakened soul, the very first and faintest thought of repentance—the very first longing for reconciliation and pardon—the very first breath of life that vents itself in "God be merciful to me a sinner,"—is most surely the work of God's Holy Spirit and of nothing else. I consider the grand feature of Quakerism to be the individuality of true worship—the aversion from all worship by proxy—the direct communication of the soul with its Maker through Christ alone. Such combined individualities make up the best and truest public worship. Nor will that worship be silent: vocal utterance of confession—of entreaty for pardon—acknowledgements of the mercies and the love of God—praise and thanksgiving to Him,—will complete and crown this public worship. If this in any congregation is rarely the case, the fault is not in the system, but in those to whom, if they had sought it, God would have given these precious gifts for the edification of His Church.

I know it is utterly impossible in a brief letter to satisfy

a young and earnest enquirer like thee.   I believe that few
if any such inquirers ever found satisfaction in any system
however spiritual, or however material—whether amidst the
silence of a Friends' Meeting, or amidst the music, the incense, the vestments, the eloquence, and all the appliances
to charm the sensuous nature found in some other churches.
I believe no such inquirer found either peace or rest, till
by individual application, by all the earnestness of one
who is ready to perish without it, he has sought and
obtained through Jesus Christ reconciliation and pardon
with his Heavenly Father.   Having found this—filled with
the love of Christ—private and public worship are his
delight.   The more hold he has of the substance, the
less anxious is he about the mode.   I can with all truth
acknowledge that the profession of my education has become
the religion of my judgment, of my heart and conscience;
and I find as a member of the Society of Friends, no limita-
tion in regard to the attainment of every Christian grace
and gift, and the acceptance of every Christian doctrine.

I know, and I rejoice in knowing, that there are multitudes
thronging the road to Heaven of other names and professions;
but I believe I shall best promote—not merely my own salvation—if I may say so—but the universal cause of Christ,
by remaining in this small enclosure of the great sheep-fold.
But I would judge no one who in all sincerity of heart
believed that he had found his own proper allotment in
another quarter.   To the young I would only add, be not
hasty.   Try whether in the profession of thy education there
is not ample scope for the young and earnest Christian—for
him, who, having accepted Christ as his Saviour, can look to
God, not as an offended sovereign but as a reconciled and
most merciful Father—one to whom he can now confidingly
go and confess his faults, his infirmities, his transgressions,
sure of pardon for his Saviour's sake.

Thus the work of sanctification proceeding day by day—
love to Christ increasing—it will be passing strange if he
does not find service for Christ to do : to tell of His love—to
invite others to partake of the same blessings.   Many in the
Society of Friends are doing this.   Would that many more
would yield their hearts to do the same.   Silent Meetings
would cease.   The voice of exhortation and prayer and
praise would again be heard within the walls of ——— and
——— Meeting houses.   I long to see "Yorkists" coming
forward in this glorious work.   I know of several who have
so come forward.   May it please our Heavenly Father to
increase the number.

———————

3rd mo. 24.—On the 21st I completed my Sixtieth year.
How solemn the thought—the three-score over and gone !
Few of the ten may be mine.   May I seek with renewed
earnestness and watchfulness and prayer, to be ready at a
moment !

Failing physical power—memory less dependable ; an idea
presented and if not laid hold on immediately, gone past
recovery ; less elasticity of spirits ; more easily depressed ;
these are some of the symptoms of three-score.   May the
remnant, whether few or many, be increasingly dedicated.
I believe I desire to serve ; I pray to be enabled so to do.   I
pray that my service may be appointed and ordered for me—
that my faith and love may be increased.

To his brother Samuel.

5 mo. 16, 1861.—I did not like to leave home without a
line to thee, for thou art very often in my thoughts and art
remembered in my prayers.   For amidst anxieties about
myself, that as I draw nearer and nearer to my journey's

end, I may know the work of preparation for an eternal
state to be carried on, I do not forget those connected with
me by the ties of nearest relationship.   Whilst at times
enabled to trust that through our Heavenly Father's mercy
in Jesus Christ our Saviour, I may, notwithstanding utter
unworthiness meet acceptance at last, I cannot but earnestly
desire the same good hope for thee, and many others whom
I have known and loved.   As our lines of life differ, so do
our temptations and besetments; and all of us have need
again and again to adopt the poor publican's prayer, " God
be merciful to me a sinner."   And it is a blessed thought,
and a very blessed truth, that no such prayer as that is ever
breathed in vain.   I am turned sixty : thou art approaching
that mark : it is time for us both to be in earnest to give
diligence to make our calling and election sure.

8 mo. 4.—Anxious and troubled about the future, I went
to Meeting with little capacity for enjoyment.   A prayer
was offered which did not seem to help me.—Towards the
close of the meeting F. Thorp spoke on " they that seek Me
early shall find Me," addressing himself chiefly to the little
ones.   This seemed to open up some little spring of life, and
I ventured to commend the little ones present for the especial
blessing of our Heavenly Father's love.   My own spirit was
tendered, and the clouds that hung over me parted so as to
admit a gleam of light.

*   *   *   The vacation closes to-night—the thirty-third
vacation ! possibly the last to me before either my services
here end, or the long vacation from earthly service begins.
Oh that by the grace of a merciful Saviour—preserving—
keeping—sanctifying—redeeming from day to day, it may
be a matter of indifference to me whether one or the

other event await me—that indifference which is comprised
in "Thy will, not mine be done." Grant me, Heavenly
Father, a more trustful spirit.

8 mo. 11.—I have been lately perhaps over anxious
about the future. I have made *that* a subject of frequent
prayer, desiring to trust it entirely to the Lord—to Him
who has appointed my locations hitherto from my youth up.
I wish to trust Him entirely. I pray to be guided and
directed solely by His counsel. I want to be as a little
child in His hands. I pray for an enlightened judgment in
this matter, and that I may not be permitted to err. If the
time is approaching to sever my connection with the School,
all I ask is light upon my path—light to point out where
my few remaining days may be spent, where I may best
serve, if permitted to serve Him, whom amidst all my
wanderings and waywardness I believe I love. May I
to-night with a thankful heart accept the invitation, "Casting
all your care upon Him, for He careth for you."

8 mo. 12.—Drank tea at Bootham with the members of the
Senior Class. I addressed them before we parted on responsibilities, duties and privileges—their power to help us—points
in which they could especially do so—language—private conduct—courtesy—politeness—the power of *silent* disapprobation
—the duty of more active remonstrance against evil. Sketched
the tale of the little book "A Word in Season"—the young
man who so politely not only stopped profane language in
a railway carriage, but whose interference was blest to the
conversion of a gentleman much older than himself. His
expostulation was,—"Will you have the kindness not to
swear." So might a schoolboy say to another, "Will you
have the kindness to stop that kind of conversation." We
had a very pleasant evening.

10 mo. 27.—It is very late, near midnight—but I do not like to let a day of renewed mercy and favour pass unrecorded. I can look back upon some of these records and as I read them, say, "Thou hast been my help,"—and then perhaps the prayer may arise, "Leave me not neither forsake me, O God of my Salvation." Help asked for and granted, in Meeting, at Bootham, and in my own evening reading at home, has been again my experience : the spirit of prayer has been bestowed.

11 mo. 1.—To-day the little memoir of Richard E. Tatham is published. I have thirty copies, most of which I intend to distribute to young friends. Before sending away a few this evening, the thought occurred to me with much sweetness, to pray that a blessing might go with every volume. I retired to my room, and on bended knee preferred this prayer in the name of Jesus. How many things we may make subjects of prayer! Happy they who make this discovery in early life! Happy even they who make it though late—who make it at all—who make it ere it be too late!

11 mo. 3.　*　*　* A little incident toward the close of the day encouraged me. One of the elder boys—one over whom I have watched, and for whom I have prayed—and who was the object of the care and love of my sainted R., followed me from the school, and in a simple way expressed to me his feeling of the privilege of our First-day evenings. I said a few kind, encouraging words to the beloved young man.

11 mo. 24.　*　* In the evening after special private prayer, I was enabled to address the boys very solemnly on a very solemn subject. I recommended them to make the subject of the evening's address a matter of special, individual prayer

K

that night, in faith that the promise made to two ("if two
of you shall agree") would be verified to sixty, promising to
join my prayer to theirs for them. Heavenly Father, be
pleased to bless them and answer their prayers, and permit
me to pray for them, and hear us for Jesus' sake.

11 mo. 30.—Address to the boys on First-day occupations,
&c.—frequent change—interval of relaxation. I had stood
for some time talking with two of the teachers. Loud rising
conversation, &c., were proceeding in the schoolroom. At
length they all assembled. I queried whether if all they
had said within the last twenty minutes were taken down, it
would be congruous or incongruous with the purposes of the
day. I had no reason to believe it was *out* of harmony with
those purposes. I was glad of these signs of freedom. I
feared the sudden hush—arising often out of the consciousness that there was something that would not bear light—an
appearance as plainly indicative of conspiracy as if conspirator
were labelled on the back.—Happy to see no such signs here.
This led to a review of the duties of the day—the reasonable-
ness of requiring a few verses of Scripture to be learned.
My desire that First-day might be to them in recollection a
pleasant day. Referred to the dying declaration of dear
J. H. Walpole of the happy First-day evenings spent at
York. My prayer that such might be the retrospect of every
one present.

12 mo. 8.—Last evening kneeling by my bed-side I was
enabled to pour forth prayer for the senior class, and for
those who leave us finally this winter, with more of earnestness and feeling, and with a sense of access in the name
of Jesus exceedingly precious. To-day in Meeting, John S.
Rowntree, once a York scholar, spoke with much feeling on
the text, "They watch for your souls as they that must give

account;" expressing his sympathy with those who for long
years had been so watching, perhaps discouraged at little
fruit.   My spirit was greatly contrited with the love of Christ
in remembrance of the favour of last evening.   I felt as
though my prayer had been heard and would be answered.
I felt too, reluctant as I was to speak of this coincidence,
that I must try to bring it before the senior class this evening.
I sought and found a suitable opportunity.   I told them the
circumstances—my motive for telling them—to encourage
them to unite with us in prayer for themselves.   A very
solemn feeling seemed to spread over us; and I said, "I
believe some of you can unite in prayer now to the same
end."   I kneeled down and was enabled once more to pour
forth earnest, heartfelt petitions for this beloved company.
A solemn, quiet tone seemed to prevail with them the rest of
the evening.

12 mo. 15.—In the evening I gave one more brief parting
address.   "We have already been reminded to-day that this
is our last Sabbath of the session.   At its commencement we
endeavoured to set before you the blessedness of three great
practical duties—Christian virtues eminently for school boys
to cultivate,—truth, kindness and purity.   From time to
time as the months and weeks have passed away, we have
endeavoured to encourage and confirm you in the practice of
these as well as of all other Christian virtues.   And we have
prayed with you and for you, and encouraged you to pray
for yourselves, that truth and kindness and purity might ever
be your characteristics; that so when the day should come,
which now at last has come, bringing our sabbaths to a close,
not one remorseful thought might oppress the heart of any
one amongst you in looking back on the half-year in reference
to these duties."

Silence and solemnity seemed to deepen; and I said,

"It did not seem to me when I first opened my mouth that it would be required of me vocally to express our sense of the mercy and goodness of the Lord to us during the session, but I feel that I cannot consistent with peace of mind omit it. I trust some of you can unite with us in this." I then kneeled down, and returned thanks for the mercies temporal and spiritual showered upon us, and prayed that the Divine presence and blessing might go with those who go, and rest upon those who stay : and that seeing we might never meet together again in time under our present relationships—that through our Heavenly Father's mercy in Jesus Christ our Lord, we might meet together before His throne in Heaven, there to join in an endless song of praise.

In Fourth-month, 1862, under the apprehension of religious duty, and with the encouragement of his Monthly Meeting, John Ford attended the Yearly Meeting in Dublin, and visited the schools in Ireland conducted by Friends. In this service he was joined by his cousin, William Tanner, of Bristol, with whom he was closely united in the bonds of Christian fellowship. In the following autumn, again liberated by their respective Monthly Meetings, they visited most of the Meetings composing London and Middlesex Quarterly Meeting, and had many social gatherings and meetings for the young, as well as other more private service.

6 mo. 17, 1862.—Having analysed the character papers I spent a few minutes at reading time in commenting upon them. The prevalence of truth—the few exceptions—some of the exceptions explicable on grounds indicated by other

characteristics. Noticed the variety of employments—the mention of kindness to schoolfellows—the rare instances of associations not for good—the opposite—several whose influence over others and over each other was decidedly good—the belief entertained that with several, in the Senior Class especially, this good influence arose out of their having measurably given their hearts to their Saviour. F. Thorp read a short Psalm, and I ventured on thanksgiving and prayer. I shook hands with each as they filed out. ———— hastily withdrew his and buried his face in his hands: he sent word by one of the teachers that he wished to see me in his bed-room. I went, and had a few words of parting with him. He came a very little boy—was most kindly cared for by my dear R. After causing me deep anxiety by his conduct, latterly there has been cause of rejoicing in the change apparent in him. So ends one more session. "Non nobis, &c."

In giving a brief outline of a tour taken during this summer, John Ford writes :—

At Evesham I heard that my very earliest surviving friend, Thomas Pumphrey, had died on the 31st of Seventh-month. * * * * My dear friend had sent a message of love to me from his dying bed. On the 10th of Sixth-month last I accepted an invitation to assist at a festival at Ackworth on dear Thomas Pumphrey's sixtieth birth-day. The proceedings were of a most interesting character. In T. P.'s speech he particularly referred to me as one of his oldest friends, our association as children, our common ancestry, our companionship at school, and at length our duties running in parallel lines, the bonds of true friendship ever drawing us more closely together.

At the solicitation of Thomas Pumphrey's family,

John Ford consented to prepare a Memoir of his departed friend. It was published in 1864.

To ———— (a young man).

10 mo. 17, 1862.—I have often thought of thee since I left ————. I gratefully remember the hospitalities received at thy father's house and thy own particular kindness. The story of thy varied experience of life during thy absence from home deeply interested me. Now if any apology is needed, these must be my apology for writing to thee. I want to express the desire which I feel so truly that I cannot avoid expressing it, that now, having seen much of the dark side of human nature in various forms, thoughts of the solemn responsibilities of life may begin to have due place with thee.

All the associations of my life have been with youth : the result of this has been enlarged sympathies with them, and an ever increasing desire (if so I may be enabled) to help them, if it be only to point to the path of peace and happiness.

It was impossible (to me at least) to be acquainted with thee, even for so brief a time as my visit afforded, without perceiving qualities of head and heart that greatly interested me, and raised in me desires which I now venture to convey to thee, that all these—the energy of will—the executive ability—the affections—the costly knowledge of the world—may all be made subservient to thy own highest interests. I have no doubt there are times when these desires have a place in thy own heart. I want thee to yield to them—to cherish them : yielded to and cherished, they will lead thee where they have led many others—to the foot of the cross. I need not interpret this phraseology to thee. I long that thou shouldst realize for thyself, all the benefits, all the sweetness of going *there*—knowing all past transgressions for ever blotted out, and ability granted to pursue

henceforward the path of peace.   And *that* is a bright path.
The life of the young Christian is a joyous life.   There is
room in his path for the expansion of all his faculties, of all
his peculiar gifts and talents.   The energy of his will, his
executive ability, his power to influence others will find
ample scope.   His joyous temperament will commend his
profession ; by his lively yet chastened wit he will show that
Christianity is no dull, morose affair, but that the young
disciple of Christ *is* and has a right to be, one of the most
cheerful and happy of men.   It has been well said—and
there are living proofs of the truth of the saying—"there is
no more beautiful, no more blessed sight upon earth than a
youth devoted to Christ."

And thou art yet young—with position, means, and talents,
and many other advantageous circumstances.   Come then at
once, and take the road I have endeavoured to point out to
thee.   If it should prove painful and difficult for a time, thou
hast already shown qualities that are not daunted by pain
and difficulty—and be assured, dear ————, that before long
the ways of wisdom will be found to be ways of pleasantness
and all her paths peace.

———————

To ———— (to the same young man).

10 mo. 25, 1862.—I do not wish to burden thee by
writing, or in any way to lay upon thee the obligation of
replying, but thy letter of the 21st, I can most truly say,
deepened the interest I had already felt for thee, and left me
no alternative, (with a peaceful mind at least,) but to write
to thee again.   The naturalness and the truthful air of thy
letter, the condition of thy health, and above all the sense of
want which it seems to indicate—the longing for peace with
God—all these sentiments led me to desire and to pray too,

that I might be enabled to point out to thee a little further, the road to peace. I know it is little we can do to help one another, but it pleases our Heavenly Father to use human instrumentality and to bless its use.

I read with painful interest and yet not without a hopeful and cheering thought, thy query, "Am I fit to die?" With like feelings also I read thy reflections on the past. I have said "hopeful and cheering," because I believe that the very first dawn of the light of the Holy-Spirit in the heart, is given us to convince us of sin. Under this conviction, we have in Holy Scripture abundance of authority and encouragement and loving invitation to go to our Heavenly Father, and earnestly to plead for pardon in the name of Jesus. I have no doubt that the parable of the prodigal son is perfectly familiar to thee. So it has been to thousands who never felt its fitness and beauty, till a deep personal interest brought it home to their hearts, and the spirit of God sealed the instruction there.

Men are apt to talk of little and much in reference to their transgressions against the Divine law; but these distinctions disappear when we come to see ourselves as we are seen of God. *Then* even those who to human apprehension have least erred from the way of peace, can without cant or hypocrisy (but with solemn conviction of the truth of the confession) confess themselves fallen, sinful and helpless— pronounce themselves utterly unworthy, and throw themselves just as they are, like the poor prodigal, on the mercy of their Heavenly Father in the name and for the sake of His dear Son, who died for our sins, and paid the price of our redemption with His most precious blood. So coming, we have the promises of our Lord Himself that He will in no wise cast us out. I want thee to come. If any suggestion arises in thy mind that thou art not fit to come, and thus to apply for pardon, reject it as a temptation of the evil one. Go just as thou art. If prayer seems difficult, ask for the ability to pray. Ask for the grace of repentance, ask earnestly—importunately. Remember the declaration, " If we confess our sins, God is faithful and just to forgive us our sins, and to cleanse us from all unrighteousness." He is *faithful* because he has promised; and His promises are yea and amen for ever. ·He is *just* because Christ Himself has paid the penalty of our sins—of mine—and of thine. We have but to ask and to have. "Ask and ye shall receive," is His own blessed declaration. An unbeliever on hearing the simplicity of the Gospel plan set before him is said to have replied, "This is too *good* to be *true*." Millions of redeemed spirits in heaven and tens of thousands of believers on earth, can testify that it is as *true* as it is *good*.

It is not a vague indefinite trust in the mercy of God that will suffice us. We must seek that mercy under a deep, heartfelt sense of our need, and in simple reliance upon the sacrifice of our Saviour—the blood shed for the remission of sins. Seek that, dear ———, and thou shalt assuredly find : and then the all important query, "Am I fit to die ? " shall receive a joyful and affirmative solution. And then if restored health should be granted thee—fit to die, and fit to live—a happy life may be thine. If early summoned away, a happy death—a happy translation to a better inheritance will be thine. An entire stranger to thee till within the last few weeks, do I need to apologize for the freedom with which I write ? Thy kind and frank letter of the 21st inclines me to think I need not. Whilst it will be pleasant to me to hear from thee, I beg that thou wilt not feel under any obligation to write, especially, if still unwell, writing should be wearisome or fatiguing to thee.

4 mo. 19, 1863.—Two weeks have passed away since I wrote. Why do I write? I am too prone to take desponding views of myself—to think how much I might do, how little in comparison of others I am doing, if I am doing anything for my Lord—feeling often how much more I might know of the peace and joy of believing than I do know. With these views I sometimes can reap a little comfort, a little renewed trust and faith and love, a little contrition of spirit, by reading a brief record of past mercies. Did the psalmist know something of this when he said " This is my infirmity ; but I will remember the years of the right hand of the Most High " ? * * * On Fifth-day I accompanied —— in soliciting for new Subscribers to the Bible Society. It appeared in the course of conversation that we had both prayed for a blessing on the undertaking before engaging in it. We had good success. We were both prepared to unite in " Thank God," as we parted at the end of our morning's work.

4 mo. 26.—Some lively and earnest longings for holiness and conformity to the will of Christ, not for a ground of trust but as evidence of love, have been mine to-day, accompanied with tenderness of spirit and access in prayer. It is evening with me. Oh for a peaceful sunset—a humble, quiet, confiding trust! Even if it be but to lie at His feet weeping—no one was ever repulsed, no one ever perished there !

> " Not one object of His care
> Ever suffered shipwreck there."

To —— on leaving School.

6 mo., 1863.—I need hardly tell thee in reply to thy enquiry, that "Truthful" in its highest form stands opposite thy name in the report: and believing as I do that thy truthfulness is not the result of mere expediency, but that

it is the result of the love of Christ in thy heart, I trust it
will be to thee, as it is to me in observing it, cause of thankfulness to our Father in Heaven. The love of Christ in the
heart is the only sure ground of allegiance to Him. In
regard to other manifestations of character, I can hardly
speak of them freely without the risk of ministering to
feelings allied to self-complacency. Those who are gifted
with pleasing qualities both of head and heart, such as attract
the esteem and love of acquaintance and friends, have special
need to be careful in the choice of their associates. Possessed
of the power of pleasing, they do not like to offend. It is
not easy to say *No*. Keep then, dear ————, a tender
conscience. Resist the first temptation to violate it, whether
from within, or by the solicitation of others. As the best of
all possible helps to this, be constant in morning and evening
prayer. Leaving behind a good name at School, and
carrying away with thee the esteem and love of many (of
my own I can assure thee), may the ending of a happy
school-boy life be the beginning of a course to be marked in
every stage by that ever-increasing happiness, which the love
of Christ and a life evidencing that love—and that alone,
can procure.

———————

6 mo. 27.—Nearly four years have gone by since I
watched the last peaceful sigh of my sainted treasure. * * *
Longing for rest—striving yet often vanquished in the
strife—lonely yet not always alone—sometimes cheered by
the felt presence of Him who can sympathize even with
loneliness—cheered too by recollections of the departed—
cheered by the hope of re-union—separated perhaps even
now by a very thin veil. Help me, Heavenly Father, for
Jesus' sake in this sore conflict. Undertake for me, blessed

Saviour! Oh that I might know Thee to be unto me wisdom and righteousness, sanctification and complete redemption. Grant me the cleansing, purifying, sustaining, preserving grace of Thy Holy Spirit, now and for ever. Amen.

8 mo. 6.—School formally opened this morning. Treated on the usual topics—Truth, the character long sustained by the school—the effects of truth and candour in the minds of those who have to govern—how it propitiates—and how justly—for everything is to be hoped for from a delinquent who speaks the truth—it is the first step towards that self-conviction which is the legitimate end of school discipline. Kindness—remarked on the many set down as kind in the review at the vacation—let it continue to be the characteristic of the school. The moment any one sees a school-fellow pained by word or act, desist—and never shrink from a kind apology for offence whether intentional or not. I spoke strongly and plainly on the avoidance of act or word that could in any degree lower the moral standard in the mind of a school-fellow, or call up a blush on his countenance. Cultivate that chastity and purity of thought that would shrink from uttering or hearing anything that could impair the sentiment. Guard against innuendos : most unclean ideas are but too often conveyed by this means in very clean language. Guard yourselves and one another in this particular. Let your bedrooms be sacred places—unassociated in after life with a single thought of evil—associated as in the minds of some York Scholars, with recollections of prayer. The responsibilities of elder scholars. The power of all of us to contribute to the general happiness. The duty of old scholars to set nothing but what was right and good before the new—of the new, to furnish no new contributions to anything wrong. These were some of the prominent topics of the opening address.

To a Gentleman of his acquaintance.

8 mo. 19, 1863.—I have long had it on my mind to tell you how much I enjoyed my visit to ———, and how much that visit deepened the friendly interest I felt in my kind host. I have delayed writing, because it seemed that if I wrote I should wish to refer to our conversations at the breakfast table, as well as on other occasions, when topics of deep interest were discussed, the importance of which demanded more time and thought than I could give immediately on my arrival at home. In entering upon them now, I trust implicitly to the candour· and courtesy with which, when our views differed, any presentation of my own was always received.

We agreed in our belief in the Divine authority of Holy Scripture—in the essential deity of our Lord—and in the duty and the efficacy of prayer. These are some of the great truths of Christianity. There are two others equally important—the doctrine of the atonement—and that of the necessity of a change of heart—the one set forth by our Lord in His declaration that He came to give His life a ransom for the many; the other in His words to Nicodemus, " except a man be born again he cannot see the kingdom of God."

I remember on one occasion you made the remark, " God is Love ; and I cannot believe that He created intelligent beings with a knowledge that they would exist for ever in endless misery." I also believe that " God is Love," and that He *did not intend* any of His intelligent creatures for such a destiny ; for I believe our Lord when He speaks of a condition of penal woe as " prepared *for the devil and his angels*". Into the origin of evil we need not go: it is not revealed. The origin of evil to man *is revealed* : it did not originate with him ; it came from external agency. If asked, why capable of evil ? Why susceptible of temptation ? The

answer seems to be that an impossibility of transgression is
incompatible with the exhibition of obedience. The will is
one of those resemblances of man to God, implied in his
being created in " the image of God." The attribute of will
implies freedom to choose. Man in the exercise of his free
will listened to the tempter, transgressed and fell. The
declarations of Holy Scripture and the individual experience
of every one of us, establish the truth, that we inherit a
nature prone to evil, and that we all have sinned. Suppose
we admit all this, and yet reply, " True, but ' God is Love ' ;
therefore He will pardon." True also ; but God is just. He
has made known His laws. Law cannot be broken with
impunity : anarchy would ensue : distinctions between right
and wrong would be lost ; and yet God *will* pardon ; " As I
live saith the Lord God, I have no pleasure in the death of
him that dieth ; " and therefore He has provided a plan by
which " God can be just and the justifier of him that believeth
in Jesus."

I now come to the great truth expressed by the Apostle
Paul in 1 Cor. xv. 3, that " Christ died for our sins according
to the Scriptures." It would occupy time and paper almost
indefinitely to quote all the passages which enforce and
illustrate this truth ; and moreover it is needless to one who
is as well read in Scripture as my friend. The passages to
which I refer show that the penalty of our sins has been
paid—our redemption purchased—and that a sacrifice, atonement and propitiation for *our* sins has been offered to God
(and accepted by Him) by one who, mysteriously combining
in His person perfect deity and perfect manhood, very God
and very man, suffered for us as one of us—and, as one with
God—gave infinite value and efficacy to the sacrifice. He
thus became the " propitiation for our sins, and not for ours
only, but also for the sins of the whole world." Let us

admit all this, and infer, " well then our pardon is purchased
and is secure." True !—but with one more truth superadded—we secure this by faith in Christ—the reality and
efficacy of our faith is proved by our love—our love by our
allegiance—and our allegiance is manifested by our daily
life and conversation.

And now we come to that other great truth, the necessity of
a change of heart ; for our ability to manifest our allegiance
consists in that change wrought in us by the Holy Spirit of
God. By this, new motives—new affections—new hopes—
are implanted in our hearts. Love, joy and peace take the
place of anxiety, distrust and fear. The man thus changed
no longer lives to himself, but to Him who died for him and
rose again. We must be " transformed by the renewing of
our minds." Without this change heaven would be no
heaven to us. Blest with all temporal blessings, the man
thus changed holds them all as a steward. His new affections
leave him still all his love for his friends, heightened and
intensified by the belief—the sure and certain hope—that the
bonds of friendship are of eternal duration : and above all he
can look to the end of this transient life as the beginning of
a blissful eternity. Thus then we come to the axiom with
which we set out, that " GOD IS LOVE," that by this love
pardon, reconciliation, and peace are freely offered to us in
Jesus Christ. And the believer may assure himself that no
place of penal woe is prepared for him. The abode prepared
for him is quite another thing : " In my Father's house are
many mansions—*I go to prepare a place for you.*"

I may well be asked, " Have you yourself realized all
this ? " I answer with Paul—immeasurably below him
nevertheless in the measure of attainment—" I count not
myself to have attained ; " and (modifying his words) I
would add, " this one thing I (strive to) do, forgetting those

things which are behind, and reaching forth unto those things which are before, I press toward the mark for the prize of the high calling of God in Christ Jesus."

Excuse this long letter and the freedom I have used in writing—and pray accept it with all its imperfections as evidence how sincerely I am your grateful and affectionate friend,

JOHN FORD.

P.S.—When a man has reached his grand climacteric as I have nearly,—sixty-three,—he may hope to be excused if he shrinks from delaying to a future day what appears as a present duty. This is my case. Often whilst penning the foregoing I have been reminded of one similarity in our circumstances—you have lost a friend whom you long and and hope to meet again. I too have lost one of even a dearer name than that of friend, and the same hopes and longings animate me. One object of my letter is the earnest desire that the hopes of both of us may rest on the alone sure foundation. I pray that so it may be!

---

8 mo. 23.—" But above all, let me mind my own personal work,—to keep myself pure, and zealous, and believing—labouring to do God's will, yet not anxious that it should be done by me rather than by others if God disapproves of my doing it." Thus wrote good Dr. Arnold on Saturday evening, June 11th, 1842, within two days of completing his forty-seventh year : on Sunday, June the 12th, after two hours' illness he died. I am fifteen years older than he was at the time of his death. To-day, these his last recorded self-musings have occurred to me with an earnest desire that I may have them for my own experience. I think I have measurably attained to the condition of being glad at witnessing the

services of others—not *anxious* that I should share them if
God disapproves of my doing so.

9 mo. 6.—Read to the school a short extract from "Harrow
Sundays." "Ask God's blessing each morning upon what is
to befall you that day, &c." The deep, silent attention with
which it was listened to, led me to express my belief that
many times we had together experienced, both here and in
the Dining-room on First-day evening, the presence of our
Saviour by His Spirit, solemnizing our spirits. This belief
made it still as it had ever been to me, a pleasant task to
minister to school-boys, permitted in some measure perhaps
to encourage and to help them, if it were only to point out
to them the path of peace and safety. Expressed my belief
that there were many among them who knew something of
the love of Christ influencing their hearts, producing returns
of love to Him, and helping to testify of their love by their
allegiance :—that I earnestly desired the encouragement of
these, and that all might be like-minded. If there were any
who thought I drew too fair a picture—that they would
pardon me, and earnestly try to realize it for themselves.
That I was about to be absent for three or four First-days—
that I knew I was leaving them with those who loved them,
and whose hearts were often lifted up in prayer for them—
that I should often remember them especially on First-day
evening, and would that they might *so* remember me. A
very solemn silence ensued; and after a brief pause I once
more prayed with them and for them.

To his brother Samuel.

9 mo. 10, 1863.—I am again going to unite with my dear
cousin, William Tanner, in religious service in the Quarterly
Meeting of Durham. Whilst anxious that I may know for
myself a preparation for a time that cannot be very far distant,

and desirous to be found trusting in Christ as my Saviour both from the penalty and the power of sin, I find myself called upon to invite others to seek after the same blessing. Not seldom do I think of thee and pray for thee that thou mayst so come to Christ for thyself, as to know thy sins forgiven for His sake. It is now the eleventh hour with both of us. Neither of us have any plea to offer for acceptance at last but the unmerited mercy of God in Christ Jesus, and that is freely offered to all of us if we will but earnestly ask for it and accept it. That this may be the happy experience of both of us is the prayer of thy affectionate brother.

---

11 mo. 14.—How precious are the moments—how refreshing—when the tendering influence of the love of Christ distils like the evening dew on the longing heart. Some little experience of this has been mine this evening. It is not always so. To kneel morning and evening—at times without any glow of devotion—seemingly without ability to pray, is my condition; and yet not doing it as relying upon it—not satisfied with it as perfunctory—not thinking of it in the smallest degree as a claim for favour—but often and often feeling as a poor, erring child waiting in silence for a Father's morning blessing—longing for it if but little earnestness is felt in asking for it—not liking to begin the day or to encounter its duties and its trials and temptations without at least trying to put myself in the way for a blessing,—I dare not, I cannot intermit the practice. I can sometimes venture to take comfort, even in times of emptiness and incapacity, in the thought, "Thou God seest me—Thou knowest my wants, my weakness, my infirmities of flesh and spirit," and thus silently appeal and wait for help in the name of Jesus.

And so on retiring at night, I cannot intermit the practice
of again kneeling, again seeking to put myself in the way of
asking for pardon and peace, and committing myself to the
protecting care of my heavenly Father in Jesus' name.   If
it be not often that I enjoy the precious sense of heavenly
love, contriting my spirit, renewing my faith and love and
allegiance—I feel as though I would yet go evening by
evening even as a child to his father, depending upon his
father's love ; although he should not always, or even not
often, receive sensible demonstrations of it.   And then how
precious are those times when kneeling empty, lifeless, poverty
stricken—scarcely faith enough to kneel—fearing it is mere
habit—half disposed to listen to the evil suggestion to give
it up, to turn into a prayerless bed to a prayerless sleep—
how precious even then, before we rise, to find this lifelessness
departing, access granted, ability given to pour out the over-
flowings of a full heart before Him—to know that He has
inspired, and hears, and will answer our prayer.

11 mo. 30.—To Ackworth to-day to attend the sub-
committee.   Among other duties was that of seeing a few
scholars, three boys and four girls, newly entered.   After
one or two members of the Committee had said a few words
of counsel, I addressed them on not being afraid to show
their colours—neither being afraid nor ashamed of doing what
they believed to be required of them, nor yet of abstaining, even
in the face of custom to the contrary, from doing what they
felt was wrong.   I instanced the subject of prayer, illustrating
it by the results I had seen of faithfulness in this matter.   As
I went on I believe my own spirit was helped.   Oh if I was
permitted to help this little company—permitted to help even
one of the little lambs of Christ's fold, what a blessed privilege ; overpayment tenfold for any cost of any kind in going
on this errand this day.   Of all the privileges of the gospel

few are sweeter—very few so sweet as union of spirit and
sympathy with the piety of a child. The thought that " of
such is the kingdom of Heaven" is inexpressibly precious.
I shall long remember, perhaps never forget the sweet
feelings accompanying this very little service.

12 mo. 31.—The evening of the old year, his expiring
hour from eleven to twelve, and the early minutes of the
new, were spent as in earlier days they were sometimes
spent by me, in "watching unto prayer." The year 1863
is just expiring. The minster bells are ringing him out.
To me the year has been one of multiplied mercies. Oh
that more adequate returns had marked its course, more of
grateful, willing service. And yet I know that whatsoever
service has been permitted, whether more or less gratefully
or cheerfully rendered, only in Christ can his poor unprofitable servants be complete—only accepted in Him.

The moment is full of memories of the past. The ever
dear one—dear as ever still—who has entered on her heavenly
rest—the two much loved and faithful friends of earlier and
later years, Joseph Rowntree and Thomas Pumphrey—
many who in the ordering of Providence have been placed
under my care—have been brought before me. During the
year just going out I have had more enjoyment of prayer ;
have used the privilege more frequently and for a wider
range of requests : for many a trifle, so called, I have asked
for help and guidance ; for many a little favour, for many a
preservation from blunders and mistakes (having raised a
secret aspiration for help), a brief but earnest thought of
thankfulness has been offered.

2 mo. 4, 1864.—This afternoon I had a visit from an
interesting young man with whom I had become acquainted
slightly, many months ago. He spent the evening, and

seemed to enjoy scientific conversation relative to the stereo-
scope, microscope, polariscope, &c., some of the phenomena
of which were new to him.   *   *   After he left, a feeling
of regret—almost of condemnation, came over me, that I had
not *made* an opportunity (seeing that none very manifestly
occurred), for a word on a Saviour's love. ·

6 mo. 5.—In the evening at Bootham I believe I was
helped in addressing the boys in the school-room, and in
vocal prayer especially for them at Reading time. When
thus favoured to feel the love of Christ, flowing through
one so utterly unworthy, toward this beloved company, I
can make the grateful acknowledgment, "The lines are
fallen unto me in pleasant places." Childless, (so it has
pleased my Heavenly Father I should be,) yet loving the
young with deep natural affection, I can indeed rejoice when
permitted to feel that holier affection—the love of Christ—
sanctifying and intensifying the natural love.

To his brother Samuel,

(who had recently met with a severe accident).

8 mo. 4, 1864.—Four years ago I was summoned to
Sheriff Hutton with the news, that thou wast thought to be
dying. I hastened over and found thee apparently in great
danger. Thy life was then mercifully spared; and my prayer
was then, and many a time since has been, that our Heavenly
Father in His mercy would lead thee to deep, sincere,
heartfelt repentance. I have assured thee often, and I can
again assure thee, that it is not too late to seek for mercy.
I want thee to look upon this accident as another invitation
to review the past, and avail thyself of the opportunity, by
earnest prayer in the name of Jesus, to know all thy past
sins forgiven. Independently of this accident, there are
other signs of failing health and strength. Neither to

myself nor to thee, in the natural course of life, is it likely that many more years can be allotted: the probability is that there may be but very few—not years—but months remaining. I am not writing as though I needed not such counsel myself—but as one who has felt, and still feels, the need of pardon, and who can at times feel that pardon is secure for all the past. But this does not satisfy me. The more I know of the sweetness of pardoning mercy, I cannot rest satisfied with possessing this myself. I long that all who are dear to me, especially by the ties of blood and affection, should be partakers of the same blessing—that they may know for themselves how it can sweeten life—give comfort and resignation amid trials and suffering, and fill the heart with glowing and glorious hopes of happiness when this mortal life and all its trials shall end.

It would be a sorrowful thing for me, if in a time of extremity, when thy powers of life were failing and death seemed near at hand, were I to hear thee saying, as some have said when alarmed at the prospect of eternity, "Why did you not tell me, and warn me of all this before?—whilst there was time and opportunity to seek for repentance and pardon?" It is in no accusing spirit that I write, but with all the earnestness of Christian and brotherly love, that I want to encourage thee to seek for thyself that mercy so freely offered, even at the eleventh hour. Remember the gracious promise of our Lord, "Him that cometh unto me, I will *in no wise* cast out." Ask for ability to pray—Ask for the Holy Spirit to help thee to pray. If no answer to prayer should come *speedily*, do not be discouraged. Our Lord bids us be importunate in prayer. "Create in me a clean heart, O God, and renew a right spirit within me," is a very fitting prayer —a prayer often made and answered.

9 mo. 18.—Addressed the school in reference to the sermons
and prayer at Meeting—their solemnity. Our responsibility
in thus hearing the Gospel preached, and being present at
worship owned by the Divine presence and blessing. Have
we profited? Are we profiting by it? Has the love of
Christ more place in our hearts? Are we more His than
we were a week ago? We may apply tests to ourselves—
kindness—gentleness—and love—scrupulous truthfulness—
these are some of the evidences which we may seek for in
ourselves. I believe there are those amongst you who never
knowingly or wilfully inflicted pain either of body or mind
on a schoolfellow. I can imagine no more beautiful or
blessed sight than a company like the present, were every
one seeking to realize the Christian in all his conduct. Let
not then the gospel messages such as we have heard to-day—
to use a common phrase,—" go in at one ear and out at the
other;" but let us resolve that with the help of the Holy
Spirit of God we will seek to realize the beauty of the
Christian character. And let none of us be discouraged if
we seem to fail of realizing all that we long for. Let us go
again and again for pardoning mercy and grace to help us
to overcome : if so, then the life-long conflict will end in
victory at last through " Him who hath loved us."—The
deep silence at the close of these remarks seemed to indicate
the spirit of prayer granted to us—and to this I gave
utterance.

10 mo. 17.—I availed myself of an opportunity of handing
to ——— a balance of account sent by his father in paying
his bill—to offer him a word of counsel. I told him I had
thought much of him, partly through long acquaintance with
many of the family, and especially in remembrance of his
two brothers who had been York scholars; and that I hoped
he was trying to be a good boy. I had nothing to upbraid

him with, but I wanted to encourage him to try earnestly
for the remaining part of the session. His looks betrayed
considerable emotion. I reminded him of the peace accompanying the effort to be good, to keep a conscience void of
offence. It seemed that this was pretty much the message
I had for Christ to him. I parted from him not without
hope : my prayer for him now is that the very simple
message may be blest to him.

About this time the consideration of retiring from
the Superintendence of the School engaged John
Ford's attention. After noticing a correspondence
on the subject with some of his friends, he states in
his Journal the conclusion arrived at.

12 mo. 4.—It seems right for me at present to take no
action, but carefully to observe any pointings towards an
opening for it. I have made it a subject of frequent prayer,
and have sought to trust it as regards time and mode, to Him
who has hitherto umistakeably directed my steps and chosen
my allotment—from Worcester in 1815 to Rochester, from
Rochester to York in 1828, and to a most happy marriage
in 1837. Not less wise and not less kind, even though full
of sorrow, the event of Seventh-month 2nd, 1859. And now
alone ! in the *evening*, my desire and my prayer are that the
same loving hand may guide my steps, appoint my service
and my place of service. " Thou *hast been* my help ; leave me
not, neither forsake me, O God of my salvation."

The compilation of a Hymn Book specially
adapted for young persons now occupied John
Ford's leisure. He engaged in an extensive correspondence to ascertain the views of others as to

what particular hymns were desirable to be included in such a collection. The result was a volume which appears to have met with favour, as the little book, " Selected Hymns," has gone through several editions.

2 mo. 27.—Long interview with ———, reported for repeated acts of disorder : this combined with a recent affair with one of the Teachers occasioned a reference to me. After much patient labour,—reticence, reserve and obstinacy—if that was an ingredient—gave way : sensible that he had been in the wrong both in act and in mental condition—sorry for it—*really* as I believe—intending to strive earnestly to be more guarded. Thus the true ends of discipline appeared to be attained. I introduced the Teacher to him, and cordiality and kindness seemed to be restored. He expressed to him as he had to me the above sentiments. I appealed to him as a young man ; (he is in his 17th year). Difficult as he seemed for a long time, the conference ended with an increased rather than a diminished estimate of his whole character. He needs very careful handling. I had prayed for wisdom for myself, and a yielding heart for him in this matter.

4 mo. 23.—Whatever may be the fate of these records, whether I burn them myself, or commission others to burn them for me, or whether they be burned without a commission,—of this I have no doubt, they have been inestimable aids to me. Sensitive, and as a consequence often tending to despondency, I find my faith and hope and love from time to time renewed, rekindled, confirmed, by being thus enabled to "remember the years of the right hand of the Most High," the " times of refreshing from the presence of the Lord "—times of sweet communion with my Saviour.

I dare not indulge in the morbid anatomy of thoughts and feelings, by a record of temptations yielded to or resisted. I know them but too well. But the loving kindness of my Lord through all the past, I am too apt, in the cloudy day to forget, and thus to live below the privileges even of a poor, erring, sinful believer such as I am; and so I record them still.

6 mo. 17.—On retiring to my bed-room this evening, I was very unexpectedly favoured with a most memorable season in prayer. I had nearer access than usual to the mercy seat—was enabled in something like living faith, to pour out my heart to the Lord in Jesus' name. All my earnest longings—all my little wants—all my many fears— I seemed at liberty to bring them all as to a loving Father. Oh the preciousness of such seasons! I cannot give up stated times of prayer—but oh the difference when such favours as these are granted!—No distrust—no coldness—all earnest, confiding love. Oh for that state when this shall be not the exception, but the ever abiding condition of the happy spirit.

7 mo 4.—I left for Ackworth. The examination of the girls in Scripture again fell to my lot—a pleasant task, refreshing to the spirit by the sweetness and readiness of this beloved company, numbering not a few of the lambs of Him whose almost last parting command was that they should be fed. The Educational Meeting was held on Sixth-day and numerously attended. I read a paper on " Penalties," a subject I have long had on my mind; it seemed to be well received. This looked like another *last time*. Much was said about younger men coming forward: I wish they would, and that they might be enabled to come with a little self-distrust—with modesty and humility, not with self-confident dogmatism.

John Ford's professional life had now extended over more than fifty years. It had been his earnest desire not to retain his position as Superintendent of York School longer than, in the opinion of his friends, the Institution would be benefited by his remaining at the head of it. He often expressed a dread of retaining office after capacity for effective service had gone, and shrunk from the idea of its being thought,

> "Superfluous lags the veteran on the stage."

Feeling satisfied that the right time was now come to withdraw from further service, he tendered his resignation in the following letter.

To the General Meeting of the York Quarterly Meeting's Boys' School.

20 Bootham, 9 mo. 25, 1865.

Dear friends,

After giving the subject the most careful and serious consideration, I have been led to the conclusion that the right time has come for me to resign the post of Superintendent of the School. I therefore wish to close the connexion on the 31st of the Twelfth-month next ensuing, when I shall have completed thirty-seven years of service.

In the Sixth-month, 1857, in consequence of the declining health of my late dear wife, the Committee accepted my proposal of leaving the house in Bootham, and residing at a short distance, retaining the post of Superintendent, my friend Fielden Thorp being appointed Resident Head Master. In 1862 I tendered the resignation of my office, if, in the judgment of the Committee, the time of final retirement had arrived. The Committee expressed their belief that the interests of the school would be served by my occupying the post awhile longer. And now, in finally tendering my resignation, I wish to express my unfeigned satisfaction in the belief that the school will not suffer thereby, and that my dear friend, Fielden Thorp, is fully prepared to undertake the duties of Superintendent and Head Master. In reverting to the eight years of our joint labours, I cannot speak too highly of his courteous and cordial co-operation. Nothing has been permitted, at any time, to interrupt harmonious action. To sever a long connexion, under circumstances so favourable to the school, is cause of reverent thankfulness.

Well aware of many imperfections, mistakes and failures in the past, I can acknowledge that they have met with the kind and charitable construction of my friends; and that I have been enabled, from time to time, to take them to the foot of the cross, for the pardoning mercy and sustaining grace of a compassionate Saviour, and thus to find my strength and trust renewed. To the Committee, among whom I have numbered some of my dearest personal friends, I have been largely indebted, for their kind, most efficient and constant support and counsel. Nor am I less bound gratefully to acknowledge the hearty co-operation, as well as the kind recognition of service—of numerous parents, and the continued attachment of young men once under my care. In conclusion I may say that the interests of the school will ever be dear to me. My prayers will be for its prosperity, and that the blessing of the Most High may richly rest upon the labours of the Committee, the Superintendent, and the various officers, that so, by their joint efforts, the scholars may ever be trained, not only in sound learning, but above

all, in the knowledge, and fear, and love of their Heavenly
Father and their Redeemer.

JOHN FORD.

EXTRACT FORM THE ANNUAL REPORT OF THE COMMITTEE OF
YORK QUARTERLY MEETING'S BOYS' SCHOOL, 9 MO. 1865.

We believe the School to be in a sound and healthy
state. That this should be the case, is felt to be a cause of
special gratitude at the present time, when our dear friend
John Ford has signified his intention of shortly retiring from
the Superintendence of the School. He has held this office
since the Quarterly Meeting assumed the management of
the Institution in 1828. Since that date, 670 boys have
entered as Scholars. Many of these are now reaping the
benefits of the education therein received, and will unite with
the Committee in those warm feelings of thankfulness and
satisfaction, with which they recur to the long period during
which John Ford has been enabled to discharge the responsible duties of his position. In the prospect of his retirement,
whilst we cannot but feel regret at the close of our official
connexion, we are not insensible to the claims he has for
release from this field of service, and we earnestly desire that
the Lord's blessing may richly rest on his future lot, and
that he may long be permitted to witness the sucessful pro-
secution of the work, to which so large a share of his best
energies have been devoted.

To REBECCA THOMPSON. (Bridgwater).

11 mo. 13, 1865.—My resignation was accepted; and I
am thankful in believing that I have not overstayed the right
time—and that the right time has come. And yet I cannot

forego the pleasures of a long professional life without regret. "The warm precincts of the cheerful day," (if I may apply Gray's beautiful language to the association with young life which I have so much enjoyed), seem to claim "a longing, lingering look behind."

---

11 mo. 19.—In Meeting this evening, using as I trust a little faith, I spoke on the text, "Be not weary in well doing." The concern seemed to be to encourage those who might at times feel discouraged by the strong demarcation sometimes insisted on, "You are in Christ, or you are not." True enough—and yet capable of being so presented as unduly to discourage. The work of grace is a gradual work, and because not all accomplished at once, but many a conflict yet to come, therefore we must not conclude that we are not in Him;—"First the blade, then the ear, &c.;"—and yet this we are too apt to do, and our enemy is but too ready to avail himself of our despondency and to second it. Our reply to him is, "I know I am a sinner, and yet I may and will come again and again for pardoning mercy and sustaining grace. Get thee behind me." I referred to the hymn, "'Tis a point I long to know;" and though the prayer of the last stanza may sometimes be adopted,

> "Let me love Thee more and more,
> If I love at all, I pray,"

there are times when the believer can get beyond *that*, times when under the influence of the descendings of Heavenly dew—the Holy Spirit of God—access is granted us into the very presence chamber of the King in the name of Jesus, and we can gratefully and humbly make the Apostle's appeal, "Lord, Thou knowest all things; Thou knowest that I love Thee."

11 mo. 26.—I would commemorate this evening a most precious season of private prayer. It seemed as though I was enabled to trust my Saviour for sanctification, as I *have* already trusted him for justification. I was enabled earnestly to plead that He would undertake *this* for me, enabling me to maintain the conflict, trusting in Him and in Him alone for ultimate victory.

In Twelfth-month, 1864, a Royal Commission was appointed to enquire into the education given in some of the principal Schools in England. Though the powers of the Commission were largely confined to endowed schools, the Commissioners were desirous of obtaining information respecting other educational establishments, and John Ford was invited to attend before them. His evidence is published in the Commissioners' Report.

12 mo. 10.—Indisposition—and at times extreme fatigue consequent, as well as multiplied engagements, have interfered with these records. To-night I may tell again of special answer to prayer. Each recurring First-day evening bringing the *last* nearer and nearer—this evening being probably the last but one—deepens the sense of responsibility: so before going into the school-room I kneeled once more in the lecture room, and there was enabled to ask with some earnestness and a deep sense of need, and some renewed faith in prayer in Jesus' name. I asked of my Father in Heaven that He would condescend to go with me and be with me, and help me in addressing once more the assembled school; and now, as heretofore, I think I can say, " I know He does answer prayer, for He has answered me."

To-morrow if all be well I go to London to give evidence
before the Royal Commission of Education.   I have prayed
and still pray for that same most blessed and most effectual
guidance and counsel and help.   I know and feel in my very
heart at this moment that I am utterly unworthy, and yet
in the name of Jesus I may come.   I am entreated by
Himself to come.   Oh that I could make more return of
love !

12 mo. 16.—" Sufficient unto the day is the evil thereof."
But for the desire to accept profitably this truth, I might
look forward to to-morrow with over anxious thought.   If
all be well I give my last Scripture lesson ; and in the
evening I take for the last time my post in the school-room,
where for many years I have been accustomed to stand and
address the assembled School.   This has been to me the most
precious part of my First-day services at Bootham ; for there,
many times after preparation by previous prayer, I have
been enabled to set forth the beauty and safety of early
dedication of heart to Christ.   So I will still trust in the
help heretofore granted, and try to look hopefully to to-
morrow.

12 mo. 17,—First-day evening.   Nor have I been disappointed.   Throughout the day it seemed as though I could
not give my thoughts to the subject of taking leave in the
evening ; therefore once again in the Lecture-room alone I
prayed for help and counsel.   I heard a few of the juniors
repeat portions of hymns, and then addressed the School in
substance as follows :—

"I referred briefly this morning to the fact that I was
giving my last lesson of Scriptural instruction.   There is
something solemn in doing a thing for the last time, but
especially so when the act is the last of a long series, involving

the highest responsibilities, as that does in which I am now engaged for the last time, after a long service of 37 years.

"Standing before you here week after week on this evening, I have sought earnestly and prayerfully from time to time to warn and counsel and encourage you, as ability might be granted me, in all that concerns your highest interests for time and for eternity. To-night I have no new thing to say ; but you will pardon me if for a few minutes I occupy you with a few words of personal concernment. This day has been one of very solemn thought to me. I am closing a service of infinite responsibility—responsibility such as I dare not look back upon were it not that, conscious of numerous imperfections, mistakes and failures, I have sought from day to day to take them where I have counselled you to take yours—to the foot of the cross—there to plead the name of Jesus, to ask for the renewed application of the all-cleansing blood of sprinkling—and there I have found pardon and peace, and renewal of strength and trust for daily service. But for this I should not have stood before you here this evening. But having sought so to do, notwithstanding anxieties, difficulties, sore trials and distress, I can now look back upon a happy professional life. For this I am deeply indebted to kind and able colleagues. To my dear friend ————— my grateful recollections are most justly due: for more than twenty years I have had his invaluable services. Nor am I less indebted to my beloved friend, your Superintendent and master, Fielden Thorp ; for nearly twenty years I have been permitted to enjoy his friendship. For eight years we have stood in relations to each other not devoid of liabilities. But it is a peculiar happiness to look back upon the connexion as one of constant courteous and most cordial co-operation, and one the harmony of which nothing has been permitted for a moment

to disturb.   To my younger colleagues, in whose earlier
training I have had some share, I am also indebted for kind,
efficient and affectionate support.   Scarcely less is the debt
I owe to you, my young friends on my right,—the senior
scholars.   Year after year I have seen on those forms youths
who have well sustained the character of the school, not
only in the intellectual and moral aspect, but in its higher
aim as a place of Christian education.   I have seen from
year to year those seats vacated and re-filled, and never as I
believe more worthily filled than now.

   " Excuse me if I refer for one moment to a matter more
exclusively personal to myself.   I cannot part from all the
pleasant associations of many years without pain.   More
than six years ago it pleased the Almighty in His inscrutable
wisdom and love to remove from me, one who for twenty-two
years shared my toils, and cheered me with her wise counsels
and her tender love.   You will believe how differently I
should have looked upon retirement had she been spared to
share it.   In the autumn as you are aware I finally tendered
my resignation, and my connexion now ceases altogether.
It was in prospect of this that I presented each of you with
a copy of the little Hymn Book which I compiled last
summer.   I mention it now, because it was intended as a
parting present, in hopes that thereby I might occasionally
be remembered by each of you with no other than friendly,
kindly feelings.   And may I ask of you occasionally when
assembled here on First-day evening to bear me in your
remembrance, in your prayers ; it will cheer my somewhat
solitary lot to believe that I am so remembered.

   " I have said that mine has been a happy professional
life.   One peculiar happiness I have yet to notice—that of
leaving the school in so happy and prosperous a condition—
leaving to my successor, able, efficient, affectionate teachers,

who love their office and the objects of their care; and leaving
too that which especially makes a school a happy community,
kind, intelligent and loyal school-boys.   For my beloved
friend, Fielden Thorp, I cannot express a better wish as
regards his position than that, whenever by the course of
time or by other causes he may withdraw from his post, he
may leave as I do without an anxious thought for its future.

"Many a time at this hour in this place, I reverently and
thankfully express my confident belief, we have been favoured
with the overshadowing of our Heavenly Father's love.
May this through long years to come be the happy experience
as York Masters and Scholars meet together here.   That so
it may be, may all of you, in words which I used last First-
day, seek and cherish and live in the personal love of a
personal Saviour."

Fielden Thorp followed and in most kind and touching
terms referred to our past connexion.   At reading time I read
the 145th Psalm and then, "Finally brethren farewell, &c,"
at the close of the Epistle to the Corinthians.   I afterwards
engaged in prayer for F. and A. J. Thorp, for the teachers,
the scholars and the servants; and thus ended this formidable
looking day.   I might well say at the end, "What shall I
render unto the Lord, &c."

SECTION V.

EVENING OF LIFE.

In the early part of 1866, soon after withdrawing from his professional duties, John Ford spent some time in visiting his friends in the Midland Counties and West of England. On his return home he writes as follows :—

3 mo. 2, 1866. * * I was permitted much enjoyment in these visits, and in looking back on them find nothing to mar the recollection. * * * One bright, clear, frosty morning I seemed capable of enjoying as I did forty years ago all the profuse beauty of nature ; " the incense breathing morn," kindling even as it did in early years, thoughts too deep for words—love for the author of all these beauties, both as God and Saviour—crowned with thankfulness for this renewed capacity, this freshness of spirit, recipient of such chastened pleasure.

On my return to York I was so kindly welcomed at Bootham, and so lovingly at Union Terrace, that all the clouds that had seemed to gather over York melted away, and all I needed was a more grateful heart.

To ONE OF HIS SCHOLARS WHO HAD RECENTLY GONE
TO A SITUATION.

2 mo. 10, 1866.—I heard that thou wast gone to ———, and now I suppose thou art beginning to be accustomed to thy place and its duties. I trust thou art doing all thou

canst to please thy employers and to be very useful.   It will
give me great pleasure, (few things would give me more)—
to hear that thou wast getting on well.   Don't be discouraged
by mistakes and failures, but rather let them serve as stimulus
to new exertions.   The way to excel in business is to give
the mind thoroughly to it.   *   *   *   *   *   *
And now dearest ———, do try to be good, always truthful,
willing and obliging, and do not forget some good counsel,
often repeated but never out of place—*never forget to pray.*
Ask morning by morning thy Heavenly Father to help thee
to do all that is right and good,—to keep thee in time of
temptation—to comfort thee in trouble.   Ask Him to help
thee to love thy Saviour, and ask Him to do this for Jesus'
sake.   I long for thee to be a good, prosperous and happy
young man.   Be careful in thy choice of companions ; and
if any one should tempt thee to do wrong, give up his
company.

On First-day evening, 3 mo. 11, at F. Thorp's request I
took my old post in the school-room and addressed the boys
after the old fashion : their marked attention was very
grateful.   I have free access to the school.   My earnest
desire is that I may be enabled to use this liberty in service
for Christ, and that in the ability which He may give, I may
occasionally still be permitted to feed the Lambs of His fold.

4 mo. 15.—In the evening Fielden Thorp invited me again
to my old First-day evening post in the school-room, and I
addressed them, asking their permission to suppose myself for
a moment in my old character.   I spoke of the half-year
as half over—the value of retrospect—the opportunity of
persevering in well doing, or for amendment if need
were.   The pleasure of a retrospect of school when by

daily watchfulness and prayer the school-boy had sought to
approve himself a disciple of Christ—that good soldiership
now, was the best preparation for good soldiership in the
sterner conflict of life.

Last Fifth-day, 6 mo. 14, was an eventful and noteworthy day, one I had looked forward to almost with dismay.
About fifty old (York) scholars dined at the De Grey Rooms.
I was their guest. After dinner they presented me with a
screen containing under glass 257 portraits of old scholars,
also a silver inkstand, and an address accompanied by a
cheque for six hundred pounds to be invested in an annuity.
I replied partly extempore, chiefly by a written reply. I
would I had a more grateful, loving heart to my Father in
Heaven for His protecting grace that has kept me to this
day. Had it not been that I have sought and obtained His
pardoning mercy from time to time for all my unfaithfulness
in the discharge of the solemn responsibilities of thirty-seven
years, intense sense of unworthiness would have marred all
the pleasure of the day, if it would even have allowed me to
touch what was so kindly offered. But having, as I have
before acknowledged, known the pardon of all these mistakes
and omissions, I could again acknowledge that mine had
been a happy professional life, and that I could thankfully
accept these tokens of the esteem and love of more than
three hundred old scholars.

To Rebecca Thompson.

8 mo. 2, 1866. The account of the proceedings of 6 mo.
14, printed by the Committee of the Presentation, will have
informed thee of the particulars of that interesting occasion.
To myself it was almost overwhelming. The kindness and
the munificence of the old scholars took me by surprise. I
did not know that I had so large a place in the affectionate

remembrance of so many. Perhaps the most touching part
to me was the graceful and grateful tribute to the memory
of my sainted R., paid by two or three of the speakers.
One, a warm-hearted youth, spoke with intense feeling of her
kindness in sickness and in affliction, he having partaken of
it in both. The money gift was very opportune, enabling
me to continue my duties as a Steward, nearly if not quite
on the same scale as heretofore: this, otherwise, I could not
have done in York. The screen containing the photographic
portraits, when opened out, presents an array of intelligent
and useful men and youths—(not a few of them, I believe,
avowed servants of Christ) very pleasant to look upon,—not
the less pleasant, because, not reproachfully, but kindly, I
can imagine them looking upon me.

The deep interest which John Ford took in the
Castle Howard Reformatory for Juvenile Criminals,
is manifested by repeated notices in his diary. He
was appointed on the Committee of the Institution
in 1855, and remained a member till the time of
his death. He frequently availed himself of the
opportunities afforded by the Committee Meetings
at the Reformatory, to address the Inmates collec-
tively, as well as to have private interviews with
individual boys in difficult cases.

7 mo. 12.—I attended a summons to the Committee at the
Castle Howard Reformatory: no other member attended.
I remained the usual time, dined with Mr. ———, and had
an interesting conversation with him on the theological
aspect of the present day as manifested in its literature,

sermons, biographies, &c. His son, an Oxford student, was present. I endeavoured to give the conversation a course that might be instructive to him. In the morning I had a few words with a boy of twelve recently admitted. Mr. F. gave him a very good character. The cause of his committal is very doubtful as regards any criminality on his part. His fine, open countenance was a strong contrast to some of his harder associates. I said a few words to him, and gave him a little book. Mr. F. introduced me to a very different character, a lad of eighteen sentenced to seclusion, described by Mr. F. as exceedingly hard. I had two or three minutes conversation with him—he seemed more moved than I expected, told me he had shed many bitter tears when alone in his cell. I reminded him of the force of temptation supposing he was restored to society ; asked him if he knew where to apply for help : did he pray ? Yes he did. I recommended him to tell Mr. F. that he would as once before try to conduct himself well—to make a frank acknowledgment. He said he would try to do better. On parting, I said, "Now give me your hand, and try to be a good fellow." He gave me his hand, and seemed much moved. I would commend the three youths—the Oxonian, and the other two, the gentle and the hard, to the care and notice and love of a compassionate Saviour, even now as I write.

9 mo. 9.—I find I am near the end of this volume. How near am I to my journey's end ? *That* need concern me not, provided "I am His and He is mine." Sometimes turning my thoughts to the life beyond the end, I feel as I pass along from day to day an intense craving for objects of affection and care and help and love and sympathy. I try to find and to cherish such objects—perhaps too exclusively among the young, feeling a pleasure in it second to none but the sense granted at times of Christ's love to me, or of my

poor love to Him. I call to mind gratefully times when I have knelt and prayed with and for many a beloved school-boy in sickness, in sorrow or under convictions for sin—occasional visits to sick chambers, and some to poor offenders, found in seclusion in my visits to the Castle Howard Reformatory. These stand out with a distinctness beyond almost all other events or incidents of my recent life. Seeing it is so, I think (must I say speculate) at times on what similar service may be mine, when the earthly journey is ended and its opportunities for service all over. Service there will yet be, for " *there* His servants shall serve Him ! " Oh what joyful commissions may there not be, to minister in some way, beyond human comprehension to conceive—to the poor, the sick, the sorrowful, the penitent, the solitary ! Heavenly Father, I ask Thee to fit and prepare me yet more and more thus to serve Thee here, that such service if it be Thy will may be mine for ever in Heaven !

9 mo. 28.—Yesterday at the invitation of the Matron, I attended a gathering of ex-scholars at the Grey Coat Girls' School. No other gentleman was present. A clergyman had been expected but had not come. Several ladies of the Committee were present. When the ex- and present scholars were assembled I was asked to address them. I, paused a moment, and then felt it would be right to engage in prayer previously to addressing this exceedingly interesting company. I did not know what the ladies and matron would think of it, but this did not disturb me. I was enabled with earnestness to pray for and with them. I then addressed them and felt helped in doing it. I had peace and more therein. And so service of various kinds still is found for me.

Reference has been made to John Ford's friendship with William Tanner, and to their uniting in

religious services in Ireland, and in London and
its vicinity.   By William Tanner's marriage with
Sarah Wheeler, a much loved cousin of Rachel Ford,
he and John Ford were brought into closer intimacy,
with frequent interchange of visits; and for many
years they maintained a continuous correspondence.
In 1863, under the apprehension of religious duty,
they united in visiting the Meetings of Friends in
Durham Quarterly Meeting; and in the following
year they were occupied in a similar service in
Yorkshire.   Visits to the schools were a part of the
service, and they had many social meetings of a
religious character attended by large companies of
both sexes.

In Tenth-month, 1866, John Ford spent a few days
with his cousins at their residence, Ashley Farm
near Bristol.   A fortnight after his return to York
he received the sad intelligence of the decease of
William Tanner after a very short illness.   In re-
cording this sorrowful event he thus writes :—

More than brother to me, his was the most congenial
mind I ever met with : though more logical and metaphysical
and far more powerful in these respects than myself, there
was united in him a spirit as lively, genial and tender, as
ever warmed a merely human breast.   His cheerfulness, his
ready sympathy, the absence of all that was gloomy or
repellent in his piety, gave him ready access to the young,
who charmed by these attractions eagerly sought his company,
his correspondence and his counsel.   In the midst of my

sorrow I could but be grateful and glad that providentially—
contrary to my usual custom—I had so recently been at
Ashley. I greatly enjoyed his company. Besides his usual
liveliness and the brightness of his intellect, there were times
of special enjoyment in our evening and morning social
worship. After breakfast on the morning of the 26th, I
was engaged in vocal thanksgiving for the permitted enjoyment of the visit, and in prayer commended ourselves now,
and "in the unknown future, to the love and care of our
Father in Heaven in the name of His dear Son, our Saviour."

Four months only elapsed after the death of her
husband, when Sarah Tanner also was summoned
away, and laid in the same grave in Sidcot Burial
Ground. A few weeks before her decease she had
placed in John Ford's hands her late husband's
manuscripts, for the purpose of publication. The
compilation of the Memoir of William Tanner occupied much time during the rest of the year, and the
volume was published in the Spring of 1868.

1 mo. 16, 1867.—I have spent some time to-day in closing
my accounts for the year 1866. At the close of 1865, the
last year in which I received a salary, my income exceeded
my expenditure. * * * * * My desire is to devote
the surplus to cases and causes consistent with Christian
stewardship. I have prayed to be preserved in a liberal
spirit in this stewardship, and for wisdom rightly to discharge
it.

1 mo. 23.—Nearly two weeks of continued frost have
had a very depressing effect upon my health, and consequently on my capacity for work or for liveliness of

spiritual perception. And yet perhaps this very circumstance
may have aided in intensifiying a few precious moments of
access in prayer. * * * This evening, much of the day
having been spent alone, the cold keeping me within, I was
looking through " Lyra Anglicana," a Hymn Book recently
sent me by a kind friend, when I met with one new to me,
the sweet refrain of which is, " Son thou art ever with me,
and all that I have is thine." The last two lines, indeed
the whole piece greatly moved me—

" I shall hear, through the lapse of ages, when the stars have ceased to shine,
  ' Son, thou art ever with me, and all that I have is thine.' "

A little bright momentary gleam of heavenly light seemed
to warrant my appropriating this glorious expectation, and
left a sweet calm on my spirit—poor and contrite yet trusting.

8 mo. 21.—With several young men, watched the planet
Jupiter when all his satellites were invisible: three were
passing over his disc, one was eclipsed by the planet. On
the 27th and 28th again at the Observatory in the Museum
Gardens. My desire not to yield unduly to diminished
energy, not to become an idle, self-involved old man, induces
me to note some of these engagements. It helps to keep
alive in me the desire to be usefully occupied, especially in
any thing in which the interests of the young are concerned.
The memoir of my dear cousin William Tanner finds me
employment almost every day.

8 mo. 23.—I do not get on well when I omit to note the
passing events of the evening of life, the blessings, the
mercies, the conflicts, the pleasures allotted, accepted and
enjoyed. This evening I resumed my ecclesiastical lessons
at the Mount School. I was most kindly received, and was
told that my young friends expressed their pleasure when
they heard that the lessons were about to be resumed. At
the close they repeated in concert, " Rock of ages cleft for

me." The recitation and the Scripture reading refreshed me. I think the occasion was owned. I made a few remarks on the Scripture and hymn amidst, I think, a sweet solemnity. This little event has cheered my spirit and revived a little, faith, hope and love. I am thankful that this little service, which brings me into pleasing association with the young, is still permitted me.

To Rebecca Thompson.

8 mo. 28, 1867.—I entirely agree in the sentiment, that it is not wise or well, either as regards ourselves or the world at large, to look despairingly. Despair paralyses, hope impels to action; and I am glad to find that my dear friend, thy husband, continues with unabated active interest, to promote the religious welfare of the many. If the gospel message is to find access and acceptance with these, it must go through disinterested channels, divested of all pecuniary motive, on the part of those who convey it. The Society of Friends will maintain and strengthen their hold upon the many, by virtue of the non-payment principle. It gives them a power, which from various indications, I think they are using with something of the freedom of earlier days— *going* to the poor, the ignorant and the vicious, meeting them more in their own way and condition, and setting before them in simple terms, the story of the life and love of Christ. And even if it should not result in filling our Meeting Houses, or extending the boundaries of our own particular part of the Church of Christ, let us rejoice in the belief that by the Divine blessing upon these various efforts, not a few may be gathered into the *one fold* under the *one Shepherd*.

---

11 mo. 2.—This evening in F. Thorp's absence I presided

at the evening reading at Bootham, and yesterday evening
I was also there and conducted the recitation of texts. I
greatly enjoyed the renewal of the old occupation : I addressed the boys briefly both evenings and felt my own spirit
refreshed.   Opportunities for little services still occur. I
have undertaken for some months to register the meteoro-
logical phenomena as observed at the Museum, and have
superintended and recorded the transits taken at the observatory of the Yorkshire Philosophical Society. This occupation
has the advantage of taking me out regularly every morning
and sometimes in the evening, and is a wholesome break in
reading and writing.   I recently prepared a short paper on
Reading, for the Albert Soirée last Third-day, and I have
spent several hours in preparing one on the Reformation, to
read at Doncaster on the 26th.   Besides these, there is a
lesson on Ecclesiastical History every Fifth-day evening at
the Mount School, and though I have accumulated much
material, I occupy considerable time each week in re-modell-
ing the lessons and introducing new matter. The preparation
of the memoir of dear William Tanner and the correspondence connected with it, demands much time and thought.
*   *   * I have attended several times, the Committee of
the Castle Howard Reformatory held at the school. My
four years service on the Ackworth Committee ended last
Seventh-month.   The committees of the Blue Coat Boys'
and Grey Coat Girls' Schools, and attendance at the Council
Meetings and Monthly Meetings of the Yorkshire Philosophical Society serve also to vary my engagements.   *   *
I occasionally annotate from various sources an interleaved
New Testament; and mostly have some book in reading
connected with biblical literature.

John Ford's scientific pursuits, especially Geology,

Astronomy and Meteorology, gave him a deep interest in the proceedings as well as in the Collections and the Observatory of the Yorkshire Philosophical Society; nor was he less interested in the extraordinary assemblage of Roman and Mediæval antiquities collected and in situ in the Society's beautiful grounds and Museum at York. He greatly valued the opportunities afforded him as a member of the Council, of associating with men of high literary and scientific attainments. Amongst these may be enumerated, John Philips, F.R.S., the Geologist, in his earlier days Curator of the York Museum, and who subsequently held the Professorship of Geology in Oxford University;—Charles Wellbeloved, the learned author of " Eburacum ;"—William Vernon Harcourt, Canon of York, one of the founders and an early President of the British Association;—John Kenrick, eminent as a classical scholar, and author of Histories of Egypt and Phœnicia;—and Robert Davies, F.S.A., whose antiquarian researches have thrown much light on the early and and mediæval History of York.

The following notice of John Ford's connexion with the Yorkshire Philosophical Society appeared in the Annual Report for 1875 :—

" Mr. Ford came to reside in York in 1828, and from that date took a deep interest in the various objects and in the welfare of the Society, having been elected a member so far back as the year 1834. For many years he was an active

member of the Council, and one of the vice-presidents. The
Society is more especially indebted to him for his services as
curator of Meteorology. His records of daily observations in
connection with this department extend over more than forty
years. We are glad to add that since Mr. Ford's decease
these records have been presented to the Society, and are now
deposited in the library. Mr. Ford was also much interested
in the study of Astronomy, and as long as his health permitted he was in the habit of using the instruments in the
Society's observatory."

---

11 mo. 17.—At F. Thorp's request I supplied his place at
the school in his absence. In the evening I addressed them
for a few minutes. "I wish to offer a few words of encouragement to you. I cannot believe that there are among you
those who are wilfully, unconcernedly living in sin. I have
always found pleasure when addressing you as now, in the
thought—the firm belief—that not one among you had
become hardened in sin, but rather that though failing at
times and falling through the force of temptation, still from
time to time there was raised in your hearts the earnest
longing for better things—for purity and all other Christian
graces. I want you not to be discouraged by the past;
there is a future before you, let it be full of hope. There is
One looking down upon you, watching over you—not with
the severe aspect of a judge but that of a loving Saviour,
who longs to have you for Himself. Thus leading a life of
watchfulness and prayer, you may lay up a store of happy
recollections of school-boy days, as many at Bootham have
done before you. I have a note from one in which he speaks
with affection of his school, and says, ' I shall always look
back with pleasure to York School, and to the corner in

"Number 1" where I first poured out my soul long and earnestly to the Lord.' It is not often that we know what passes in the heart and mind of a schoolboy, but occasional glimpses such as this give one faith to believe that in many a bed-room besides the corner in 'Number 1,' has been a schoolboy's place of prayer, of pouring out his soul before the Lord." A deep, solemn silence followed. I believe the spirit of prayer was granted, and once again I kneeled on the schoolroom floor, and gave utterance to earnest, heartfelt prayer for the preservation from all inroads of the enemy for this beloved company—and that for Christ's sake our Father in Heaven would make them all His—now and for ever. Oh that a blessing might largely rest on the services and mercies of the day. To-night I can give thanks for the help granted, surmounting as it did feeble health and failing powers.

To ———

12 mo. 12, 1867.—I sit down to pen a few thoughts on the subject of thy last letter, under an almost painful feeling of incompetency, and yet with an earnest desire that in pondering upon the great truths involved, I may be helped myself, and may, at least, not hinder thee. To take thy letter as it lies before me.—I have referred to the sermon of dear William [Tanner] mentioned by thee; and I find it does in some measure meet thy need. He says, "The new Covenant is distinguished from the old by the larger and fuller appeal to the affections and understandings of mankind, and by the higher influence which it should bring to bear alike on heart and mind." "There were mysteries indeed in their teaching [that of our Lord and His Apostles] to the full conception of which it was impossible for the mind of man to rise." These are two important points—the appeal

N

to our love and yet mystery. I believe these two are most practical considerations—the appeal to our love, to influence our conduct—the appeal to our faith, " without which it is impossible to please God."

Before I proceed with thy letter, I will give thee a short passage from a very profound thinker, Bishop Butler, which seems something like a resting place to me. "Why and how it was necessary that the innocent blood should be shed for man's redemption, or how or in what particular way it has the efficacy assigned, I do not find that Scripture has explained. It is our wisdom thankfully to accept the benefit without disputing how it was procured."

I now return to thy letter—"the difficulty of not seeing in the sufferings of our Lord an equivalent for the eternal sufferings of millions." I observe thy remark, "I do not want to see it equivalent." Nor need we. No such doctrine is contained or implied in Holy Scripture. The statement that God could not pardon unless His Son suffered in the sinner's stead—a statement made by some Evangelicals (so called), seems to me little short of blasphemy. Thy own summary, immediately following this shocking sentiment, is a plain and concise account of one very important *part* of the truth. "There is *a sense* in which our Saviour actually bore our sins"—suffering and sorrow and pain and desertion and death. Thy comment upon it is one which every one who has tasted the preciousness of pardoning love, could endorse. "The thought of this has wonderful power; it seems to announce and to seal the news of God's pardoning love."—Most true—most beautifully and practically true! Then follows—"Still I suppose there is more than I have grasped in our dear Saviour's death." Yes, there is :—just the *how* and the *why* of Bishop Butler. And it seems to me, that the pride of the human intellect on the one hand, or its presumption on the other, has given rise to two attempts to explain the how and the why. The Socinian rejects or explains away "redemption through His blood" (Col. i. 14), "propitiation for our sins" (I. John ii. 2). Other theologians undertake to make all clear and plain: they see in the sufferings and death of Christ a full equivalent for all the eternity of woe due to me as a sinner—no mystery—nothing left to the province of Faith.

There is yet another attempt to bring Salvation by the death of Christ down to the level of the human understanding:—it is perhaps the most specious of all, ascribing Salvation to the regenerating influence of the love of Christ in the heart, produced by the exceeding beauty of His moral character.

To thy enquiry, "if the Scriptures do not mean this" (the equivalent theory) "what do they mean respecting Christ's death"? I should be disposed to answer such an enquiry by passages from Holy Scripture that *need* no explanation. I believe "that Christ died for our sins," I. Cor. xv. 3—that "He is the propitiation for our sins," I. John ii. 2—that "we have redemption through His blood" Col. i. 14, (already quoted)—that we are "redeemed with the precious blood of Christ," I. Pet. i. 19—that He "bare our sins in His own body on the tree," I. Pet. ii. 24—that "Christ suffered for our sins, the just for the unjust," I. Pet. iii. 18. I could multiply such passages indefinitely, and ex animo, in heart and conscience, endorse them all. Then if questioned what do you infer from this or that, I should resort to Scripture again; as for instance, I infer, "that God was in Christ reconciling the world unto Himself." The inquisitorial "what do you infer," has made an apostate church in ages past "drunk with the blood of the Saints," and would do so again but for a more extensively enlightened public opinion. I need only refer to what is called "the sacrament of the altar," the Roman mass, struggling for pre-eminence again, all based upon a false inference from Scripture—"this is My body."

I will now as I promised give thee a few thoughts of other men. "If there be any hope of redemption from this consciousness of sin—this separation from God—this discord in himself, universal in the history of man,—the most thoughtful will feel the most fully, that it must be only by a method which involves in it a full recognition of the evil, and which, probably, will involve as great a mystery to the intellect in the solution, as in the problem: all the light coming through the same moral portion of man's nature, which is the chief region of his misery and the only one of his sin. And that great practical solution of this awful problem given us in the Bible, comes to us under precisely such an aspect of *mystery*, as a Revelation which may justly be termed transcendental—*wholly incapable of being explained,* but yet *not incapable of being believed.* * * * * The mere pardon of sin by an absolute act of the Divine will can never seem to the spiritually minded man, so satisfying as that grand act of voluntary self-sacrifice, which is the centre of the Atonement of Christ, and which not merely vindicates the majesty of God's Law, but also displays His character of love in such an aspect as to be most attractive and subduing to the heart of man. The great act of atonement through Christ does, above all that we could conceive, produce in the heart that believes it, a deep consciousness of sin and of its infinite evil, but at the same time, by the gratitude which it inspires for the deliverance from such evil, it produces also a living self-surrender of the whole man to God. A new spirit is infused by which the sinner is not only reconciled but renewed—not only released from the punishment due to transgression, but made meet for re-union with the holy and happy portion of God's universe, and for increasingly closer communion with Himself. * * * * The moment a man truly believes in Christ as his redeeming Mediator with God, he feels that his sinfulness *may* and *will* and *shall* grow less in him even day by day: that it shall have no more dominion over him, now that he is under grace—but that what no law could have done—subdue his heart unto a loving obedience—God, sending His own Son as a sacrifice for sin, has done and shall do, until he is more than conqueror over all the enemies of his soul." (Fredk. Myers.)

Once again the writer whom I quote reminds his readers, "This atonement of Christ which lies at the very centre of the Christian religion, is to be received by *Faith* rather than by the *understanding* : it cannot be fully *explained* either in its *causes* or its *consequences*."—But I must come to a close. I have not satisfied myself with my *manner* of setting forth the truth as I hold it; I shall doubtless fail in this to satisfy thee—but I *am* satisfied with that child-like acceptance of the Truth which is sometimes granted me, in which I can from my very heart say,

> "I do believe, I will believe
> That Jesus died for me:
> That on the cross He shed His blood
> That I might happy be!"

O my dear friend, it is in moments such as these when the Holy Spirit of God bears witness with our Spirit that we are His—that plans and schemes and creeds of *man's arranging*, are less than nothing—lose their importance—cease to trouble us, and we can repose on our Saviour's love in full confidence, and trust our all to Him for time and eternity. May this be evermore the blessed experience of my friend and myself.

P.S. I have reviewed thy letter again. I do not think
that pride has anything to do with thy distrust—(not of
Scripture truth—but) of the received modes of explaining
these truths. Possibly there is in thy mind a longing for
more insight—more of comprehension of the " how and the
why," than the human intellect, under its present limitations
is capable of attaining to—more perhaps than would be
profitable, if attained. Tennyson, after a few stanzas giving
a desponding view of man and his destiny, finishes with this
line :—

" Behind the veil—Behind the veil !"

And then possibly, but not till then, we may find all mysteries
solved ; among them these : " Why is evil permitted in a
world governed by omnipotence and love, and whose material
frame-work is a wondrous display of Law and order and
beauty and life ? "   " Why, in the moral world, Transgression—disorder—pain and death ? "   " Shall evil and its
consequences be *eternal ?* "   I do not know !

---

1 mo. 12, 1868.—Five weeks have passed away since I
wrote last. Alone as I often am, unwell,—absent from our
evening Meeting ; not for mere occupation of time, but
seeking a little renewal of faith and hope in the contem-
plation of many continued blessings, I write again. I feel
at times so weary, so little power of exertion, as to make me
fear lest I should allow diminished health and strength, the
loss of wonted elasticity of mind and limb, to make me an
idler in this late evening of life. So if I enumerate little
services, it is to help me to believe that I am striving against
that unhappy, profitless condition. *   *   *   *   For myself—poor, very poor, and sometimes depressed, I can still
speak of " times of refreshing from the presence of the Lord,"

in answered prayer, in anxieties for others alleviated, and
permission at times granted to speak for Christ and His
Truth.

Oh at times to feel as I do, that I do indeed love Him—
.that He is my only refuge, (other have I none) that I can
trust Him for time and eternity—this is peace—sometimes
joy. I have read much in the last few years, and have
recently read much in writings which are thought by many
not orthodox, especially on the Atonement as ordinarily
described in formulas of doctrine. These have not in the
smallest degree shaken my faith, or weakened my entire
acceptance of this doctrine as set forth in various ways in
Holy Scripture. One thing I think I have learned from
them—the fitness and the safety of expressing and setting
forth this doctrine in the words of Scripture. The result of
further thought on this fundamental article of a Christian's
creed, convinces me that in simplicity of statement and in
variety of illustration, Holy Scripture furnishes a most ample
supply. Accepting this Scriptural setting forth, I think I
can sometimes say with that Christian philosopher, George
Wilson, "I rejoice that I have a creed with which I can
(Christ helping me) face death and eternity, and which
makes this life often a joyous worship and always a patient
endurance."

At times when sitting down to a lonely meal as I often
do, I am comforted, sometimes beyond words to express, by
remembering the gracious assurance, "Behold, I stand at
the door, and knock; if any man hear my voice, and open
the door, *I will come in to him, and will sup with him, and he
with Me.*" What a glorious guest!

I feel increasingly the uncertainty of continuance here.
I am outliving my contemporaries. Not a day passes but
this thought is with me. As one result I have been slightly

looking over and burning hundreds of letters, not only mere
business ones, but many full of memories of much enjoyment
in the affection and intelligence of the numerous youthful
writers, many of them in my earlier days most intimately
associated with me when schoolboys, and maintaining for
several years a most affectionate correspondence as young
men. The writers of not a few have I believe obtained,
through their Saviour's atoning mercy and infinite love, an
inheritance in that better land where through the same love
and mercy, when the time comes, may I rejoin them and
many more dearly loved—there to unite in all the fulness
of love for Him through whom alone we enter there.

3 mo. 21.—I am sixty-seven years old to-day. Whilst I
can truly say, "surely goodness and mercy have followed me
all the days of my life," and whilst I long and pray for a
more grateful heart, I still find life a warfare—a painful
conflict—sometimes even to the conviction that "to depart
and to be with Christ" would be far better; and yet amidst
the conflict, enabled, with a little renewal of faith, to commit the keeping of my soul in well doing, unto a faithful
Creator. I see conditions of holiness—of conformity to the
Divine will in all things—every thought brought into captivity
to the obedience of Christ—to which I have not attained,
and yet earnestly longing for it, and in distress, but not in
despair, I utter the petition "Undertake for me." I have
known from time to time, plenary pardon for all past sins,
through that blood which cleanseth from all sin, and have
felt the love of Christ to me and a love to Him in return
that moves me to tears. I have, nevertheless still to deplore
coldness and lifelessness—prayer without the spirit of prayer,
and yet again enlivened by "times of refreshing from the
presence of the Lord," and then can say with F. W.

Robertson, " I feel the beauty which I cannot realize :—robe
me in Thine unutterable purity."

In Ninth month, 1868, in company with his dear
friend, Isaac Brown of the Flounders' Institute, Ackworth, and with the concurrence of York Monthly
Meeting, John Ford paid a visit to the Schools of
Friends and to some of the Meetings in Ireland. A
brief account of this visit is given in the following
letter.

To Rebecca Thompson.

11 mo. 9, 1868.—I must tell thee a little about our visit
to the Schools and some of the Meetings in Ireland.—It
was a very laborious time. We attended sixteen Meetings
and had eleven conferences with Friends in a conversational
way, exclusive of the visits to the public schools. We were
only twenty-three days between landing and re-embarking.
On our return home we were enabled to look back peacefully
and thankfully on our service. Sometimes together (and
often each alone) we asked for direction and help in our
work, and for a blessing upon it, and we could at times rejoice
in answered prayer. We found much progress in Christian
work for the benefit of the Society, as well as for the poor,
the ignorant and the vicious, since a visit to Ireland in 1860.
We were especially pleased with the evidence of life among
our younger Friends in Dublin. We had a Meeting of a
social character soon after landing. At the close, several
young men came round us, and expressed a wish that we
would meet them again on our return from the South. We
gladly assented. They sent out invitations to " the workers
and those who wished to encourage Christian work," to meet
us at tea at the Meeting House on the 7th of Tenth-month.

More than one hundred Friends met.   After an hour's
interchange of conversation on various modes of Christian
usefulness, a psalm was read, followed by solemn silence;
'this was broken by several offerings in prayer.   It was a
finis to our service in Dublin for which we were indeed
thankful.   Here and there we met with some of the honestly
over-cautious, who looked with apprehension on change and
progress: our counsel to our younger Friends was to avoid
as much as possible offending these, and to seek in a prayerful
spirit to use the various means and opportunities for promoting
the cause of Christ in themselves and in those around them.
One of the pleasantest things of the journey was the warm
greeting I met from my old scholars.   Four of them, all
from different families, were. on the quay at Kingstown to
welcome me.

The following extract from John Ford's diary
has reference to a visit paid whilst in Ireland to a
young man apparently on his death-bed.

There are some happy moments when the truth as it is in
Jesus, in all its completeness, in all its beauty, is presented
to the mind with a force which scatters to the winds all false
philosophies, all the refinements of logic that would disturb
our faith; the heart and soul triumph over them all.   That
glowing, earnest, loving spirit is not about to be annihilated,
or "absorbed into the spirit of the universe," whatever that
may mean.   No! the blood of Jesus Christ has cleansed it
from all sin: the Holy Spirit has taken possession of His
earthly temple.   The weakness of the enfeebled mortal frame
is over-mastered; the very countenance radiant with the
peace of God, told of a sure and certain hope of a joyful

resurrection and a glorious eternal life. It was a moment in which it seemed that I realized in all its fulness the sentiment of Dr. Arnold often quoted by me at Bootham, " There is no more beautiful, no more blessed sight on earth, than a youth that is rich towards God."

12 mo. 31. * * The year just closing has again thinned the ranks of my dearest friends. In the Fourth-month Edwd. Smith, and in the Seventh, John Pease, were summoned away by very brief illness. The very prayer of my heart is that this increased and increasing loneliness, this departure of " friend after friend," unreplaceable by new earthly friendships, may help me to seek day by day to draw nearer and ever nearer to the friend of sinners—the friend that sticketh closer than a brother—to Him who is not ashamed to call us brethren—to Jesus the Mediator of the New Covenant: even so, Amen ! * * * * A continuous cough in a temperature below 48° or 50°, seems my regular winter companion. How soon and how quickly this might assume the form of a summons, I know not; that it may do so, I do know. Not without " times of refreshing from the presence of the Lord," I am nevertheless often walking rather by a modicum of faith, than by the lively feeling of this presence : and though sometimes failing and foiled, yet still desiring and striving, and praying for help to maintain the fight.

3 mo. 19, 1869.—I feel at times as though mine were a useless life, so that I am glad when any service calls me out. I could not now at sixty-eight meet the demands of daily compulsory work as at forty-eight and fifty-eight; but I look back on the times of compulsory, daily, regular occupation notwithstanding their responsibilities and difficulties and nightly weariness, as times of enjoyment

and privilege, contrasted with the incapacity of feeble health
and the dangers of desultoriness.   And yet at times I can
take a more cheerful view—perhaps a healthier one, of my
present circumstances of health and occupation—lively thankfulness that a blessing on the working days of life has provided
abundantly the alleviations for the closing hours : and I
desire to enjoy with a grateful heart, the permitted repose
of evening, without on the one hand being too anxious to
work, and on the other, careful, watchful, and frequent in
prayer to be preserved from slothful ease.

6 mo. 20.—Whatever other records are omitted through
lack of opportunity, lassitude or weariness, answered prayer
must not pass unnoticed.   To-day in feeble health, partly
due to the depressing cold weather and the remains of previous
illness, I have felt very incapable of any exertion or exercise,
mental or spiritual.   Thus passed the morning and afternoon.
Before leaving for the evening Meeting I knelt in prayer,
first for the blood of sprinkling over all the past—then for
the Saviour's presence and love,—then that if it were His
will that I should serve, that He would be with me to give
me subject and utterance.   With my spirit tendered before
Him I went to Meeting.   Soon I found the spirit of prayer
granted.   I knelt down, and with more sense of freedom
and earnestness than usual, I gave utterance to thanksgiving
and praise, and to various petitions for varied individual
needs.   After an interval I spoke for some time, with a
grateful sense of help and with that freedom which *help*
confers.   I quoted "What would ye that I should do for
you ?"   I applied the question as put then and there by a
loving Saviour to each condition present—a loving Saviour,
able, omnipotent and all willing to supply all our needs.   I
left the Meeting humbly thankful.

6 mo. 22.—I had a brief visit from an old scholar, formerly a loving schoolboy. Following a little impression of religious concern, I found liberty to converse with him freely, and he freely responded. "Meliora video, proboque," and the sorrowful context, was the starting point of our conversation, and led to words of Christian encouragement under a glowing sense of the love of Christ. This love was I believe inclining the heart of this young man not only to see and approve, but to long to follow. He spoke touchingly of the transient nature of his good resolves, of his failing efforts. I spoke to him of the efficacy of persevering prayer; said I would pray for him: this he gratefully acknowledged: assured him of the love of his Saviour to him,—of this I felt no doubt. Need I doubt that He was with us, touching both our hearts? I was enabled to pour out my soul in prayer in the evening for my beloved young friend. I parted from him thankful for the opportunity and the ability granted to try to help him.

7 mo. 3.—— and —— and their children took tea with me at St. Mary's. As years glide away the probability of such gatherings grows less and less. On the 5th they all left for a visit to ——. I believe this family is to me a mercifully and graciously accorded blessing. Isolated, except during twenty-two happy years of married life, from all connected by blood even from my earliest manhood, I prize the blessing thus granted me as a most precious blessing. I try to guard against inordinate affection; I try to love them in Christ, Him first and supreme. I remember them, mention them in my prayers. I miss them now in their absence exceedingly, and I try to seek yet more earnestly for closer and more frequent communion with Him, their friend, and brother, and Saviour, and mine too, all unworthy

as I know and feel I am. I am reminded whilst writing, of
the words of Augustine of Hippo, " Blessed whoso loveth
Thee (Christ) and his friend in Thee ; for he alone loses
none dear to him, to whom all are dear in Him who cannot
be lost "—an ever present Saviour and friend and brother !

11 mo. 11.—Castle Howard Reformatory. I have not
unfrequently desired to have an opportunity of addressing
the poor boys. I attended the Committee this morning.
The business was over by noon, and the boys were at their
dinner. All the gentlemen had left except W. W. We
went into the dining-room and conversed with some of the
boys. Just as dinner was ending I asked Mr. Fish if I
might say a few words ; he said he was just coming to ask
me to do so. At the Scripture reading at home this morning
I read from Matthew xviii., " Jesus called a little child, &c."
This brought to mind the company at Castle Howard Reformatory. Alas ! how unlike the little child ! and I think
this determined me, not without a prayer for help, to seek an
opportunity to speak to them. I began as I did once before
by questions, requesting only individual answers, and these
only in a whisper from each whom I might ask. The questions
were asked aloud, and in reply to most of them many hands
were held up in token of readiness to answer. It soon
appeared that their attention and interest were quite absorbed. The series of questions, led to the conclusions—
that they knew when they had done wrong—their conscience
told them—that they were not happy in doing wrong—that
it was better to be found out, than successfully to conceal
their wrong doing—that concealment tended to harden the
heart, and to repeated sin—that the Holy Spirit of God
taught their consciences, and that the Holy Scriptures taught
them. All these answers and many more were given by

individual boys, and repeated aloud by me, and were illustrated and commented upon.

The answers to questions on the facts and teachings of Holy Scripture denoted careful teaching, and that their memories were fairly stored,—that all that God created was very good, man included—that he became evil by disobedience—that the act of disobedience was taking that which he was forbidden to take—that it is sin which separates from God—that all have sinned—that eternal punishment is for unrepentant sinners. This led to facts concerning our Lord, His birth, life, sufferings and death, &c.; eliciting from all in concert the glorious text, " God so loved the world, &c." I enlarged upon this, pressing upon them the great love of Christ to us and our obligation to love Him—confession—prayer and forgiveness—the Holy Spirit's help to keep us and guide us. These and other kindred truths I was enabled to set before them and press home to their hearts and consciences with earnestness and love, reminding me of some favoured times on First-day evening at Bootham.

Though I felt I had entire hold of their most earnest attention, I was not aware till my friend W. W. told me afterwards, of the deep emotion of many, evinced by the tears of some and the efforts of others to repress their tears. Deep thankfulness was the covering of my spirit then, and is now in the remembrance of the help graciously given in this little service.

11 mo. 21.—The low temperature has made my cough troublesome, and respiration out of doors difficult. I am staying away from Meeting this evening. Whilst pondering this matter at tea time, to go or not to go, and examining my motives, querying whether idleness, carelessness and love of ease were the inducements, and somewhat unwilling to

succumb to the infirmities of age, such a sense of the love of
my God and Saviour came over me—the assurance that He
is not a hard master—that He knoweth our frame, He re-
membereth that we are dust—as contrited my spirit—gave
me peace in the conclusion to stay at home, and joy in the
thought that my frequent prayer, "Forsake me not when my
strength is failing," is heard and answered. Whilst my
friends were at Meeting I enjoyed occupation in annotating
and afterwards in solemnly reading Holy Scripture. This
was succeeded by a precious season of prayer and thanksgiving—prayer for myself, for several beloved and loving
ones, for the congregation then met, for individuals by name;
and thanksgiving for admission to the throne, for communion
with Christ through His Spirit. Once more τῷ Θεῷ δόξα.*

To Rebecca Thompson.

12 mo. 6. 1869.—I fear I shall be much confined to home
during the winter. I can less and less bear the cold weather.
I sometimes recall the beautiful description of Heaven
learned in very early years in Barbauld's Hymns.—"There
the cold of winter shall not wither us, nor the heat of summer
scorch us. In that land there is eternal spring and light
without any cloud;"—and, most blessed thought of all,
"There we shall see Jesus!"

----

1 mo. 18, 1870.—Encouraged and strengthened by the
evening Meeting, I carried out a little impression of duty in
a visit to the Blue Coat School. I found the boys assembled
in a social group near the stove, and one of the younger
teachers reading a narrative to them about a boy who had
been wounded (and who died) by the accidental discharge of

* To God be the glory.

a gun. When he ended, I told them the tale of the dear Irish boy whom I visited, pointing out the blessedness in such a time to have no painful remorse of unforgiven, unrepented sin, but to be like him prepared to go, his heart overflowing with love, and nothing but praise for himself and prayer for his friends. I read to them the beautiful hymn, " The Prodigal's return." I stayed the evening services. They sang "Abide with me." At the close I gave a short parting address. I believe the love of Christ, His to us and ours to Him was felt. I rejoice in these permitted humble services with these dear boys.

2 mo. 20.—Several weeks have passed by since my last entry. During that time I have suffered from a harassing cough, interfering with rest by night, and producing prostration and incapacity for exertion of body or of mind. Between six and eleven in the evenings I have felt less of the weariness of the former part of the day. Often the spiritual as well as the intellectual life, has sympathised with the physical depression. And yet at times as last evening, the sun has shone through a rent in the clouds. A most precious time of access in prayer was unexpectedly and suddenly granted me ; it was like a burst of sunshine, with a refreshing shower spanned by a rainbow. I was indeed thankful for this.

To Matilda Sturge.

4 mo. 4, 1870.—In the *human* character of our Lord, there is to me nothing so beautifully illustrative of it as His personal, peculiar friendship for the " beloved disciple." It is like a beam of earthly sunlight on His sometimes sorrowful and often suffering lot. His susceptibility of hunger and thirst and weariness and pain, His tender sympathy, His tears—all

o

assert His human nature, but it is on the sorrowful and suffering side : whilst His friendship, (His friend leaning on His
bosom at supper) may lead to the thought of His participation
in some of the highest order of pleasures granted to earthly
life. It seems to bind Him to us, and us to Him by even
a closer bond than His participation in our sufferings and
sorrows. It seems as though even His oneness with the
Father (His "yet I am not alone ") did not prevent Him
from seeking and enjoying the sweets of human friendship.
*   *   *   *

I suppose that like most other lovers of literature thou
hast read Tennyson's last—" The Holy Grail."—The reading
of it has led me to look again at his other " Idylls of the
King."   Dean Alford has written a very able and interesting review of the whole series, in the "Contemporary Review"
for January.   I was pleased to find in that Review a passage
quoted as beautiful and instructive, which, when at Bootham,
I had quoted in an address to the boys.   It speaks of the
change in the countenance indicating the prevalence of the
higher and nobler—the Christian motives and impulses, in
the heart and mind.   I have marked these changes with
infinite pleasure.   There is something exceedingly beautiful
in the expression of a young face, when the heart is brought
under some measure of the love of Christ.

To Rebecca Thompson.

8 mo. 2, 1870.—Thy letter came in the midst of our
Quarterly Meeting engagements.—With us as with you, the
barriers of exclusiveness are breaking down. Selfishness in
Churches may be as injurious to a Church, as it is to the
individual man, " the wretch concentred all in self." *Our*
testimonies, *our* numbers, *our* interests, *our* members, are

phraseologies giving place in some measure, to words and thoughts and doings, that take the wider range of the *Church of Christ* and the multitude not yet within that safe enclosure. Inasmuch as any of our testimonies are essential truths of the New Testament, let us stick to them, and seek to spread them far and wide : and we may be glad that some of these,— most of them—are far less exclusively *ours* than they were. * * * I apprehend that a large amount of mistaken Christian zeal has been expended on sentiment, [as distinguished from *conviction*,] traditions, conventionalities. * * * Thou enquires kindly about my health. Having entered my seventieth year, I have much to be thankful for in that respect ; though I feel, and have felt for the last two or three years, greatly diminished ability to encounter bodily fatigue. My earnest desire is that I may not lead an idle life, but that work may yet be assigned me adapted to advanced years. Such work I continue to find in and around home, occasionally visiting our smaller Meetings, as well as some not within our Monthly Meeting.

To Isaac Brown (Kendal).

9 mo. 6, 1870.—I hasten to reply to thine which I read this morning with emotions of reverent thankfulness. The prospect of the service had been subject of frequent prayer ; and though the probable lateness of the season had made it appear formidable, I had come to the condition of willingness trustfully to face all that it might bring, if the right time were come. And now I can accept thine as another answer to prayer, shewing so clearly, as it appears to me, that it is *not* the right time, and that the postponement, if it should prove only postponement, is not the result of my own willing or contriving. I shall gladly look out for openings and

intimations of service, such as I named to thee in my last, not implying long absence nor long journeys.

I can form, I apprehend, some idea, though perhaps but a faint one, of the engrossing and painful, as well as exhausting labours past and prospective in Lancashire and Cheshire which fall to thy lot, such as I am sure would need an interval of rest and refreshment as a preparation for the far pleasanter work of seeking to "lay our spirits alongside the *unadulterated spirits of the young.*" My heart nearly overflowed at my eyes, as it responded to thine, as thou describes this "sweet and soothing service." I felt it to be so, last First-day evening, when towards the close of a sermon not especially addressed to the young, I turned to them (the large majority of the assembly) as unadulterated with a long-continued course of sin—conscience not yet hardened—ears and heart still open to the Spirit's gentle pleadings. I could but assure such of their Saviour's love, and invite them to give their hearts to Him in all the glow of early affection—inviting them to make their daily lessons and even their amusements, service for Christ. The latter, in order to refresh and invigorate their bodily health and mental powers, that thus learning and science might be successfully cultivated and consecrated to Him.

To Matilda Sturge.

9 mo. 10, 1870.—I read thy contribution to the Examiner with much interest, and have looked at it again. If I differ at all, it is in reference to "the dawn preceding the rising of the Sun." I see in the condition of the Roman, Grecian and Jewish world, circumstances most aptly described by the Apostle as denoting that the "fulness of the time" was come. The old systems of religion (with the exception of the

pious manifestations of Judaism in a very select few), were
utterly worn out. Greece and Rome were at the very zero
of moral degradation (see Romans i.). The great rulers
and teachers of the Jews, paid to virtue the tribute of that
hypocrisy which our Lord so sternly denounced. On the
other hand Rome had brought the nations together under
one head ; Greece had furnished a universal language ; and
Roman roads and Roman ships were ready to carry the good
tidings to every land. In regard to conclusions, I say
Christianity has *not* failed. With all the wickedness which
we feel, and see, 'and hear of, I nevertheless believe that
from Eden down to the present day, there never was so large
a number of the human family, as now, in harmony with the
mind and spirit of Christ. I think " the better and brighter
day " will not prove to be so remote as to involve periods
intervening comparable to the rate of geological changes
in the past. Holy Scripture appears to intimate that the
strife between good and evil, and the triumph of the former,
will be completed by some decisive display of Divine
Power. But with thee I say—" let us contribute our little
aid, &c."

12 mo. 21.—For most of the time since the 6th ult., I
have been often very incapable, sometimes quite lethargic,
sometimes comatose, and occasionally a wave-like sensation
sweeping across the head with every pulse, like the old school
head-aches. These things remind me daily of the increasing
frailty of the earthly tent. I cannot say that the ever present
thought day by day that my " three-score years and ten " are
nearly completed (only three months short of it to-day) alarms
or disturbs or depresses me. I feel at times that I know in
whom I have believed and can trust all to Him. Yet

longing and earnestly praying for more and more conformity to the mind and spirit of Christ, more of purity and
holiness and faith and love, I can adopt the beautiful language in the reply of Christian to the enquiry of Prudence,
"What is it that makes you so desirous to go to Mount
Zion?" He replies, "Why, there I hope to see Him alive
that did hang dead on the Cross; and there I hope to be rid
of all those things, that, to this day, are in me an annoyance
to me; there they say there is no death, and there I shall
dwell with such company as I like best. For, to tell you
truth, I love Him, because I was by Him eased of my
Burden. And I am weary of my inward sickness: I would
fain be where I shall die no more, and with the company that
shall continually cry, *Holy, Holy, Holy.*"

To Edward Rhodes, M.D.*

12 mo. 29, 1870.—The touching details of thy letter,—
thy dear father's illness and thy own present condition, move
my warmest Christian sympathy. Oh how I rejoice even
whilst writing as I turn to thy words—that thou canst
realize the hand of Love, enabling thee to rejoice even
though in affliction and bonds. I lift up my heart for thee
as I pen these lines, that if it please our Heavenly Father
to restore thee, it may be with enlarged gifts for the service
of the dear Saviour. The alternative will be the ever blessed
service of Heaven, where His servants see His face, and His
name is on their foreheads.

Thy letter finds me a prisoner from the effects of the
severe weather, and the little resistance which threescore
years and ten nearly accomplished, presents to its influence.
Thy reference to dear William Tanner, whose portrait

---

* Edward Rhodes of Philadelphia, a young physician of great promise.
He received this letter only two days before his death.

presented by his Mother hangs before me, reminds me of
thy tender sympathy with me in his loss, expressed in thine
to dear E. H. Crosfield. I find as year after year glides
away, how dear companionships, heart friendships, are severed for a time, till the preponderance is on the other side of
Jordan.   Mine has been an extremely isolated lot in life as
regards kindred by blood: but this has been most kindly
compensated by the attachment and friendship of very many
not so connected. And now as the end draws near, I have
in my dear friends ——— and ——— (who stand to me in
the relation of adopted son and daughter) and their family
of affectionate and loving children, those on whose kind care
and love I can rely when the end comes. And why should
I hesitate to say that I have, and trust to have even to the
end and for ever and ever, the care and love of Him who
died for me, and whom (how inadequately) I love and desire
to serve.

To an Old Scholar.

(About) 1871.—I have thought so much and so often of
thee since I saw thee, that it was a great pleasure to receive
thy deeply interesting letter. It has brought me into warm
Christian sympathy with thee. Oh how it recalls my own
early days, when I read thy complaint of " little progress "—
the " road more difficult ''—" the smallness of faith "—and
" the lack of enjoyment." I trace in all this, dear ————,
indications of the true-hearted young disciple.   These
longings for more conformity to the mind of Christ, for more
enjoyment of His love, and more sense of love to Him, in
His own good time He will assuredly satisfy. How often
has the thought—so sweetly expressed by thee—crossed my
own mind—" If we could only once see and speak to Jesus,"

—followed by the thought, " I would fall at His feet, confess
my sins, tell Him my wants—that I loved Him and longed
to love Him more." And then sometimes such a sense of
His presence seemed to be felt, that I could then and there
tell Him all this, and rejoice in the renewed experience of
His love.

I *have* remembered thee and thy dear brothers in prayer,
and do still remember thee, and pray that child-like faith
may be granted thee, and that when assailed by temptation
He may be at hand to help thee, who " was tempted in all
points like as we are," and (as in Heb. ii. 18) " in that He
himself hath suffered being tempted, He is able to succour
them that are tempted."

Thy experience, dear ————, of occasional coldness in
prayer is no strange thing : I think it is a sign of love to
Christ to feel and to lament it. I have many a time been
comforted and encouraged myself, and, in times past, have
sought to comfort and encourage my beloved flock at Bootham
by the following from Dr. Vaughan's " Memorials of Harrow
Sundays : "—" Be resolute to withstand the tempter, when
he first says to you that God does not hear or will not answer
your prayer. Oh be able to say then from your own experience, ' He does answer, for He has answered me.' And
is not that true ? Oh is it not true that God has answered
us all ? Has He not, sometimes as we knelt before Him,
cold perhaps and dead, self-accusing yet not penitent, touched
our hearts with that inward impulse, which quickened and
reanimated, which gave meaning to our formal words, and
warmth to our cold and languid spirits ? Have we not risen
from our knees, humbled with that sort of humbling which
is better than any elation ? "—I would add to the foregoing
' Have we not risen from our knees with heart and eyes
overflowing with gratitude and love ?'—And if joy like this

is not often permitted, let us hail it when it is granted, as a "time of refreshing from the presence of the Lord." The Psalmist gathered strength from such remembrances, when he says, " I will remember the years of the right hand of the most High." This was a time of deepest discouragement. The seventy-seventh Psalm sets forth this despondency and its cure most wonderfully.

---

3 mo. 21, 1871.—My " three-score years and ten " are completed to-day. Surely goodness and mercy have followed—gone with me—all the days of my life. I would that with a little more glow than I just now feel, I could adopt words, familiar to me from my earliest years,

> " When all Thy mercies, O my God,
>   My rising soul surveys,
>   Transported with the view, I'm lost
>   In wonder, love, and praise."

Though bodily health and strength are waning, the unspeakable blessing of freedom from acute pain, (once my frequent portion) is granted me. The blessing of intellectual clearness is still graciously permitted. Lapses of memory of names are not much more troublesome than I find them acknowledged by my juniors.　＊　＊　＊　＊　What of the higher life? Conflict is not over—evil is not utterly expelled. "The blood of sprinkling" is needed day by day, and asked for still. The travel-soiled feet need daily washing; and so I try to come day by day, and oftener—for pardon, for cleansing, for renewing and sustaining grace. And thus not hopelessly nor doubtingly I run the race, ever looking to Jesus—I fight the fight relying on Him alone for victory; seeking for more of faith and love, more of. longing for holiness, more of the heavenly mind.

To Matilda Sturge.

4 mo. 3, 1871.—I have felt the effects of the long and cold winter, and have been more confined to the house than ever before. But I need not complain that at " three-score years and ten " the powers of resistance fail, but rather, thankfully acknowledge the measure of health granted, and work assigned, suited to circumstances. Nevertheless I have been inclined to think that the trials of inactive life are quite as great, in their demands upon patience and watchfulness and prayer, as are those of the pressure of exacted daily toil. I know that the evening of life is the allotted and permitted season of repose, but I fear lest repose should degenerate into indolence. * * * * *

Thou refers to the question of non-intervention [in the Franco-Prussian War]. If intervention implied armed force, I should have said it was not only a *crime* against humanity (human nature I mean), but a gross political blunder, said (by one of Satan's prime ministers, Talleyrand,) to be worse than a crime. In reference to the first Napoleon—are we sure that he would have needed crushing, had the principle of entire non-intervention been the rule of action in Europe ? Happily, the intervening sea, as a secondary cause, left England at liberty to settle her own affairs in 1642-8, and again in 1688. *Wrong* never turns up *right* at last. I think it *was* wrong to interfere in the affairs of France ; and now it seems the bloody game of settlement amongst themselves is to be played over again. I refer to the *first* interference and the Brunswick proclamation.

I have only just received the Report of the Dublin Conference. I shall refer to it with interest, to read thy paper. I cannot assent to some of the opinions announced at Dublin, in regard to the qualification for engaging in Sunday-school teaching. The ability and the will and the opportunity to instruct the ignorant, seem to me sufficient qualification and authorization. Many have engaged therein on no higher ground, and have found it a stepping stone to higher things—to devotion of heart to Christ. Having attained to something of this previously is certainly an additional qualification of great value. But who is to judge?

---

10 mo. 5.—In compliance with an invitation from Richard Fish, the Superintendent of the Castle Howard Reformatory, I attended the harvest thanksgiving and feast. An excellent sermon of just twenty minutes was addressed to the boys assembled in the chapel. E. V. Harcourt had provided for them a plentiful dinner of roast beef and plum-pudding. After the visitors had lunched, the boys were re-assembled, and at R. Fish's request I addressed them. I described the happy results of the training of this school to at least eighty in every hundred, out of the three hundred and thirty who had received the benefits of the school. If I could summon them all before you to-day, what would they say to you? Well dressed, earning an honest and respectable living, capable of looking any man in the face, they would tell you to profit by your instruction here—the daily reading of Holy Scripture—the morning and evening family prayers—the services in public worship—and your own prayers when kneeling by your bed-side—by the kind care and instruction bestowed upon you from day to day. They would entreat you to profit by all these—to learn habits of obedience, of truth speaking, and all other habits becoming Christian boys.—I was listened to as heretofore by these poor boys with fixed attention. I remembered them in prayer. I breathe a prayer for them now.

To an Old Scholar, who had some view of entering on
Foreign Mission Service.

12 mo. 17, 1871.—I have read thy letter again and again,
and each time with much emotion and deep sympathy.   My
very heart responded to the perfect *naturalness* of thy wish,
"for one hour's converse with Jesus."   But we must bear in
mind His words, "it is expedient for you that I go away."
A verbal, vocal command from Him would not be in harmony
in its effect upon the mind of the recipient, with the stress
which He always placed upon the exercise of *faith*.   On
the morning on which I received thy letter, one of the texts
for the day was, "Commit thy way unto the Lord : trust
also in Him ; and He shall bring it to pass."   A comment
following was, "Even in the affairs of daily life, His Providence opens up or closes our way, with no doubtful meaning
to the simple heart that sincerely asks to do His will."   I
immediately associated this text and comment with thy
letter.

I was glad to find that thou had given the little book,
and to find that it *cost thee an effort*.   These little things
that "cost an effort," are the very things to which the
promise belongs, "to be made rulers over more."

I have seen enough of ——— to enable me to understand
thy "passionate love" of such a home.   I have seldom seen
one so happy.   These preliminaries have arisen out of thy
frank and confidential communication.   I enter upon the
direct topic, not without prayer that I may be permitted to
help thee.   I think I can say as the prophet to David, "thou
didst well that it was in thine heart."   I am reminded of
what we frequently hear of the length of time between the
first impression of required service, and the attainment of
clearness as to entering upon it : a time of great trial of

faith and patience. In my own small experience, I have endeavoured to cherish the impression, to live in the spirit of prayer concerning it, and ask that by the leadings of His Providence He would make His way straight before my face. This guidance has not failed me, nor misled me. And I would say to thee, my dear young friend, cherish the impression of service—ask for an enlightened judgment concerning it. "In all thy ways acknowledge Him, and He shall direct thy paths." * * · * * *

It seems to me that as the impression remains and deepens, the time will come to take further counsel—*home first* :—then, with the sanction of home—of some of the wise, judicious and well informed friends who are interested in Friends' Foreign Mission work. * * * I note thy remark regarding marriage. Under the guardianship of Paul, it is probable that for a time, Timothy deferred matrimony. We are not informed whether or not he was ever thus united. But I think there can be no doubt that if he was, he found his *whole* nature, in all its beauty, (as sanctified by Divine grace) developed as it never had been before, and his qualifications for his mission work enlarged. It is not for nothing that the inspired book tells us of the joint labours of Aquila and his wife Priscilla.

In conclusion I would say, cherish the impression—look for its realization—wait for and pray for further clearness—watch all providential pointings—continue the careful reading and study of Holy Scripture. I shall continue to remember thee when access in prayer is specially felt.

5' mo. 14, 1872.—Tea at the Mount School. I went anxious, and came back thankful. I attended the Scripture reading, and was enabled to address the beloved company with freedom, earnestness and feeling.   I spoke of the golden period of youth, its peculiar privileges, its comparative innocence—sin not yet become habitual by a long process of hardening—conscience still tender and watchful—the freshness of youthful feeling, the power of sympathy called forth by your youthful friendships leading you to loving participation in the sorrows and troubles, the pleasures, the joys and the happiness of each other.

Surrounded here by a Christian atmosphere, familiarized day by day with the truths and the incidents of Holy Scripture, the life and actions of the dear Redeemer, the wealth of sympathy, compassion and love in His human heart, manifested in the narratives of the widow of Nain and her only son, the poor epileptic, possessed boy and his agonized father,—the Divine merged in the human when He wept at the grave of Lazarus.   Do you not love Him as you trace His character in the New Testament?   Sin and suffering and sorrow—disease and death itself calling forth all the tenderness of His love, all His Divine, creative, restoring, sin-forgiving power.   Looking to your training now in relation to your future, I am reminded of some lines by a lady-poet sometimes called the English Sappho, in which she glances at the sorrowful side of female life:

> " Her lot is on you—to be found untired,
>   Watching the stars out by the bed of pain,
>
> *   *   *   *   *   *
>   Meekly to bear with wrong, to cheer decay,
>   And, oh! to love through all things—therefore pray!"

But it has its joyous side too, in your power to double the sense of happiness by participation in the times of rejoicing—to cheer and to sustain in trouble.   Thus now with your school-associates and friends, with brothers and sisters at home, you are training for whatever relationships the future may bring. There is an incident recorded in the life of the Czar, Peter the

Great, illustrative of woman's power to soothe. He was a hasty, impulsive man, subject to fierce outbreaks of wrath. We are told how Catherine placing her cool hand on his burning forehead, soothed and assuaged his fierce spirit. This wealth of love and sympathy, the especial gift and ornament of the woman—the meek and quiet spirit,—what can it not do? I spoke of the value of prayer—the habit of morning and evening prayer—do not give up because of the feeling of coldness or lifelessness. Pray for one another; there is reflex action in intercessory prayer. Expect, look for answers to prayer, and you will be able to say, "I know that God answers prayer—for He has answered me."

To ———— (aged 14.)

7 mo. 23, 1872.—You have so many pleasant things to write about at Whitby, that you have quite an advantage over me. Ten, or twenty, or more years ago I could have told you of excursions by sea and land, climbing mountains, exploring caverns, swimming in lake or sea or river, botanizing on the hills, or studying geology in the rocks or the coal mines: but all *that* is passed. Paley, an English philosopher, whose works are still worth reading, says, "It is not for *youth* alone that the great Parent of Creation has provided. Happiness is found with the purring cat no less than with the playful kitten; in the arm-chair of age, as well as in the sprightliness of the dance." I am somewhat in the condition which the same writer describes as one not without its enjoyment—"riding at anchor after a busy life." I think it very likely that I felt as much pleasure in believing that I ministered a little to the pleasure of dear, suffering, patient ————, by quietly conversing with her a few minutes in the darkened and silent room, as thou finds in thy many *active* engagements at Whitby. Be thankful, dear ————, for the

capacity of enjoyment, for active limbs and lively spirits.
Do not forget Him from whom all these blessings come.

To the same on his Birthday.

7 mo. 30, 1872.—I do not like to let this thy fourteenth
birthday, pass over, without at least a greeting to assure thee
of my continued interest and love.   I wish it may be a
happy day, and I wish the same for every succeeding one
even to the last.   When fourteen years have passed away,
the age of childhood is rapidly departing.   The time is
coming when *less* by the force of rules and regulations, and
more by a sense of personal, christian responsibility, a boy
must seek to govern his conduct: and he will be enabled to
do this, just in proportion as the love of his God and Saviour
has place in his heart.   May this evermore increase and
abound in the heart of my dear ————.   These are solemn
words, but not, I think, unfitting in a birth-day letter of
loving congratulation.   And what I wish for thee is, I am
sure, no bar to a *happy, cheerful, sunny* life.

---

8 mo.   *   *   *   The week spent at Scarbro' was rainy
and cold.   I had much social enjoyment, but was strongly
impressed with the evidence of failing physical power.   The
well remembered enjoyments of former days still appeared
pleasant things but no bodily power responded.   Not with a
repining, but with a thankful spirit I refer to this change.
Other enjoyments—the liberty to *serve*, the ability to *serve*,
are precious, highly prized substitutes for the pleasures
passed away.   The days referred to, and the enjoyments of
those days, were often most thankfully regarded by me as
permitted relaxation from the responsibilities of school-life,
unencumbered with a single anxious, troublous thought.

To THE OLD SCHOLAR TO WHOM WAS ADDRESSED THE
LETTER, PAGE 204.

12 mo. 13, 1872.—I have read and re-read thine of the
10th with deep and affectionate interest, and have sought in
prayer for right direction in the matter for myself and for
thee. I cannot but look upon ———'s kind offer, (coinciding
as it does with thy own previous impression and prayer,) as
a kind and loving pointing of the Divine finger, towards
present duty, at least for a time. I have gratefully marked
and accepted such intimations in my own course, and can
thankfully acknowledge in looking back, that I was not
mistaken in so doing. ———'s offer seems to provide the
leisure for mental improvement so very desirable, whether
thy future work should be at home or abroad. The increased
study of Holy Scripture, increased experience in teaching
and influencing the human mind of young and old, are
excellent preparations for either allotment—home or foreign.
I am therefore glad that thou hast accepted ———'s well-
timed offer.

One step at a time, dear ———. If the next step should
be to unite in partnership with———, and then called to a
third step, to leave all and follow Christ wheresoever He may
please, I do not doubt that power to see and to take each
successive step will be granted thee. " Make thy way
straight before *my* face," was the prayer of the Psalmist. I
have used it for myself, and changing *my* into *his*, have used
it for thee. It is indeed a pleasant sight 'to see youth
desirous of devoting itself to the service of Christ. If it were
not that *there*—in that better land—" His servants shall
serve Him,"—I should regret my failing powers, and the
not far off end of my little service *here*. The young are
coming forward; I rejoice therein.

P

1 mo. 1, 1873.—New Year's Day! Shall I see another?
I would adopt in reference to the query, good Richard
Baxter's thought—

> " If life be long I will be glad,
>   That I may long obey ;
> If short—yet why should I be sad,
>   To soar to endless day ?"

Each memorial of death that has lately come to me has been
of men younger than I. The approaching end is daily in
my thoughts; it does not alarm me. I can sometimes say,
" I know in whom I have believed." I find need, and I
daily ask for the renewed application of the blood of sprinkling—the daily feet-washing. If I sometimes fear lest mine
should be a misplaced confidence, when thinking of the
solemn declaration, " without holiness no man shall see the
Lord," I turn to the Apostle's resource, " not having mine
own righteousness, which is of the law, but that which is
through the faith of Christ, the righteousness which is of
God by faith ; " and, " Therefore being justified by faith, we
have peace with God through our Lord Jesus Christ."
Though it is not often that I have seasons of rejoicing in
hope, yet my spirit is sometimes contrited under a sense of
the love of Christ to me, enkindling renewed love to Him;
and I desire to do *that* which I counsel others to do, never
to distrust His love. My prayer is still to be permitted a
little service for Him; and I am glad that I have still a
part (rightly I believe) in the ministry of the word : and I
can rejoice in the frequency with which the Gospel is pro-
claimed in our Meetings by young and well-qualified men.
Other little services I thankfully accept. If I turn to these,
it is not in a self-complacent spirit but with a thankful heart.
In moments of depression they have served me in the sense
conveyed by the Psalmist, when he said, " I will remember
the years of the right hand of the most High ! "

I sometimes turn to the possibilities of the closing scene—possible pain—possible desertion. In these I still desire to confide in the love and goodness and *wisdom* of my Heavenly Father. He does not willingly afflict. I recur very gratefully to the peaceful, painless departure of my sainted wife—" a death-like sleep, a gentle wafting to immortal life." For nearly fifteen years I have had remarkable and most merciful exemption from acute pain. Previously much had been my portion from facial neuralgia, so much so, that when it became less frequent, and ceased, many a time, remembering the extremity of former suffering, I have added to a grateful evening offering, thanks for freedom from pain. Should it again be my portion, I trust that grace and strength to bear it will be granted. Oh! I would say to-night in simple resignation, and in a sweet feeling of renewed love tendering my spirit, " Thy will be done."

3 mo. 21.—I entered my seventy-third year. My age and the condition of health, the symptoms of the taking down of the tent, do not distress or alarm me. I am thankfully surprised at times by the calmness and the peace with which I am enabled to contemplate the not far off end.

I daily number my blessings and ask for a more grateful heart. I have kind and most loving friends still left, though the number on *the other side of the river* increases year by year. * * * * I have many alleviations of the monotony of invalid life. * * * * I have a few remaining correspondents of thoughtful, active, christian minds, with whom it is a pleasure to interchange thoughts on the tendencies of the religious sentiments prevalent in the Church, and on the oppositions of men of science.

After noticing the decease of friends with whom

he had been much associated in various ways, John Ford thus proceeds under date 11 mo. 9, 1873.

These events and anniversaries remind me that the end is drawing near. Whilst contemporaries are departing year by year, amidst increasing bodily infirmity my life is still prolonged—mercifully prolonged—that the discipline of Fatherly love may prepare me for the purity, the holiness, the love and the joy of Heaven, to which so many of my associates and friends and many dear York scholars have been gathered. I look back thankfully and gratefully to the days when work was my appointed portion. How imperfectly the work was done, none but myself and He who appointed the work, and who did not withold His blessing can tell. Now to *bear* rather than to do is my portion. But yet I can speak of abounding blessings—freedom from acute bodily pain—competence to provide the alleviations of the increasing infirmities of age—the ability and the will to administer through the agency of others, to the sick and the poor— permission and freedom to assist in the vocal service of public worship, not unfrequently in prayer—and not without the occasionally expressed approval of my friends. How can I be sufficiently grateful for all these blessings ! I long for a more constantly grateful heart. Often the beautiful lines of Addison, remembered from my early boyhood,

" When all Thy mercies, O my God, "

glide through my mind with great sweetness. And yet another blessing—childless myself, I have daily the loving attentions of my adopted family and the sweet affection of their dear children. And yet another—refreshment in the house of prayer—in public worship—and in the solitude of my own room. * * * * In the early part of the Meeting I had been enabled to lift up my heart in earnest

silent prayer, and at the close of a fervent vocal prayer from
——, I uttered a half-whispered " Amen." An earnest
desire pervaded my prayer that in little things—little troubles,
little disappointments,—I might know far more than I have
done, my will brought into untroubled acquiescence with all
that befalls me that is not of sin. I long to be able to cast
all my care upon Him who careth for me, even for *me*.
After this desire for renunciation of self, whilst listening to
——'s sermon on Matt. xxv., I had enjoyment in the
ability to appropriate, with overflowing thankfulness, the
blessed words, " ye did it unto Me," in remembrance of some
instances in which, directed and guided by Him, I had been
permitted to minister to Him in the persons of His brethren
and of the lambs of His Fold. I will not apply a morbid
anatomy to these, to determine how much was the result
of the natural feelings of kindness and compassion, and of
the pleasure in the exercise. I will attribute all the praise
to Him who sends His brethren, and gives me the ability
and puts it into my heart to help them. This very evening,
whilst writing, my heart has overflowed with thankfulness
in remembrance of " the years of the right hand of the most
High," and under the contriting sense of His continued
love in Christ Jesus my Saviour. And so once again I
write, τῷ Θεῷ δόξα.

To Henry Hipsley.

12 mo. 13, 1873.—I am glad thou art engaged in visiting
Kent. I spent fourteen years of my early life at Rochester,
from the age of fourteen to twenty-eight; and there about
the middle of that period, I was enabled to enter through a
very strait gate into the narrow way: and though, with
some of Christian's experience of " the hill difficulty " and
other hindrances, I can thankfully believe I have never been

permitted to lose sight of the road or of the Leader. In
the earlier stage of the road, I passed (not unobservant) by
" a Cross and a Sepulchre." "Then was Christian glad
and lightsome." I had not thought of this when I sat
down to write, but the word "Rochester" is a *plectrum* that
strikes a harp of many strings.

---

12 mo. 25.—In looking back in the records of services
connected with Ackworth School, as well as of various others
of an active kind at Bootham and elsewhere, notwithstanding
all their imperfections, they appear to me as times of great
enjoyment, recognizing prayer for help in the services, help
most graciously granted, followed by grateful thanksgiving.
And now at times I indulge the thought of the future
blessedness of the unalloyed service of Heaven, for *there*
" His servants shall serve Him." No more hindrances from
infirmities of flesh and spirit—no more weariness of the poor
exhausted body—no more mixture of motives—the glory
of God sole and alone ! And so to-night having turned to
the past and its many mercies, I feel as though I had
gathered a little encouragement, a little renewal of faith,
hope, and love.

2 mo. 20., 1874.—Constant familiarity with the thought
of the not far off end of the journey does not disturb me.
I believe this is the result of no false security, but of a confiding, humble trust in that love which has followed me all
my life long and which will not fail me at the last, for my
only hope is in Christ my adorable Redeemer. I have come
to Him and have His promise, " him that cometh unto Me
I will in *no wise* cast out." My more than daily prayer is
for help to maintain the conflict to the end—for an increase
of faith and love and meetness for a home in heaven, through

Him who has redeemed us by His own blood. Oh for more constant love for Him, and for a more continual sense of His presence and His love.

To Isaac Brown.

3 mo. 17, 1874.—When I read of thy journeys and labours past, present and prospective, I said, "then let my dear friend give thanks every morning for the ability, the opportunity and the commission to work for his Lord." Long may all these be granted him. My opportunities for active service are very much limited by declining bodily ability. Evening Meetings, among them our Fellowship Meetings, I very seldom attend. —— in one of his recent sermons reminded such, "they also serve who only stand and wait." I look back with a kind of regretful pleasure on our little joint services. The morning prayer for help in the day's work, the evening thanksgiving for the answered prayer, seem to gild the past, and turn my thoughts to the not far off future, where *service* still awaits the servant, unencumbered, unalloyed. In the meantime I desire to be found so waiting as to be ready for any little work adapted to declining powers.

8 mo. 17.—I sent to the Editor of "The Friend" a review of the first seven chapters of Farrar's "Life of Christ." I read through the two volumes while at Scarborough. The seven chapters reviewed refer to the early life, the boyhood and the Nazareth home of our Lord. Whilst confined to Scriptural facts alone, these are set forth with exceeding beauty. The tenor of the whole narrative, from the joyous youth through the early manhood to the painful yet triumphant close, seemed often to bring my spirit into very near loving and adoring communion.

In the summer of 1874, John Ford visited Scarborough, staying with his friends, William and Mary Rowntree, by whom as on many previous occasions he was most kindly welcomed, and his every want anticipated. Difficulty of breathing as well as increased general debility made the exercise of walking very fatiguing. He nevertheless enjoyed the change, and returned home feeling refreshed. From this time the downward progress became more evident. He still got to Meetings occasionally; but the colder weather added to bodily infirmity soon compelled him to forego this privilege. The last occasion he attended public worship was on the First of Eleventh-month; and from the end of that month he was entirely confined to the house. Lethargy and weariness greatly disqualified him for reading or writing till towards evening : and almost constant internal pain prevented him from sleeping at night without the use of anodynes.

9 mo. 20.—I had nearly concluded not to go out this evening, but the genial air and a secret desire to go altered my conclusion. I went not without a prayer for help and blessing. I had no prospect of vocal service. F. Thorp rose early, quoting several verses in the 12th of Hebrews relative to the " Cloud of Witnesses," referring also to part of the enumeration of Patriarchs and Saints recorded in the eleventh chapter. To these he added the accumulated crowd of the eighteen elapsed centuries, and then the witnesses whom we ourselves had known and honoured and loved, exhorting to look as they had looked, even to Jesus, the author and finisher of their faith.

I soon rose, fearing to omit what seemed set before me to offer. I said that whilst listening to what we had already heard, I had been reminded of the cloud of witnesses gathered from among the school-boys and school-girls, who had once occupied the seats now filled by our dear young friends: that in the forty-six years since the boys' school was established more than one hundred who were once scholars had passed into the eternal world, and from the other side a like proportion. Of very many of these there was indubitable evidence, both from their daily lives and their dying beds, that they are now a part of that great cloud of witnesses. * * * * * It seemed to me that in the presentation of this portion of the ever-accumulating crowd of witnesses there was encouragement and stimulus for my dear young friends. You, as they, have had the blessing of pious parents, of loving Christian care at school— have had the privilege of faithful gospel ministry within these walls and elsewhere,—and you, as they also were, are the children of many prayers. I would ask you then to resolve, God helping you, to give your hearts to Christ to-night, even now. I echo the words uttered here this morning, and say, " Why not now ? "—Group after group, the occupants of these seats are passing away : may they continue to succeed one another for many a year to come. The boys and girls of each succeeding group will be the fathers and mothers of the future. May you, the present occupants, so live as true disciples of Christ, that the influence of the schools may be for good, and for good only, and thus be transmitted to those who shall succeed you. Nor is it to you alone that these aspirations belong, but equally to us all, so to live as that we too may be a part of the cloud of witnesses whose record already is on high. Thus may you with life before you, and we who have passed many years, like those to whom I have referred, testify to Christ in our lives and on our dying beds ; and like them, when the end shall come, pass away with His blessed name on our lips.

To Isaac Brown.

11 mo. 4, 1874.—Fifteen years ago this day my more than brother, dear Joseph Rowntree, entered upon his heavenly inheritance. I have a memorandum of one of his last expressions : " This marvellous peace ! this wonderful peace ! this perfect peace ! " With greatly increased debility and with ailments, which, though not threatening, may at a short notice develop what are called alarming symptoms, I can thankfully acknowledge a *sense* of this peace, in looking towards the close. My sole reliance is on Him who " is our peace," and of whom I can sometimes say,

> " I muse on the years that have passed,
>   In which my defence Thou hast proved ;
> Nor wilt thou relinquish at last,
>   A sinner so signally loved."

To Thomas Puplett.

2 mo. 6, 1875.—Though thy kind considerateness relieves me from all obligation to reply, there are circumstances connected with thy most welcome letter that impel me, as briefly as I can, to account for writing.—Previously to the Quarterly Meeting, my prayer had been for a blessing upon the gathering—for an out-pouring of the Holy Spirit on all—Ministers and congregation, and for myself that I might, though absent, be a partaker of the festival. This request was most graciously and abundantly granted. My room from time to time during the Quarterly Meeting became a little sanctuary. Besides kind messages and visits, on three separate occasions, ministers of the Gospel, Hannah Thorp,

my dear cousin Hannah B. Sewell, and Isaac Brown, engaged
in solemn prayer and thanksgiving, greatly to my comfort and
rejoicing.　To these I may add the kind and loving visit of
dear G. and R. Satterthwaite, full of Christian fellowship.
Then on Third-day, came thy letter.　In a wakeful hour in
the night these especial blessings came before me so forcibly,
with such an overpowering sense of a Saviour's love, that
I enjoyed a tearful jubilaté, never to be forgotten.　And then
I thought I must tell Thomas Puplett how largely he had
contributed to this.　There then occurred to me as the best
answer I could send him, some lines from Cowper's poem on
Charity, as expressive of the enjoyment I had had in this
accumulation of blessings.　They occur rather beyond
midway in the poem, with the line,

　　"When one that holds communion with the skies,"

and the eleven following lines.*　I would have copied them
as part of my letter, but I leave that to thee as I have
already reached the extent of my very small capacity for
writing.　In unabated love, thy attached friend of many
years,

JOHN FORD.

P.S.　Do not construe this letter as boastful or self-
complacent; but rather as a thankful acknowledgment of
unmerited mercies.　May not the Christian tell of his visit

---

* When one that holds communion with the skies
　Has filled his urn where these pure waters rise,
　And once more mingles with us meaner things,
　'Tis e'en as if an angel shook his wings:
　Immortal fragrance fills the circuit wide,
　That tells us whence his treasures are supplied.
　So when a ship, well freighted with the stores
　The sun matures on India's spicy shores,
　Has dropt her anchor and her canvass furled,
　In some safe haven of our western world,
　'Twere vain enquiry to what port she went,
　The gale informs us, laden with the scent.

to the House Beautiful, as well as of his imprisonment in
Doubting Castle ?

---

2 mo. 9, 1875.—S. R. called.   After a very interesting
conversation she engaged in most sweet and solemn thanksgiving and prayer.   We did indeed recognize a *third* with
us, Him who said, "There am I in the midst."   One
expression had an earnest echo in my own spirit,—"*Home* in
Thy own good time."

2 mo. 27.—Praying for entire conformity of will—accepting
all as from a Father's hand.   Tempted to complain—turned
away immediately.

The following extract is from the last entry in
John Ford's regular diary.

3 mo. 21.—Seventy-four years completed !   In the midst
of many ailments incident to old age, (free from acute pain,)
passing through a daily round of bodily trouble—sleep by
means of anodynes—needing frequent counteraction by
opposites—often oppressed with lethargy—forms of disease
increasing—others intensified—still through the cloud of the
discipline of pain (chastisement a mark of son-ship) I can
thankfully acknowledge innumerable blessings—alleviations
of physical suffering—kind and watchful nursing, * * and
above all these, in answer to daily, earnest prayer, preservation from an impatient, a repining or a distrustful
spirit, faith being granted to appropriate "My Grace is
sufficient for thee," as for Paul.

Night after night I dwell upon (silently repeating) many
beautiful hymns, and many of the most precious promises of
Holy Scripture—promises of my God and Saviour—kept

from all doubt of *acceptance* in and through Him alone, not having a single plea of any other kind. I hold as a creed, adopted many years ago, the lines in Cowper, of which these form the substance :

> " I never trusted in an arm but Thine,
>   Nor hoped but in *Thy righteousness* divine,"

with their previous and following context.* I long and pray for entire conformity to the will, and mind and example of Christ.

In First-month 1875, John Ford's strength failed so rapidly that those about him thought the end was near. But such was not the case. Months of weakness and weariness were still to be his portion·; and a long course of bodily suffering was before him, in which he was permitted strikingly to exemplify the theme which was especially dear to him—the all-sufficiency of Divine grace to support in every hour of need. The difficulty of going up and down stairs becoming very great, in Third-month a room adjoining his bedchamber was hastily fitted

---

*Since the dear hour, that brought me to thy foot,
And cut up all my follies by the root,
I never trusted in an arm but Thine,
Nor hoped but in Thy righteousness divine :
My prayers and alms, imperfect and defiled,
Were but the feeble efforts of a child ;
Howe'er performed, it was their brightest part,
That they proceeded from a grateful heart ;
Cleansed in thine own all-purifying blood,
Forgive their evil, and accept their good ;
I cast them at Thy feet—my only plea
Is what it was, dependence upon Thee ;
While struggling in the vale of tears below,
That never failed nor shall it fail me now.

COWPER'S " TRUTH."

up as a sitting-room; and here he spent many
happy hours. The extreme beauty of the Spring
and of the vegetation in the gardens seen from the
window, was a continual source of delight to him.
He looked upon them as the works of his Heavenly
Father's hand, testifying to His love and goodness.

He retired to rest early. After a few hours' sleep
he usually woke feeling much refreshed, and enjoyed
sitting up by the fire for an hour or two in the very
early morning. The comparative freedom from pain
and lethargy usually granted him in these early hours
he felt to be a peculiar blessing, and his " Matins "
(as he termed them) were the brightest part of the
day. It was then that he enjoyed his Scripture
readings in Greek and English; and Anna Shipton's
books,* recently brought under his notice, were a
source of great comfort and help to him. It was at
such times before returning to bed that he made
most of the brief records in pencil which form the
continuation of his Diary.

3 mo. 23.—Weariness and pain. Many a prayer for
patience amidst the trials of the poor body—not in vain.

3 mo. 31.—Faith not failed, but longing for light and
love.

---

* " Wayside Service;" " Asked of God;" "The Lost Blessing;" " Waiting Hours;" "The Secret of the Lord;" "The Promise and the Promiser;"
"The Watch Tower in the Wilderness," " Tell Jesus;" and " Footsteps of
the Flock."

To Rebecca Thompson.

4 mo. 6, 1875.—I thank thee very much for thy encouraging and comforting texts. How wonderfully does a visitation of illness, especially amidst the weakness of age, enhance the estimate of the priceless value of Holy Scripture—its glorious promises—its *assurances*—its setting forth of the infiniteness of our Heavenly Father's love to us, in and through His dear Son our adorable Redeemer. * * * * I should be an ungrateful receiver of blessings did I not thankfully acknowledge that I am not permitted to distrust my Saviour's love, notwithstanding intervening clouds of weariness and pain sometimes drift across the sky, and partially obscure the sun for a time.

To Isaac Brown.

4 mo. 14.—As regards the body and its varied ailments, I am many stages lower than when I saw thee last. As regards the spirit, *that* was a time of most especial favour. I have thought of it since as a brief sojourn in the land of Beulah and of intercourse with the "Shepherds" on the "Delectable Mountains." I did indeed experience the *joy* as well as the *peace* of believing, arising partly perhaps from a near prospect of *home*. And now, through the clouds of the discipline of pain, I have faith to believe that the sun is shining *above* the clouds, and through occasional rifts I see its brightness and feel its glow. I will not speak of my increasing ailments; it would be a depressing catalogue. They do not seem to point to a speedy issue. Is it wrong to long for home, with a full reservation "Thy will be done?" I *may* tell you of my blessings and alleviations and exemptions: I have no oppression on the breathing when at rest—no

head-ache—no confusion of intellect. I have numerous kind friends. * * * You know that I have a most kind and faithful, watchful attendant in my old servant, for whom I have made a life provision. I am still able to enjoy reading. * * * * My more than daily prayer is for "grace sufficient" for every hour—every moment.

* * *

4 mo. 19.—Earnest prayer for entire resignation. The future, moment by moment, referred solely to Thy keeping and direction.

4 mo. 23.—Why do I long to go home? To avoid suffering? Or for love to Christ and desires to be with Him? Oh give me this for His sake, and faith and grace to bear.

4 mo. 24.—In " The Lost Blessing," (pages 161 and 162) most precious promises brought home to my great comfort. The refrain,

> " Follow the Master's footsteps,
> Drink of the Master's cup."

Prayer for patient acquiescence for each moment—Grace sufficient. "Christ hath sufficed thee, and He shall suffice;"— sufficed in action formerly, in suffering now.

4 mo. 25.—More exalted views of Gospel ministry. Retrospect of very imperfect service. Is the present teaching a preparation for the perfect service of another life, in which " His servants shall serve Him "?

4 mo. 28.—Many an upward look for patience.

5 mo. 6, 1875.—Reading Anna Shipton's little books has impressed me with the imperfection of past services, and led me to believe that one purpose may be accomplished in the present discipline of pain,—and I have prayed that it may be so—a preparation for the more blessed service at

home in Heaven.   Another purpose is, I believe, accomplishing,—more and more meetness for that service—more and more of "wisdom and righteousness and sanctification and redemption."

5 mo. 25.—Ailments increasing.   My refuge is prayer for Grace sufficient.   Peace still—no fear—longing for Home.

5 mo. 31.—My prayer is now for help "to pray without ceasing."   Kneeling and rising are times of great pain.   He is not a hard Master.

6 mo. 1.—Whilst arranging my pillows, my kind, faithful attendant gave me that most precious text, "As thy days, so shall thy strength be."   Enabled to accept it, my heart overflowed with thanksgiving in the peace and joy of believing.

6 mo. 5.—The thought sometimes occurs that the end may be remote.   My prayer is, "in Thy own good time, Lord—hasten the day."

6 mo. 7.—Some abatement of pain in this nocturnal vigil. A poor sick child longing for *home*—peaceful and helped in prayer—therefore τῷ Θεῷ δόξα.

6 mo. 10.—Enjoyments *still*, but not in them—seen and heard from my nice day-room :—the advance of Spring— the beauty of the opening buds and flowers—the gushing rain—to-day, the rolling thunder, the bass of the great anthem, "Spring has come forth, her work of gladness to contrive."

6 mo. 17.—The happiness of the boys at Bootham,— present and impending—about to *go home* and then to be *there*, is even now (4 a.m.) sweetly associated with the thought of going to, and being *in* a home,—purchased, prepared,— one of the many mansions.   "What will it be to be there ?"

Q

6 mo. 21.—"When thou liest down thou shalt not be afraid." Not afraid now, nor when lying down at last—through Thy redeeming love, adorable Redeemer.

6 mo. 22.—The Spirit himself witnessing with my spirit that I—even I—am a *son*, redeemed by the precious blood of Christ and by that alone. To God be glory a thousand fold. Thankful for a long midnight vigil of clear intellect and abated pain.

The decay of bodily strength progressing slowly but steadily, at last confined John Ford entirely to his bed-room. He was wheeled in his chair into the sitting-room for the last time on the Fourth of Seventh-month. The lethargy which for months had been very trying to him became so much more oppressive, added to constantly increasing debility, that he could read but little, and writing was very burdensome. Then came complete confinement to bed. In addition to almost constant internal pain, the sense of extreme exhaustion, often as trying as pain, tested his patience to the utmost. Those who had known him in his earlier days, and remembered his nervous temperament, his ready excitability and his extreme sensitiveness to pain, could not but marvel at the patience and unmurmuring spirit with which he bore his days and nights of suffering and unrest. But He who gave the assurance, "My Grace is sufficient for thee,"—a promise which the sufferer loved to dwell on during the whole of his illness,—did not forsake His servant, but was ever present in the hour of need. Though the outward man was perishing, yet the inward man was renewed day by day ; and so to the last he could thankfully testify that as his day so had his strength been.

The great pleasure he had always taken in hymns and devotional poetry, proved a constant source of comfort and enjoyment.   The love of Jesus was a theme on which he delighted to dwell.   " Oh," he exclaimed one day in the earlier part of his illness, " if I should ever be permitted again to preach the Gospel in Meetings, how earnestly would I set forth the exceeding love of Jesus."

Rather more than six months before his decease, such a vivid sense of acceptance in Christ Jesus was granted, that he frequently afterwards referred to this period as being " in the land of Beulah : " and this sense of acceptance was mercifully continued to the last.   During the protracted period of pain and weariness through which he had to pass, he was never permitted to doubt that through redeeming love his name was written in the Lamb's Book of Life.   The precious sense of entire peace which was so often felt in sitting by him, was more than can be expressed.   The sting and the fear of death were removed.   In sending messages to friends at a distance he would say, " Tell them I am troubled in body, but with undisturbed peace."

As he became unable to write letters, he would request one or other of those about him to write for

him, and would make a few memoranda in pencil of
what he wished to say.   One of these, dated 7 mo.
16, is as follows :—

My kind substitute ——— most readily undertakes the
duty of amanuensis to one who each morning on awaking
feels himself a poor *sick child* under the notice of a loving
Heavenly Father, and a Saviour close at hand ; and thus
faith and hope and assurance are sustained even amidst much
debility and intervals of acute pain.   Very dear love, though
very weary and feeble.

It was touching to hear his fervent expressions of
gratitude and thankfulness for any alleviation of pain
or uneasiness.   One evening he was much disturbed
by a band of music in the street.   On the following
night he remarked that the absence of this annoyance
was a cause for thankfulness, and he felt that favours
and mercies however small should not be unacknow-
ledged.   Many a time he would say, " Take hold of
my arm—and now a prayer for a blessing on the
means used—that there may be a little alleviation for
the coming hour.—And now I will try and get a little
sleep."   Then like a weary child, when his pillow
was smoothed down, he would settle for a brief rest.
Again and again would the simple prayer arise, " If
it be Thy will—if it be *Thy* will—give a little relief
from suffering to Thy poor sick child."

One evening about three weeks before his decease
he said, " I wish to say emphatically in the presence
of you all as witnesses, that I have found the grace

of God sufficient on all occasions." He used nearly the same words more than once subsequently, adding to them the declaration that his faith and trust had not been permitted to waver.

During a time of extreme suffering on the 8th of Eighth-month, John Ford hastily sent for an absent friend who had been much with him during his illness, and who thus describes the interview.

"On going to the bed-side, he said, 'I want thee to pray for me, and with me.' And as the words were feebly uttered, 'Heavenly Father, we ask Thee for Jesus' sake,'—he interposed, 'Oh, yes! that is it, for Jesus' sake.' We asked that the Saviour would be very near through all the journey; and again he joined in,—'and to the river's brink.' We added 'and through the river.' The next words were his,— 'and to the very gates.' And when we added, 'and into the presence of the Saviour whom he so loved and served,' the dear invalid gave a most emphatic 'Amen.' His soul seemed satisfied."

In the morning of his last day upon earth, his mind wandered a little, and the power of speech for a time seemed gone. Occasionally the suffering expression of his countenance was changed for one of exceeding brightness, and his eyes had a very far-away look, as if gazing on something beyond the ken of those about him. Once when thus gazing upwards he beckoned with his finger; and when asked if he wanted something, he said, "I want to go home:" and after awhile, "Tell them to come quickly:"

then more distinctly, " He knows me better than any human eye," adding emphatically, " and I know Him." Words of prayer followed, but only one sentence could be gathered, " Thou knowest all the process to the *very end.*" Faith and patience did indeed hold out to the close. His breathing gradually became quieter till it gently ceased, and the redeemed spirit entered into the joy of his Lord.

John Ford died on the 16th of Eighth-month, 1875, aged seventy-four years and five months. His remains were interred in the Friends' Burial Ground, York, on the 19th. One of the many who loved and honoured him, and who came from a distance to pay their last tribute of respect, has given the following account of the day's proceedings.

I had the privilege of attending the interment: it took place in the Friends' Burial Ground, Heslington Road, York, a mile or so out of the city. The place is retired and rural, prettily planted with shrubs, and intersected with walks. Here and there on that occasion, some bird occasionally gave forth its sweet note ; and the afternoon sunbeams were falling brightly on the graves of the silent dead. Friends from many places, near and far off,—old pupils,—teachers who had served under the deceased as their chief,—City acquaintances,—the then pupils of Bootham School, and old servants of a former day, made their way, some on foot, some in equipages, to the place of sepulture. When the more immediate mourners had arrived with the remains, all drew around the open grave, a mixed but reverent company. The grave was the one in which Rachel Ford had been interred some years before,—a woman of no common virtues, and eminently graced with the ornament of a meek and quiet spirit. On headstones in immediate proximity, I read the honoured names of Samuel Tuke and Joseph Rowntree, two of John Ford's most loved and chosen friends. A heavenly feeling of unusual solemnity overspread the gathered throng, and fitting, teaching, soul-inspiring words were spoken in memory of the dead, and in praise of the efficacy of Christ's sustaining Grace. Years fulfilled, service accomplished, suffering over, an eternity of bliss begun, were thoughts, no doubt, that passed through many a mind.

As the company slowly moved away, Fielden Thorp, once John Ford's pupil, then a teacher under him, and eventually his successor as Superintendent of Bootham School, was seen to lead to the grave-side an aged pilgrim, who reverently looked down into that deep and narrow resting-place. This was Thomas Richardson, bravely bearing the weight of four-score years, a clergyman of the Church of England, a practical member of the fraternity of Teachers, and long one of John Ford's personal friends. Many others also passed over the newly upturned earth to take a last look at the coffin and the grave, and then there was a general adjournment to the Meeting-house in the City. A good and solemn Meeting ensued. The vocal offerings, whether of comment, exhortation, or prayer, seemed to me peculiarly fitted to the occasion,—judicious in their references, alike to the living and the dead.

After the Meeting a gathering of many of John Ford's old pupils, teachers and friends took place at the Bootham School, under the efficient direction of John Firth Fryer, the present Superintendent. We broke bread together under cheerful yet mingled feelings; and then a brief sketch of our dear honoured friend's last illness was read, which took us most touchingly through his lingering hours, his triumphs

of faith, his passage of the Jordan of death, and his ascent
to the very Gates of Heaven.

On my way to the Railway Station to return home, crossing the handsome Lendal Bridge that spans the Ouse, the
sun was seen hanging low in misty yet gorgeous splendour
over the river.   With what keen zest of enjoyment had
I known my departed friend to gaze on similar sights.
The splendid view became at once a reminder of the glorious
land he had entered, where flows a pure river of water of
life, clear as crystal, and where no earthly mists obscure the
light of Him who is its Sun.

SECTION VI.

PERSONAL REMINISCENCES.

John Ford's long professional career presents phases differing widely from each other. His earlier scholars retain impressions in some respects very dissimilar from those which are cherished by his pupils of a later period, when under the power of Divine grace and the influence of his happy marriage, the asperities of his character and the impulsiveness of younger life were softened down and brought into subjection. Thus the personal reminiscences of one may present a portrait, which however truthful and life-like at the particular period, is hardly recognised by others whose acquaintance with the original was limited to a different stage of life. With the hope therefore of presenting a more comprehensive picture than if it had been drawn by one limner only, the Editor invited the assistance of some of his friends, who either as Teachers or Scholars (or both) had been intimately connected with John Ford; and he feels much indebted to them for the kindness and readiness with which they have responded to his application. He has preferred giving the sketches separately at the risk of occasional repetition, rather than attempting to combine or condense them.

I.

REMINISCENCES OF LAWRENCE ST. SCHOOL, 1829 TO 1835.

It is difficult at this distance of time to recall the exact
condition of the School at its commencement, but if in answer
to his request the following jottings will in any way serve the
Editor's purpose, the writer has pleasure in placing them at
his disposal.

I well remember arriving at the School at its opening
under John Ford in 1829, in the old-fashioned six-inside
"Trafalgar" Coach, which set a fellow-scholar and myself
down at the door, after a journey of forty miles occupying
over six hours. I wish I could as readily recall my early
impressions of John Ford and of the School at that time ; but
as I find this is impossible, I must be allowed in attempting
to put down a few reminiscences, to give them as belonging
to the whole period I remained at Lawrence St. School.

There was, I remember, a mixed element in the School at
its commencement, some boys remaining over from the
previous régime who were not "Friends." One of these is
distinctly impressed on my mind from my having seen him,
when calling at the School prior to John Ford's becoming
the head, stripped for a pugilistic encounter. I never
remember an actual "fight" taking place in my school-days,
and this, like the free use of the cane which had previously
existed, was entirely abolished. I do not mean to say
corporal punishment was *never* used, but I only remember
one boy—and he was a most troublesome one—who after
spending some days in " ———'s Castle," (as the room he
was placed in was called), was flogged, whether for his good
or not I cannot say : and beyond an occasional boxing of the
ears I do not remember any other.

If my recollections are correct, as I believe they are, that
corporal punishment was in fact abolished, it will be readily

seen in looking back to the condition of the public mind and the practice of schools generally at that period, how far John Ford was ahead of his time in thus preferring to depend upon moral power or suasion, for the government of the School.

That he was successful in this, I feel no doubt; and I should think that the actual amount of other punishment was decidedly small. That this government was one which worked easily in all cases, or to the equal satisfaction of all concerned, it would however be a mistake to suppose. Many would have preferred "a good flogging" to the prolonged interviews or long silent sittings in the Library or in seclusion.

There was also at the period under review, what I have no doubt John Ford struggled hard to overcome, (and did to a large extent overcome in later years)—though we boys knew nothing of this and judged him hardly in consequence—great irregularity of temper, and at times much petulance was shewn. I well remember that the manner in which a certain door was shut behind him as he entered the School in the morning, was looked upon as an index of the way in which we might expect to be treated for the day; and thus whilst some carelessness or want of attention was one day treated with much good temper, and some allowance made for the stupidity or infirmity of the boy, the same offences were on another treated with undue harshness, and a class might be suddenly sent to its place, or a book sent at the head of a poor fellow stammering over his Latin or French, which it is needless to say only increased his difficulty and made the lessons an object of dread and aversion. Not that there was intentional unkindness in all this, but the uncertainty had an injurious effect on some boys, and made his reign to them one of fear instead of love. And thus it may easily be imagined that with sensitive boys or those who could not easily forget these explosions, school reminiscences were not so unmixed as might have been desired.

But it seems unjust to one whom I so heartily loved in after years, to dwell so long on the weaker side of his character, and in doing so, I can make every allowance for the difficulties he had to encounter with his warm, impulsive nature; and as is usually the case with such natures, the sunny days were really delightful ones. To the stupid boy he would explain the lesson as few others could, so clearly and kindly that he must needs understand it, and what brought tears one day, caused a smile then : for the restless or inattentive the fullest allowance was made consistent with good order, whilst the warm, hearty approval given to those who did their work well, went far to efface the less pleasing recollections of other days. Most delightful also under such influences were the excursions or long walks, when gathering around John Ford, he would be the centre of all that amused or interested us—a good joke, a good natured quizz, an apt quotation, a few lines of poetry, a race or a jump in which we were of course beaten :—then his deep interest in Natural History and his quick observation, helped to strengthen and form that love of Nature which has always been so prominent a feature in York School.

How many there are to whom the remembrance of "Langwith" in connexion with these excursions, will bring back a rush of pleasant thoughts, and make them perhaps for the moment sigh that they are not still boys, and able as then to drink in with the freshness of a boy's delight a draught of the elixir of childhood.

I have very little recollection of what may be called any directly religious influence in the school. There were not more than two or three boys who ventured to read their Bibles in public except when expected to do so on First-days ;

and I remember during the last year I was at school being taunted by the head teacher, why I know not, with "trying to be *relegeous*," as he called it.   As to John Ford's own earnest desire to promote and encourage a religious tone in the school, I have not the slightest doubt; and I can recall certain occasions, as in the instance of severe illness or a death in the school, when his earnest addresses impressed many young hearts, and sowed or helped to water seeds which have since borne good fruit.

Great as the difficulty may be supposed to be in the present day in obtaining good Teachers, it is nothing compared with the period under review; and the Teacher to whom I have just referred (not a "Friend") would not now be deemed worthy of the post he held; and in passing I cannot but note the great benefits which the Flounders' Institute has conferred upon the schools of the Society of Friends.

If this retrospect may seem to have brought out in too sharp or distinct a form the failings of one, who in after years became so admirably adapted for his post, it may not be without a service in showing how with increasing years came increasing wisdom and self-control; and if I and others may have had to bear what may be compared to the rule of a "'prentice" hand, which was not at all times wise or equal in its pressure—we cannot but rejoice that others have benefited by the experience thus gained; and whilst feeling that there were matters in the early years of his administration which may be regarded with regret, there must ever remain in the memory of his pupils, the image of one who never descended to anything that was mean or unbecoming, and who endeavoured to uphold in his life as well as in his words the high standard of Christian character put before us in the words, "Brethren, whatsoever

things are true, whatsoever things are honest, whatsoever
things are just, whatsoever things are pure, whatsoever things
are lovely, whatsoever things are of good report; if there be
any virtue, and if there be any praise, think on these things.''

JAMES. H. TUKE.

II.

In the year 1844, coming as a little boy to school at
Lawrence Street, I first became acquainted with John Ford;
little thinking then how largely my whole life would be
influenced by my intercourse with him. Great was the awe,
though mingled with a cordial feeling of esteem, with which
most of the junior scholars, myself included, regarded him.

There was a little ante-room partitioned off from the
Library in Lawrence Street, where I believe some books and
papers, shoes, slippers, and the like belonging to J. F. were
stowed; but the current tradition of the school maintained
that it was there that the cane was kept. As, however, I
never knew it to be brought out from this or any other
hiding-place, during the thirty-one years over which my
acquaintance with John Ford extended, I may use the language of the Roman Historian, and say, "de ea re nihil
satis comperti affirmare velim."

Acute physical sensitiveness was associated in John Ford's
case with a keen perception of the beautiful in nature, and
a quick appreciation of that which is lovely and of good
report in the characters of those around him. An amusing
instance of the first point occurred to me as a little boy:—
In the course of a game in the playground I had wounded
my head by a knock against a tree, so that it bled profusely,
and a school-fellow in alarm took me off to the old nurse who
then presided over the infirmary department. She, I suppose,

deemed the case beyond her skill, and forthwith fetched in
John Ford, who proceeded to apply plaster in a very skilful
style. But while engaged thus he noticed that a Dutch
clock which hung in the room was on the point of striking.
He could not endure the interruption of this noise; and
instantly clapt his hand on the pendulum and stopped the
clock.

Of his delight in the beauty of the outward creation his
frequent references to it in addresses to the boys bore witness—and not unconnected with this was his keen relish for
poetry. Some of us can remember with how much effect
he would bring out, after reading with us in the school-room
the Scripture narrative of Saul's interview with the spirit of
Samuel at Endor, the powerful lines in which Byron has
depicted the scene :—or remind us at a Meeting of the
Natural History Society, in Cowper's words, of Him
" Who gives its lustre to an insect's wing,
 And wheels His throne upon the rolling worlds."

Old scholars who knew something of the discipline of
sickness while under John Ford's care, will well remember
his kindness. Along with somewhat of sternness in manner
there was a depth of sympathy and consideration for suffering that at once gained the loving confidence of the patient.
He was once visiting for the first time at a friend's house,
where two boys were staying, one of whom was evidently in
delicate health. After they had left the room, the two were
exchanging notes about the visitor. The elder, a youth in
vigorous health, remarked, " What an eye he has ! it seems
to look right through you ! " " *I* think it is a very kind
eye," was the response of the invalid.

Very early in his career, John Ford became fully alive to
the importance of providing useful and pleasant occupation
for leisure time. Even while closely pressed with the ordinary work of the school, he devoted many hours to editing

a manuscript magazine, called *The Naturalist*, which circu-
lated among the boys.   Every York scholar must remember
the interest he took in the various pursuits promoted by the
" Natural History and Polytechnic Society," of which he
was the founder, and, up to his decease, the president.   As
long as health permitted, he delighted to attend the half-
yearly and other special meetings of the Society—where a
cordial welcome always awaited him.   He would tell us
from time to time, in his old lively way, how a botanical box
carried by one of the party when he and two of his scholars
were in Wales together, procured them an introduction to
one of the leading officials employed on the construction of
the Britannia Bridge over the Menai Straits, and a walk
over the tube in his company : or would take up the specimen
of the Ziczac (the *Trochilus* of Herodotus), and recount, to
the amusement of the youngsters, the cleverness of the bird
and its friendship for the Crocodile ;—and would add a few
words of loving, practical counsel on the employment of
leisure time.

Thirty years ago, when Greek, Latin, and Mathematics,
with a smattering of French, history and geography formed
the staple of ordinary school instruction, he was fully alive
to the value of natural science as a branch of education ;
and though the appliances now so abundant were almost
unknown, he contrived to interest his scholars by means of
lectures, in geology, physiology, mechanics, chemistry and
astronomy.   These lectures were at first often delivered by
himself, and gradually entrusted to some of the resident
teachers, whose attention had been directed to one or another
of these sciences.

As a teacher or lecturer, he was somewhat deficient in
method—but his discursiveness was to a large extent compensated for by the lively manner, awakening the sympathetic

interest of his scholars. He had a great dread of resembling Quintilian's description of the "magister aridus"—the "dry stick" as he used to translate the phrase. But I had comparatively little experience of his teaching in ordinary class work;—his influence in the moral government of the school is what lives most in my recollection of those earlier years. He was eminently successful in inculcating a high standard of truthfulness—not the mere abstention from direct falsehood, which he would characterize as a very poor idea indeed of the requirements of truth, but the avoidance of all shifts, evasions, and underhand doings—the endeavour to act, and speak, and live in perfect sincerity and straightforwardness. The frank acknowledgment of an offence went very far to secure his overlooking it, while any attempts at prevarication generally resulted in the utter shame and confusion of the offender.

In the prospect of entering the school in 1850 as a Junior teacher, I wrote to John Ford to enquire the nature of the work that would be likely to fall to my lot. After giving some details in reply as to the subjects taught in the lower classes, J. F. proceeds :—

" In replying to thy father's letter I mentioned that the indescribable part of our work was far the larger portion. To attempt to describe the indescribable would probably be a failure. To discriminate wisely between that which is merely the result of the liveliness and volatility of youth, and that which indicates moral obliquity, and to treat each accordingly ; to be yielding yet firm ; to be all things to all boys, in the apostolic sense ; to cultivate large sympathy with the cheerful spirit of youth ; to see that our humility keeps ahead of our knowledge ;—these, and many other faculties and endowments will be needed for that part of our work which I have not attempted to describe."

R

One secret of John Ford's success lay in his power of making his influence felt through his teachers. We have known very conscientious, pains-taking schoolmasters quite unable to attain this : their personal oversight, their constant presence, seemed necessary to the working of the machine ; or, if this were not the case, the under-masters were left to carry through the discipline of the school by the mere weight of their own authority, with little guidance or support from the Principal. John Ford's own experience at Rochester had shown him the importance of such guidance and support from the head-master ; and some of those who were long associated with him at York can bear testimony that he had learned the lesson well. Vividly do they remember his kind, almost fatherly sympathy with the young teacher in his difficulties and discouragements ; his readiness to interpose his personal influence and authority for the support of a sub-ordinate officer, and the relief experienced, in cases of difficulty, from transferring the responsibility to him.

Eminently characteristic is the following piece of advice ; and those who were privileged to be associated with him in the School will bear testimony how fully he carried out in his own practice the precepts he inculcated. "Watch your opportunities ; help your pupils in their little difficulties, answer every request so as to invite another, aid them in their pursuits of science, or natural history, in prosecuting their inquiries, in determining and naming their plants, their fossils, and their shells :—avail yourselves of every occasion of making yourselves acquainted with their parents and their home ; there is magic in even a small amount of this community of interest and of feeling : be the first to detect any little ailment, or indisposition, and whilst guard-ing against anything that would minister to effeminacy, or that would discourage them from bearing with manly fortitude, their portion of pain or of sickness, let them see that your liveliest sympathy is awakened, and your kindest care manifested. Above all, watch the precious moment of affliction, or sorrow, it is then that the portals of the youthful heart are open ; wisely, gently, unobtrusively, unofficiously, perhaps almost silently, seek to soothe and console them then."

Amongst the various papers written by John Ford for the Friends' Educational Society is one entitled " Influence and Authority," from which the extract just quoted was taken. Another of great value is on " The Duties and Difficulties of Young Teachers." A careful perusal of these papers will give those who did not know John Ford a fair idea of his professional character. I will conclude my remarks with a single extract from the latter, in which I cannot help feeling he was describing somewhat of his own happy experience. " Bringing to the service a sense of duty and of love ; that genuine interest and true earnestness, without which nothing worth accomplishing can be brought to a successful issue, the teacher will find that his honourable profession amply rewards its votaries. He will win the grateful affection of the young by ministering to their thirst for information, by inciting and gratifying their curiosity in the boundless fields of knowledge, as well as by checking their wayward tendencies, and attracting them to the paths of peace and safety. As years roll on, still distrusting himself, being a constant and earnest applicant for that wisdom which is from above, he will become a happy and an honoured man. Still endeavouring faithfully to fulfil his trust, he will find his power to influence others increased, and his sphere of usefulness enlarged. The affection of the schoolboy towards him will be matured into the grateful esteem of the young man, whose heart is still open to the word of counsel from him whom he learned to love in his earlier years. Not in the spirit of self-exaltation, but with self-renouncing gratitude to God for the ability which He has given to labour in His vineyard, he will sometimes be cheered and encouraged by seeing those whom he has taught, exemplifying the christian principles he has laboured to instil. To see truth and kindness and purity still the stamp of their character, and as years increase, to mark in them the consistent and intelligent advocates of the right, exemplifying that moral courage, firm yet gentle, which he strove to implant—to see them the faithful servants of Christ, consecrating to Him their talents and their learning, laying all their gifts upon His altar —this may be at times his happy experience, and he may say with the apostle, in the spirit of thankful gratitude, "what is our hope, our joy, our crown of rejoicing; are not even ye in the presence of Jesus Christ?" Though bowed down at times with a sense of poor imperfect service, confessing himself an unprofitable servant, yet trusting in his Heavenly Father's mercy in Jesus Christ, he may hope at the end to receive the crown of his labours in the approving sentence of Well done!"

FIELDEN THORP.

III.

I had the privilege of serving as a Teacher at Bootham for three years; and that, during what may perhaps be called the Augustan period of John Ford's administration,— his physical energy still large, his mind lively and vigorous, the asperities of an earlier day almost entirely worn down, and his Christian character, though, as we know, still further to be matured, even then shining with distinguished lustre.

On first crossing the threshold, I perceived, at a glance, that he was master of the place. His will and word were law: but that will was so happily regulated by heavenly

wisdom, that only on one occasion, was I cognizant of anything approaching to arbitrariness in his management of the
boys ; for which, his subsequent demeanour clearly showed
his humiliation and regret.

The assurance he gave me before entering the school, that,
" from his wife and himself I should receive all the assistance
their position and ability could afford," was well fulfilled.
Though expecting from a Teacher the right discharge of his
duties, he was truly sympathizing with him in his difficulties.
One instance is vividly before me, when, at inconvenience to
himself, he sought me out as I was sitting withdrawn from
others under a temporary feeling of much discouragement, and
poured balm into my wounded spirit. With all his kindness,
however, my three years under him never quite wore off a
feeling of restraint in his presence somewhat painful to bear,
notwithstanding his evident effort to put me perfectly at ease.

I knew scarcely anything of John Ford as an actual class
teacher, maintaining needful order, and laboriously instilling
book-learning from day to day. That part of a Teacher's
vocation, he had, at the period referred to, almost entirely
discontinued. But, as a trainer of youth, as a director of
mental effort and leisure hour pursuits, as a moral preceptor,
as an expounder of religious truth, and as an advocate of all
that is pure, and lovely, and honest, and of good report, I
I had the pleasure of knowing him at his prime.

That he had great influence over the young is undoubted :
and this influence resulted from a combination of qualifications. Love alone will not give this power : but when on
this foundation stone rests a true understanding of a boy's
nature,—a perception of his legitimate tastes, and ability to
aid them,— a vivacity that attracts the juvenile mind,—a
power of will, an honesty of purpose, a readiness of expedient
all exerted on a boy's behalf,— a sympathy with his joys

and with his sorrows,—the gift vividly to pourtray and to recommend what is right, and equal power in denouncing what is wrong,—mental acquirements, which, if not profound, are yet varied, and amply sufficient to command respect,—a disposition not blindly, but hopefully, to look on the brighter side of a young delinquent, and whilst faithfully pointing out his errors, not always upbraiding him,—and when from the basement to the very topstone of this goodly column is mingled the unyielding mortar of true Christian interest,— then a teacher, under the Divine blessing, is signally gifted for tutoring and moulding the minds of his precious charge. And those who knew John Ford in his full and mature development, will readily admit, that these endowments were bestowed on him in no ordinary degree.

His method, stated without detail, was threefold:—daily mingling with the boys, and so exerting an almost unfelt but powerful influence;—private, loving labour in its many forms;—and public exhortation; in which he addressed himself with remarkable skill, to school-boy needs, virtues, failings, dangers, or privileges, as the occasion might require. His style in these addresses was peculiarly his own; and I cannot doubt they often left many of his young audience fired with a true desire to tread the road he had been depicting, to climb those heights of mental or moral excellence which his graphic language had clothed with brightness, or to walk as disciples of that gracious Saviour, whose love, from practical acquaintance, he could so winningly proclaim. The teachers, too, participated in the benefit of these exhortations: delivered, as they mostly were, on the Sabbath evening, they often acted as a stimulus to my own mind, to discharge to the best of my humble ability, the various duties of the week.

THOMAS PUPLETT.

IV.

In reviewing the professional career of our late friend, it must be remembered that he did not enjoy the advantages of training now open to those who pursue the profession of teaching. The extreme difficulty of obtaining trained helpers was one of the most formidable difficulties in his early years as a schoolmaster. No one rejoiced more than John Ford when the establishment of the Flounders' Institute, the enhanced estimate of the teacher's office in the Society of Friends, and the opening of the door to university honours, began to attract to the profession larger. numbers of our talented young men. The meetings and publications of the Friends' Educational Society, founded in 1836, exercised a powerful influence in advancing the cause of education, and in promoting the change of feeling we have referred to in respect to the profession of teaching. Along with Samuel Tuke, Josiah Forster, William Thistlethwaite, Thomas Pumphrey, Joseph Rowntree, and others, John Ford took a prominent part in the gatherings held for a series of years on the day succeeding the Ackworth General Meeting for the discussion of educational subjects. His review of the History of the Association, his essays on Influence and Authority, and on the Duties and Difficulties of Young Teachers, remain to attest the quickness of his mental and moral perceptions, as well as the felicity of his style, and the aptness of his illustrations when handling topics that called forth his special powers. John Ford was a warm admirer of Dr. Arnold, and often quoted him. Their characters were, however, widely dissimilar. Dr. Arnold governed Rugby as a powerful statesman might have governed a great province. John Ford's mind was cast in another mould. His *forte* was not in logical or sustained reasoning. He attained his position as a schoolmaster from the natural

force of his will, combined with strong sympathies, warm
emotions, and an almost feminine sensitiveness of the per-
ceptive faculties.

The progressive nature of the work of Divine grace was
conspicuously illustrated in the life of our late friend. With
advancing years Christian experience mellowed, softened,
and tranquilised his character. It will be in the remembrance of some of our readers how, in one of the last
Educational Meetings, having counselled the young teacher
to be no striker, he avowed the wish it were possible for him
to recall every instance when he himself had transgressed
this rule.*

JOHN S. ROWNTREE.

V.

As a School-boy my knowledge of John Ford extended
over the seven years which I spent at Bootham, entering at
nine years of age. I shall ever look back to York at that
period as a School where boys were well and considerately
treated. Their best interests, spiritually, morally, intellect-
ually and physically considered, were well looked after; and
the principle of honour fostered in the happiest manner.

John Ford never either caned or birched; and the moral
influence which he had with the boys was I believe far
more effective than corporal punishment. We not only
respected him, but we feared to grieve him. No boy will
forget the grasp of his hand when there was "nothing up;"
nor will any boy forget the awe of being summoned to the
Library as a culprit whether for wilful disobedience or other
aggravated offence. After leaving the offender in the Labora-
tory alone perhaps for an hour or two, he would take him into
the Library, and seating him by his warm fire would kindly

* Extracted by permission from a leading article in " The Friend."

and in a gentle and fatherly manner remonstrate with the boy. Such a course generally attained the desired end, and John Ford had rarely to do more. But if needful to resort to an ultimatum, he would show a hardened offender a letter written to his father expressing his (J. F.'s) extreme regret in having in the interest of the school to dismiss the boy. I do not remember this ever failing to bring a boy to his right mind—thus rendering it needless to post the letter.

John Ford made the Bible a book which was really attractive to us boys. His lessons on Scripture History, enriched by most interesting details and illustrations from Dr. Robinson, Lieutenant Lynch and other Eastern travellers, specially caught the attention of myself, and hence they were always looked forward to with pleasure. He took great pains in their preparation, writing copious notes.

My sunny memories of York School would not be complete without referring to one beloved and esteemed by all— Rachel Ford. Tender and loving as a mother, it was the greatest of pleasures to take a picked rose, the best in our little garden, up to the parlour and offer it to her; though she might have many infinitely better, she would always receive it kindly and courteously, and give it an honourable place.

After leaving York, up to the time of John Ford's death, I ever esteemed it a privilege to meet him, or to call on him, and again realize the grasp of his hand and see his cheery countenance,—the countenace of a Christian now gone to his reward, whose memory is ever fragrant, and whom I can truly say, whether as a boy or man, I esteemed and loved.

THOMAS WHITWELL.

VI.

I was indeed grieved to hear of dear John Ford's death,

though I do not know why we should grieve that one like
him should, after finishing a long and useful life, be taken
to his reward.   For myself I cannot tell how much I feel I
owe to him.   Whatever I may do will be largely owing to
the training which he gave me at York.   He had in a most
wonderful way the faculty of exciting enthusiasm in boys,
and giving them a healthy, honest and manly tone, teaching
them to look at life as a place in which there was something
to do, and that that something had to be done well and
courageously.   It would be hard to estimate the depth of
his influence in forming the minds of the present generation.
I for one shall always hold him in most affectionate remembrance.

JAMES BACKHOUSE WALKER.*
(Hobart Town.)

After the contributions of so many well able to
form a correct estimate of John Ford's life and
character, the Editor may feel excused from adding
much, especially as he can endorse to a large extent
the views advanced by the various writers.

It was my privilege to be associated with John
Ford as a Teacher in York School for nearly a
quarter of a century;   and the close friendship
which existed between us was broken only by his
death.   He had largely relinquished regular teaching before my time ; but for a few years he continued
to take classes in one or two subjects.   Whilst there
was a want of exactness in his teaching, his earnestness and animation made the lesson interesting to
most, and compelled even the careless to learn ; yet

* From a letter addressed to Elizabeth Backhouse, Holdgate, near York.

it was at the expenditure of so much physical energy that however advantageous it might be to the learners, it was evident such an exertion could only be maintained for a limited time. The trait which impressed me most throughout the entire period of my acquaintance with him, was his force of character. He seemed born to command. He constantly reminded me of the Centurion of Scripture; " I am a man under authority, having soldiers under me: and I say to this man, Go, and he goeth; and to another, Come, and he cometh; and to my servant Do this, and he doeth it." This force of character remained to the last. To it, when brought into subjection to Divine grace, in conjunction with his intense sympathy for the young—extending as it did even to very little children—may be largely attributed his success as an educator. To these qualities must be added his manliness and straightforwardness. He despised all underhand dealing; and espionage had no place in his system. The high standard of truthfulness which he upheld in his addresses to his scholars, was maintained in all his relations in life.

The readers of these pages will have noticed how deeply John Ford lamented the irritability and impulsiveness which marked his earlier days. They will have noticed too as years rolled on how these besetments were brought into subjection. To those who were intimately acquainted with him for a long

series of years, the gradual toning down of these
asperities under the powerful influence of Divine
grace, was very instructive.

If there is one point more prominent than another
in John Ford's practice as exhibited in his diary, it
is his prayerfulness. Page after page reads almost
like a practical commentary on the injunction, " In
every thing by prayer and supplication with thanksgiving let your requests be made known unto God ;"
and often did he realize the fulfilment of the accompanying assurance, " the peace of God which passeth
all understanding, shall keep your hearts and minds
through Christ Jesus."   Thus living in the love and
fear of God, drawing his supplies of help and
strength from Him, he was enabled to be an " am-
bassador for Christ " and to feed the flock committed
to his charge : and now through the love and mercy
of that Saviour on whom alone all his hopes were
placed, he has entered upon the higher service of
Heaven which he anticipated with such delight, for

" THERE HIS SERVANTS SHALL SERVE HIM."

William Sessions, Printer, 15, Low Ousegate, York.

www.ingramcontent.com/pod-product-compliance
Lightning Source LLC
Chambersburg PA
CBHW031344020726
47499CB00005B/1391